honey
on
your
mind

Published by Amazon Publishing
P.O. Box 400818
Las Vegas, NV 89140

ISBN-13: 1612183735
ISBN-10: 9781612183732

honey
on
your
mind

Waverly Bryson Takes New York

---

by maria murnane

amazonpublishing

I dedicate this book to every reader who has offered me kind words, either in person or online, at one point or another. Your collective support and enthusiasm has convinced me that writing is what I need to be doing with my life, no matter what, and for that, I will forever be grateful.

And to Terri Sharkey, for being you.

prologue

I hung up the phone and stared at it. My hand was shaking.

Did that really just happen?

I sat there for a minute, then took a deep breath and stood up. I set the phone on my desk and made my way toward the kitchen to get a glass of water, my throat suddenly dry. I couldn't really feel my feet on the hardwood floors, but I could feel a small buzzing in my ears. I blinked a few times and shook my head as I walked.

Did I really just say yes?

I poured a huge glass of water and plunked myself onto the couch in the living room. I slowly gazed around the apartment I'd lived in—*loved* living in—since graduating from college more than a decade ago. I'd never thought about it before, but at that moment, I realized I'd spent my entire adult life here. The place had changed quite a bit from the early days, when I'd roomed with my college friend Whitney, to my "big decision" to keep the two-bedroom place on my own when she got married a few years later. Over time, I'd gradually ditched the IKEA furniture for a more grown-up decor, and recently I'd even bought a few plants—although they'd quickly fallen victim to my black thumb. There was just something about this classic Victorian apartment nestled in the middle of quaint Pacific Heights, something *more* than rent control, that had made me think I'd stay here forever.

It wasn't just the apartment or the neighborhood that had cast a spell on me; it was…*San Francisco itself.* It's difficult to pinpoint exactly what it is about the city's magnetism that captivated me, but San Francisco has a way of making you think there's no other place worth living. After ten years, I was still entranced by it, and I had never even considered leaving.

But apparently I was about to do just that.

I set my glass on the coffee table and leaned back into the couch. I closed my eyes for a moment, then opened them and stared at the ceiling.

Did I really just agree to move across the country?

I bit my lip.

What have I done?

chapter one

"I can't believe you're giving up this great apartment," Andie said. "Do you know how many people would kill to live here for so cheap?"

I squinted at her. "You can't believe I'm giving up this *apartment*?"

She laughed and took a sip of Diet Coke. "I mean, I can't believe you're *moving*. You know I'm totally going to miss you."

"Thank you. That's much better."

She rolled her eyes. "Please, we've been over this like a thousand times. You know I hate you for leaving me."

"I know, I know. I sort of hate myself right now." I looked around the nearly empty living room, the families of tiny dust bunnies skittering across the hardwood floors. The whole place looked much smaller now than in my memory of when I first saw it. Had it already been ten years since college? Part of me could still remember what it felt like to move in…my first real apartment…my first real job…my first taste of real life.

My thoughts drifted from the past to what lay ahead—and the woman who, albeit inadvertently, had made it all happen.

Wendy Davenport, ugh.

Several months earlier, my good friend Scotty Ryan, a features reporter for the *Today* show, had invited me to appear on a Valentine's Day segment about love and dating. At the time, I was writing a newspaper column on those topics, so it was a good fit, not to mention great exposure. Overall, the appearance had gone well, despite the fact that I was unexpectedly ambushed by Wendy, who also had been invited to appear. I hadn't known it at the time, but Wendy had been jockeying for a position as a TV talk show host. She showed me up on stage by asking some pointed questions about my *personal* love life that I wasn't prepared to answer at all, much less before millions of people.

Since then her syndicated advice column, *Love, Wendy*, had been turned into a full-blown TV talk show on NBC, and they'd made Scotty the executive producer. Shrugging off our rocky introduction, Scotty thought I would make a good addition to her show, and he was higher up in the decision-making food chain than she was.

Then came the phone call that changed my life.

It was a part-time gig, but part-time in TV pays the rent. It would also give me a financial boost to get my online project, Waverly's Honey Shop, off the ground. In a moment of inspiration, I'd recently launched a small line of T-shirts, tote bags, and other products with fun slogans about trying to figure life out (my personal favorite was I KNOW NOTHING, BUT AT LEAST I KNOW THAT), but it was stalled until I could improve my cash-flow situation.

"Waverly? You still there?"

I blinked. "Sorry, yep, still here. What did you say?"

"I asked when you're going to meet up with Paige."

I closed my eyes and scratched my forehead. "Um, I know the answer to that. I really do."

"So it's on your calendar?"

I opened my eyes and nodded. "It most certainly is. It's just that my calendar is currently located in a box somewhere, a box whose location is currently uncertain."

"You'll love her. She's by far the nicest person in my family. In fact, she's too nice."

I raised my eyebrows. "Nicer than you?"

She coughed and took another sip of her drink. "Yeah, right. Like you or anyone I've ever met would use the word *nice* to describe me."

I laughed and reached for a broom propped against a wall. "Good point. I'm really looking forward to meeting her."

"You know, now that I think about it, she might give you a run for your money in the 'bad date' department."

I turned around. "*Excuse* me?" I'd yet to meet anyone who could match my repertoire of dating horror stories.

"You'll see. I told you, she's a bit too nice for her own good." She pointed at me. "And as *you* know all too well, missy, nice girls get dumped on a lot."

I opened my mouth to protest, but we both knew she was right. I considered myself a nice person, and though I had a boyfriend now, my romantic history was, shall we say, *checkered*.

As I stood there holding the broom in silence, Andie finished her drink and took another look around. "So are you all packed? The taxi's coming at the crack of dawn, right?"

My eyes wandered across the room until they came to rest on a tangle of black cables sticking out of the wall. I still didn't know what half of them were for. I nodded. "I'm actually not bringing all that much with me. I realized once I started going through my clothes how I never wear most of what I own anyway. So I'm pretty much going to start over after I'm settled. It's a good excuse to go shopping in New York, don't you think?"

"Definitely. Did you end up sending all your furniture with the movers?"

I began to sweep. "Most of it. I sold some stuff on craigslist and gave some to Goodwill. I figured it would be fun to do a bit of decorating when I get there. Maybe hit some antique shows, flea markets, that sort of thing."

She put a hand on her hip. "Look at you, all Brooklyn hipster already. I'm impressed."

I laughed. "Brooklyn Heights is *hardly* the hipster part of Brooklyn. It's basically cute brownstones surrounded by cute coffee shops. And guess what? I got my new landlord to paint the walls in—"

She interrupted me. "Don't tell me. Various shades of green and blue?"

I narrowed my eyes. "How did you know that?"

"Hello? You've only been saying for years that you wanted to paint your walls various shades of green and blue."

"I have?"

"OK then, someone clearly hasn't been listening to herself. Anyhow, part of me is a little jealous of this big adventure of yours. I've always wanted to live in New York."

"Really? I didn't know that."

"Yeah, Paris, London, and New York. I've always thought they would be fun places to live at some point. I mean, look at all the action in my life right here, and San Francisco is a *fraction* of their size. Can you imagine how much trouble I could get into if I left here?"

"I'm afraid to even think about that."

She nodded. "Oh, you'll be thinking about it soon enough. Believe me, my dear, now that I have a couch to crash on, I'll be coming to visit you on a regular basis."

"You'd better."

She rubbed her hands together. "Oh, I will. Now let's go to Dino's. McKenna's probably arriving soon, and I'm starving."

I leaned the broom against the wall and picked up my purse from the floor. "Sounds good. I think this place is clean enough that I should get my security deposit back."

As we left the nearly empty apartment, I tried not to look back.

• • •

"The usual?" Andie barely glanced at me as she flagged down the waiter. We always ordered the same thing, so I just nodded in agreement. Within seconds, a frosty pitcher of Bud Light appeared on the table between us. They knew us well at Dino's.

I picked up the pitcher and poured us each a glass, then slowly looked around the restaurant. "I'm really going to miss this place, Andie."

"And this place is really going to miss you. But *you*, my friend, are on to bigger and better things, so let's be adults and deal with it." She raised her beer for a toast.

I sighed as I clinked my mug against hers. "Believe me, I'm doing my best."

"So Jake's meeting you there?"

I nodded with a smile at the thought of seeing Jake again, especially of seeing his blue eyes again. "He's going to help me unpack and get settled. He flies in Friday afternoon, and the movers arrive Saturday morning."

She covered her heart with both hands. "So romantic. At least you'll be living on the same side of the country now."

"Yeah, that should make things a lot easier. Not that I don't like Atlanta, but I'm getting sick of those long flights, not to mention the airplane hair." Jake and I had officially been a couple for six months, but it had been nearly a year since we first kissed and almost two since I'd met him. He'd been living in Atlanta that whole time—which meant an awful lot of bad in-flight movies…and flat airplane hair.

"Totally understandable. Airplane hair blows, especially when a hottie like Jake's waiting for you on the other side of security. She took a sip of her beer, and then gestured toward the entrance. "Hey, there she is."

I turned around to see an uncharacteristically disheveled McKenna approach our table. I stood up to give her a hug, but she stiff-armed me.

"I have fresh baby puke on me. You'd be wise to keep your distance." She looked exhausted.

I laughed and sat back down. "It's nice to see you too."

McKenna plopped into a seat next to Andie, whose eyes bulged at the post-baby boobs. "Holy hell, woman. Have you registered your cannonballs with the police department? You could do some serious damage with those things."

McKenna hung her purse on the back of her chair. "Always a comedian. I'm sorry for being late. Hunter was stuck in surgery, Elizabeth was having a fit trying to latch on, and I just couldn't get out of there. Then, of course, I hit traffic on the bridge. You know how it goes."

Andie picked up her beer and smiled. "Actually, I don't know how it goes, because I, as you know, am blissfully childless and live right here in the city. Did I mention I took a nap this afternoon?" She yawned and stretched her tiny arms over her head.

McKenna laughed. "Suck it."

"I'll leave that to your daughter," Andie said.

McKenna laughed again. "I hate you right now. I'm laughing, but I'm hating."

Andie took a sip of her beer. "Hey now, *you're* the one who got married and pregnant. It's not my fault that I'm well rested and having regular sex."

"Still hating you," McKenna said.

"So Elizabeth's not sleeping through the night yet?" I asked.

McKenna shook her head. "It's brutal. I adore the munchkin, I really do, but I've never been so sleep-deprived. Even in my early days of investment banking, it wasn't this bad. Who would have thought such a small person could wreak so much havoc?"

"She's not that small," Andie said. "She's sort of a chunk, if you ask me."

McKenna put her hand over Andie's mouth. "Seriously, could you shut it? I don't want to do something that will get me arrested."

I tried not to laugh. "Thanks for making the effort to come into the city, Mackie. It means so much to me that you're here on my last night."

Her face went soft. "Oh gosh, Wave, are you kidding? I wouldn't have missed it for the world. I still can't believe you're going to become a New Yorker."

"You and me both. But I just felt like I couldn't turn this opportunity down, no matter how scary it is."

She nodded. "Definitely, there's no way you could have said no. I'm going to miss you to death, but I'm so excited for you."

I interlaced my fingers in front of me. "I'm terrified, but I agree."

"I feel like I'm about to start the next chapter in The Book of Waverly—if I ever had the time to read anything besides the side of a diaper box, that is."

"Hello? I'm trying to eat here," Andie said.

McKenna ignored her and put her hand on my shoulder. "I'm so proud of you, Wave, I know how hard change is for you, but I think this will turn out to be the best thing you've done for yourself in years."

I raised my eyebrows. "Better than when I finally grew out my bangs?"

Andie sipped her beer. "And thank God you did. No one with a cowlick should *ever* have bangs. Those things were totally crooked."

"Thanks for the reminder," I said.

"My pleasure." She reached for a fresh slice of pizza. "So tell us more about the new job. When do you start?"

"In two weeks."

"I can't believe you're going to work for that woman after the way she treated you," Andie said. "Talk about a bitch."

I sighed. "I know, but I don't think I'll be working *with* her all that much, to be honest. I'll just be taping a segment for two shows a week, three if it goes well. If I'm lucky, maybe I won't have to interact with her at all."

"A control freak like that? I doubt it," Andie said.

"So the rest of the time you'll be dealing with getting your honey products off the ground?" McKenna asked.

"Yep."

Andie pushed her hair behind her ears. "That and learning how to act normal on TV. We know how well that went last time."

I winced at the memory of my one previous television appearance. Not a *complete* disaster, but hardly a smashing success. "This is true, and I promise to get better. As for the honey products, Waverly's Honey Shop may be a breakout phenomenon in our little world of three, but if I want to kick it up a notch, I really need to, well, kick it up a notch. I'm so glad Andie's cousin is going to help me with that."

"At least the TV job will help you pay for it," McKenna said.

I nodded. "Thank God. Bootstrapping my little business is turning out to be a lot more expensive than I thought it would be."

"I can't believe everything worked out this way," McKenna said. "It's almost like it was meant to be."

"I know, talk about perfect timing," Andie said.

I picked up a piece of pizza and thought about the rent-controlled apartment I'd just given up. "I hope you're right, my friends, because otherwise I just made a huge mistake."

chapter two

At dawn the next day, in a surreal haze of excitement, disbelief, and denial, I said good-bye to San Francisco. I locked up my apartment for the last time and hesitated before slipping the keys under the door. I couldn't help but wonder if I was making a mistake, but I knew it was too late to turn back now. I ran my fingers over the number that had marked my address for years.

Am I really doing this?

I turned and walked slowly toward the lobby. I could see the taxi waiting outside.

After standing by the front door for a few moments, I finally decided it was time to let it go.

As the cab slipped away in the early morning sunlight, I waved silently at the building I'd called home for so long. Then I turned to face forward, trying to shift my focus to the adventure ahead.

• • •

"It's beautiful, Waverly, I'm really impressed." Jake ran his hand along the crown moldings in the living room and looked up at the high ceilings.

"Isn't it great?" I walked around and began to point. "I thought I could put the couch here, the TV here, my bookcase here, and my desk here. What do you think?" I'd downsized to a one-bedroom apartment, so my living room was now going to double as an office, as well as a temporary warehouse for all my Honey products. To date, I'd been fulfilling the few orders I got with sporadic trips to the post office, but I hoped all that would change once I met with Andie's cousin, Paige.

He nodded and put his hand on the wall. "That'll work. By the way, I really like the colors you chose."

"I know, aren't they great? Isn't it all great? I've always wanted to live in an apartment with walls in various shades of green and blue. I can't believe I—"

I stopped talking and put my hands over my mouth.

"Oh my God, wait, that reminds me. I have a joke to tell you."

He laughed. "Do you *really* have to?"

I pointed at him. "You be nice. Wanna hear it?"

"Is that a rhetorical question?"

"Maybe."

He walked toward his suitcase. "I'll let you tell your joke if you let me give you something first, OK?"

My eyes brightened. "Give me something?"

"It's nothing big, just a little housewarming gift." Next to his suitcase was a medium-sized shopping bag. He picked it up and handed it to me.

"For me?"

"For you."

I opened the bag and looked inside.

It was a plant.

A plastic one.

I laughed and pulled it out. "Are you trying to tell me something?"

He put a hand on my shoulder. "Just trying to stop the carnage. I've seen what you can do."

I squeezed his hand and set the plant down. "Thanks for the vote of confidence. So are you ready for my new joke?"

"Do I have a choice?"

"Of course not. So there are these two green olives just hanging out on an olive tree, chatting about their day, when all of a sudden one of them plummets to the ground." I pretended to be an olive plummeting downward.

Jake nodded.

"So the one on the ground is just lying there on its back, stunned, and the one still safely attached to the tree yells down to it, 'Are you OK?'"

Jake nodded again.

"And the one on the ground yells up at him, 'OLIVE, OLIVE!'"

Jake didn't say anything.

I held my palms up. "You get it? *O-live, I'll live?*"

He smiled. "Oh, I got it. I'm tempted to jump out the window and plummet to the ground myself, but I got it."

"Hey now, you *know* that was funny." I pushed his shoulder.

"Don't quit your day job, Miss Bryson. So what were you saying about your walls?"

I was about to reply, but when I looked into his eyes, I momentarily forgot what I was going to say. Jake's eyes, an intense blue that put my walls to shame for even trying to associate themselves with the same color family, had a way of doing that to me. I needed to come up with a new color to describe them. Plain old *blue* just didn't seem sufficient. *Hot-guy blue? Babe-ilicious blue?* Nothing seemed appropriate.

"Waverly, you there?"

I blinked. "Sorry, spaced out for a second. Um, so anyhow, I was about to say that I can't believe I found a neighborhood *and* an apartment I love as much as what I had back home. I swear I'm never moving again though. Moving *sucks*."

Jake looked at me as if he were going to speak, but instead he turned to check out the walls again. The landlord had done right by me, and the colors gave the place a fun personality that shouted *Look at me! I'm a super-cute New York apartment!* I adored it.

I'd chosen to live in Brooklyn not just because it was cheaper than Manhattan, but also because, to be honest, I was a little afraid of Manhattan. I'd been there several times over the years, and while I liked to think of myself as reasonably sophisticated, I secretly felt overwhelmed by the crowds, the shrieking of ambulances, and the constant chaos in general. Brooklyn Heights was neither scary *nor* sleepy. In fact, it was charming and clean, with tidy rows of brownstones and a village-like coziness that made me feel instantly at home. During the weekend I'd spent there looking for an apartment, I was pleasantly surprised to see that the main street teemed with more foot traffic than most neighborhoods in San Francisco. And it was right on the other side of the iconic Brooklyn Bridge, just one subway stop away from the infamous corridors of Wall Street in Lower Manhattan.

"So how'd you sleep on that thing?" Jake pointed to the blow-up mattress in my empty bedroom, where I'd just spent two uncomfortable nights.

I put my hands on my lower back and grimaced. "Let's just say I've aged a bit since Wednesday. An air mattress may feel like a normal bed at the beginning of the night, but at some point you inevitably wake up lying on the ground, surrounded by mattress."

He laughed and slid his arms around my waist. "Want to give it another try?"

I looked up at him and raised my eyebrows. "You mean *now*?"

"I mean *now*. What do you think?"

I glanced at the mattress, then back at him. My cheeks flushed.

"I think…I think I could be convinced."

He smiled. "Well then, let me convince you."

He took a step toward me and gently placed one hand on the back of my neck. I lifted my head as he leaned down to kiss me, his lips warm and soft. I wrapped my arms around him and kissed him back.

"You smell so good," I whispered, suddenly feeling a little tipsy.

He briefly nuzzled my neck before straightening up and taking a step backward. He stared at me for a moment, the look in his eyes speaking for him, then pulled his T-shirt over his head and tossed it onto the hardwood floor. I admired his strong chest and abdomen. He was nearly thirty-six years old, but he looked like he could still be playing college basketball.

"Come here," he said softly.

I inched toward him. He gently pulled on the spaghetti straps of my tank top, then slowly removed it and lobbed it in the general direction of his T-shirt. He put his hands on the small of my back and pulled me toward him. We began kissing again, and I reached for the top of his jeans. I unbuttoned them and began to slide them over his hips with both hands.

Then I stopped.

"Are you going commando?"

He nodded.

I laughed. "Is this new? I've never seen you like this."

He shrugged. "It's fun once in a while. Sort of liberating. Plus, I like to keep you on your toes." As he said this, his jeans fell to the ground, and he quickly kicked them away, along with his flip-flops. I was wearing a jersey skirt, which took approximately one second for him to remove. I pushed it with my bare foot toward the growing pile of discarded clothes.

"This is sexy," he said softly as he kissed my shoulder.

"Mmm."

"*You're* sexy," he whispered, nuzzling my neck.

"Mmm."

We kissed some more, and as the heat began to spread through my entire body, I couldn't think about anything other than how attracted I was to him. We both started breathing harder, but we didn't stop kissing.

He unhooked my bra and lightly threw it on top of the clothes pile. The look in his eyes, which were locked onto mine, made it clear that neither of us wanted to be standing up anymore. He pressed his body against mine and began to move us toward the mattress.

When my foot touched the bed, I reached down with one hand and eased myself onto my back. I looked up at him, standing over me, his wavy brown hair falling into his beautiful eyes.

I reached my arms up to him.

"Now it's your turn to come here," I said softly.

He smiled and nodded.

Then he kneeled on the mattress.

He slowly began to lower himself on top of me.

Then his weight blew a huge hole in the mattress, and together we sank to the floor.

He collapsed on top of me, totally cracking up.

"Nice," he said, still laughing.

I started cracking up too. "How...ro...man...tic...but...I... can't...breathe."

• • •

The movers arrived early the next morning, and Jake and I spent the weekend getting everything unpacked and sorted. By the time Sunday night came around, we were exhausted. But at least we had my sturdy queen-sized bed on which to collapse. After the air mattress experiment had literally exploded in our faces, we'd spent Friday at a boutique hotel down the street. Jake insisted on paying. He always did.

"So tell me more about the job." He played with my fingers as we lay side by side on our backs, gazing up at the old-fashioned ceiling fan in my bedroom.

"To be honest, I'm pretty much going to be drinking from a fire hose. I don't know *anything* about how a TV show works, but Scotty said it's a lot easier than it looks, and that I'll learn as I go."

"Just don't plan on telling any of your jokes on the air."

I lightly pushed his arm. "Shut up. You know you love my jokes. Scotty's convinced that the viewers will respond to what I have to say, so he's excited to get me out there, even though I'm a total rookie."

"And what *do* you have to say, exactly?"

I laughed. "Honestly? I have no idea. *Honey on Your Mind* was always such a hodgepodge, you know? An entertaining hodgepodge based on hilarious reader e-mails, but a hodgepodge nonetheless. So I guess I'll be free to report on whatever's *on my mind*, so to speak."

He laughed. "So they really haven't given you any direction?"

"Not yet."

"Not even a list of topics to cover?"

"Nope."

"So what exactly are you supposed to *do*?"

I put my finger on his chin. "You ask a good question."

He laughed. "You really up and moved across the country without a formal job description?"

"Apparently I did. I guess I'm just trusting that Scotty will take care of me."

"You *do* realize that's a little crazy, right?"

"Good point. But we've already established that you think I'm crazy, so are you all that surprised?"

"Actually, I am. I guess your craziness never ceases to surprise me."

I pushed his shoulder again. "Be nice."

"But seriously, what's the plan?"

I shrugged. "I guess we'll see what happens at that first meeting. It should be illuminating, to say the least. I'm sure Scotty will point me in the right direction. After all, he convinced the higher-ups at NBC that I'm worth a paycheck, right? He must have *some* ideas floating around in that pretty head of his."

"Did I ever tell you that I've seen the show?"

"You've seen *Love, Wendy*?"

He nodded. "Just once, after you got offered the job. I stumbled across it on a road trip. I was ironing my shirt before a pregame meeting and turned on the TV." Jake was the head trainer and physical therapist for the NBA's Atlanta Hawks.

I propped myself up on my elbow and looked at him. "So what did you think? Was it cheesy? I'm not sure what to make of Wendy's style, especially given all that hairspray holding her blonde helmet in place. If she's not careful, she could easily catch on fire around an open flame."

"It's actually not bad. I was surprised, given how you'd described her to me. I expected her to be wearing a tiara or something."

I raised my eyebrows. "Really? You didn't think it was that bad? In the only episode I saw, she was talking about all the beauty pageants she used to compete in. After that I couldn't bring myself to watch again."

He laughed and messed up my hair. "It was fine, really. Maybe she's not as bad as you think."

"I hope you're right. If nothing else, it means so long, erratic print column and near poverty; hello, TV version and regular paycheck."

"Nothing wrong with a steady paycheck. So tell me, what's on your mind right *now*?"

I nuzzled my head against his chest. "You mean besides the fact that I'm never moving again?"

"Yes." He gently caressed my cheek.

"To be honest, it's not suitable for family-oriented programming."

"I like the sound of that." He lifted my face to his, and I immediately forgot all about Wendy Davenport.

chapter three

Early Monday Jake flew back to Atlanta. The hectic NBA season was just getting under way, so I felt lucky that he'd had a free weekend to help me get settled. For the next few weeks, however, I was on my own. Or at least I was sleeping on my own. My friends Kristina and Shane lived on the Upper East Side of Manhattan, and of course, there was Scotty, so I wasn't *entirely* by myself. Funny, though, how you could feel alone in a city of eight million people.

I had a week before my first day at *Love, Wendy.* In between countless trips to Target for everything from a shower curtain to a coffee pot, I was planning to meet Paige Murphy, Andie's cousin. A career sales rep, she was willing to help me get the products I sold online at Waverly's Honey Shop into brick-and-mortar stores.

Since Paige lived downtown, she suggested we meet for happy hour at a place called Harry's, one of the many old-school pubs in the financial district. It was easy to spot her when I walked in, not just because she'd described herself over the phone, but also because she was pretty much the only person in there not wearing a suit. Talk about a Wall Street stereotype. It's hard enough finding *anyone* who wears a suit to work in San Francisco, much less in a packed pub downtown on a Monday. In San Francisco on Monday evenings, everyone's either walking a dog, going for a run, or at Pilates.

Paige stood up from the barstool and gave me a hug as I approached her. "Waverly, it's so great to finally meet you in person. I've been hearing about you for years." Her smile was warm and genuine.

I sat down next to her. "Hearing good things, I hope." I suddenly realized that if Andie and I ever had a falling out, she could ruin me forever.

She laughed and stood up to get the bartender's attention. "Of course, all good. Now what can I get you? It's on me."

I picked up the drink menu and scanned it. "How about a Blue Moon with an orange slice?"

"Sounds great. I think I'll have the same." She ordered the drinks, then sat down and faced me. "So how are you liking New York? What a huge move to make by yourself. I'm impressed."

I smiled. "So far, so good, but I don't think it's completely sunk in yet that I actually *live* here. It was just so unexpected, and everything's moving so fast."

"Get used to it. Everything in New York moves fast. God forbid you're a slow walker, especially on the subway platform. You can seriously get taken *out*."

"I'll try to remember that."

She reached down and pulled a large binder from her bag. "OK, let's get down to business. I have all sorts of plans for your Honey products, so I hope you're ready to get busy. Are you?" She opened it across her lap.

I stared at the binder. "Wow, Andie said you were on top of it, but I think she sold you a bit short."

She laughed. "Oh yes, I don't mess around."

Over the next half hour, Paige explained where she thought the Honey products would be a good fit, as well as her strategy for developing both local and national accounts. She also discussed the most cost-effective production network to support orders, which, until then, I'd been fulfilling piecemeal out of my apartment with sporadic trips to the post office. Compared to what she was describing, I was a retail preschooler, barely out of diapers.

"Are you following me? Am I going too fast?" She stopped and put a hand on my arm. She didn't say it in a mean way and was clearly only reacting to the look on my face, which apparently displayed what I was thinking: *I am totally in over my head!*

I blinked. "I'm following. I just didn't realize how much was involved in, um, in getting a product on the shelves." Until now, the T-shirts, tote bags, and other items that made up Waverly's Honey Shop had only an online presence.

She smiled. "That's OK, no one ever does. But that's a *good* thing, because if you did, would you have made the effort to create all those cool products in the first place?"

I laughed. "Probably not."

"See? That's why you have me. Don't worry, you're in good hands. I've been doing this for years, and while it's never easy to launch a new product, I think your Honey line has potential."

"Really?"

She nodded. "I don't take on product lines I don't believe in. I learned that lesson once. It's just a huge waste of time for everyone." She reached into her purse and pulled out a Honey Tote that said IS IT WORSE TO BE FAKE OR BITCHY? on the front and HONEY, JUST FACE IT. IF YOU'RE ASKING, YOU'RE PROBABLY BOTH on the back. She pointed to it. "*This* is the story of my life, right here in black and white."

I smiled. "That's my best seller. And I don't believe that's the story of your life. Andie says you're the nicest person in her family."

"She really said that?"

I nodded.

"Andie's so sweet." She finished her beer and set it on the bar, then looked at her phone. "Listen, I hate to drink and run, but I have a date, so I need to leave soon. I'm sorry."

I raised my eyebrows. "You're seeing someone?" Given what Andie had said about Paige's dating history, I figured she was single.

She shook her head. "It's a first date. It'll probably be the last too, but you've got to try, right?"

"You've definitely got to try. How did you meet him?"

"Actually, I haven't."

"Set up?"

"Sort of. It's through a matchmaking service."

"A matchmaking service?"

She nodded. "I figured I'd try putting my love life into the hands of professionals, because whatever I'm doing clearly isn't working. You know what happened with the last guy I dated?"

"I have a feeling I'm about to find out."

She leaned toward me and lowered her voice. "I spent the night for the first time at his apartment, and right before we went to sleep, he gave me a brand new toothbrush."

"OK…"

"And then the next morning, he said he was just going to throw it away, so I might as well take it with me."

I winced. "He really said that?"

"He really said that."

"He didn't say you could keep it there?"

She shook her head. "Nope."

"Ouch."

"Exactly."

"Did you like him?"

"Unfortunately, yeah, I did." She looked...sad.

I made a sad face. "Did I already say ouch?"

"You did. Thanks."

"Ugh, I'm sorry, Paige."

She waved a hand in front of her. "It's OK. I'm used to it by now."

"So that's dating in New York?"

She shrugged. "That's dating in New York. At least my version of it. Which explains my recent decision to let the pros take over."

"Sounds like a smart idea to me."

"Andie tells me you have a serious boyfriend. Josh something? Jake? Jared?"

I took a sip of my beer. "Jake. McIntyre. He lives in Atlanta."

"How long have you been dating?"

"Officially about six months. But I went through my own share of dating hell before I met him, including being on the losing end of a broken engagement. So believe me, I feel your pain."

She nodded. "I've heard stories from Andie about the slim pickings in San Francisco, but there's no way it's as bad out there as it is here."

I raised my eyebrows. "Want to try me?"

She laughed. "Is that a dare?"

I laughed too. "I guess so."

"OK, it's on. Can you beat that toothbrush story?"

"I think I can."

"OK, let's hear it."

I paused to think for a minute, then nodded. "OK, I once went on a date with a guy who told me over dinner that I'd be more attractive if my boobs were bigger."

Her jaw dropped. "No."

I nodded and looked down at my chest. "I think I was even wearing a padded bra at the time."

"Wowsa. OK, I see that, and I raise you a guy who—*after one date*—suggested I lose a few pounds before he'd be 'up for seeing' me naked."

I pushed her shoulder. "No way! For real?"

She nodded. "For real. He even e-mailed me a link to a special Jenny Craig was running."

"Oh my *God*. What an asshole."

"Yeah, that wasn't fun. Can you top that?"

I paused. "That might be hard, but I think I can. Just give me a minute." I closed my eyes to concentrate. I knew there must be *something* in my memory I could pull out. I'd yet to meet anyone who could compete when it came to my pre-Jake dating disasters.

Think, Waverly!

I kept my eyes closed for moment, and then it came to me.

Yes!

"OK, OK, I've got one. I had a first date once that went well. We had dinner and then went for a walk. I kissed him a little bit, but nothing serious."

"OK…"

"And then the next day he sent me a text message…"

"OK…"

"Actually, it wasn't really a *message*."

She raised her eyebrows.

"It was a photo. *Just* a photo. No message."

She kept her eyebrows raised. "And?"

"The photo was of himself…no shirt on…with one hand holding the camera…and the other hand…down his underwear."

Her eyes got big. "No *way*."

I nodded.

"There's no way that really happened."

I pulled out my phone. "Oh yes it did." I scrolled through the photos and showed it to her.

"No *way*." She said again as she looked at the picture. "That's totally his package. I can't believe it."

I laughed. "Yep, right there for the whole world to see through a thin layer of cotton."

"Did you reply?"

I shook my head. "Before I got a chance to do anything, he sent me another text."

"Another photo?"

"No, this one was a message that said '*Wanna see it?*'"

"He did *not*."

I laughed. "Oh yes he did."

"What did you do?"

"I replied that *no*, I did *not* want to see it."

"Wow, that's off the charts, Waverly."

I grinned. "I know. Did I win?"

"I think you just did. She pulled her own phone out of her purse and looked at it. "And I can't play this game any longer because I've *really* got to run now, or I'll be late."

"Good luck. I hope your date tonight doesn't make our list."

"I hope not too. It was so nice meeting you. I'll be in touch soon about the Honey products, OK? I promise to take good care of you."

I smiled. "Sounds good to me. I'm so glad to have you to help me with this."

"Oh gosh, it's my pleasure. Plus, if I do my job right, we'll both make out like bandits." She put the binder and Honey Tote back inside her bag and slung it over her shoulder. "Welcome to New York, my new friend. We're glad to have you."

She gave me a quick hug and was gone.

I pulled out my phone as soon as she left and was happy to see a timely new text from Jake:

Back in Atlanta, but wish I were still in Brooklyn

I smiled at the message. I'd certainly come a long way from the guy with one hand down his boxer briefs.

• • •

When I'd come to New York in the past, I'd always taken cabs, since my company was paying. But truth be told, I'd also been a bit overwhelmed by the sheer enormity and complexity of the subway system. Now that I was living here, though—not to mention paying for my own transportation—I was determined to master it. So, on the morning of my first meeting at *Love, Wendy,* I anxiously followed the masses down into the Court Street stop.

At Union Square in Manhattan, I stepped off the train and stood on the platform for a moment, taking in the madness. Then I looked overhead and studied the signs to find the correct uptown route before I plunged into the swarming crowd. Along the way, I strolled by an eight-person jazz band and what appeared to be a fully functioning police station. *Underground.* On the final leg of my journey, I avoided the scary smiles of a few *The World Is Ending* pamphlet pushers, steered clear of a couple of sleeping/passed out people, and finally descended another stairway to reach the correct uptown platform, which was teeming with commuters moving in all directions. In the middle of the chaos, a man with dreadlocks down to his waist calmly played a Jamaican steel drum.

It wasn't even nine o'clock.

As I waited for the connecting train to arrive, I wondered if anyone actually *lived* in the subway. It certainly seemed possible. I figured it was only a matter of time before someone made a reality show out of it.

• • •

I arrived at NBC with time to spare. Scotty had been traveling the entire week before, so we hadn't connected more than briefly by phone. That meant I was essentially walking into my first day blind—and desperately hoping I wouldn't crash into anything.

I checked in with the receptionist at the front desk, who directed me to HR to fill out some paperwork before I was to join the team at ten o'clock. When I was done with that, I still had time to kill, so I played with my phone for a while and pretended to look busy. Finally, I decided to make my way to the conference room. As I walked down the crisp hallways, I half expected a security guard to appear out of nowhere, grab my elbow, and escort me from the premises.

I couldn't believe how nervous I was.

I arrived at the meeting about five minutes early. There was only one person seated at the huge table, and he looked about seventeen, so I figured he was an intern. He appeared to be playing a game on his phone. I smiled at him and sat down at the opposite end of the table, wondering if he was an executive's kid. I pulled out a notebook and looked over at him again. He didn't raise his eyes from the screen.

OK, then.

A few minutes later, the room began to fill up. People arrived in pairs or threes, chatting among themselves. No one paid me much attention, so I focused on breathing deeply and trying not to sweat too much. Then Scotty walked in.

Thank God. A familiar face.

As soon as he saw me, he trotted over to give me a big hug. Apparently, it's OK to hug at the office in the world of TV.

"Waverly! It's so great to see you. Welcome to NBC. Welcome to New York!"

"Thanks, Scotty. It's great to see you too. I can't believe this is really happening." I kept my voice low.

"I'm so excited to have you on board. You're going to do just great."

"I'm totally nervous," I added in a whisper.

He squeezed my shoulders tightly. "Don't worry for a minute. Let's grab coffee after this, OK?"

I nodded and sat down as he walked to the front of the room. "Ladies and gentlemen, I'd like to introduce the newest member of the *Love, Wendy* team, Ms. Waverly Bryson."

Everyone looked at me. I smiled and tried to make eye contact all around, but it felt a bit forced. I hoped no one noticed how uncomfortable I felt.

"As you may already know, she'll be hosting a new segment called *Honey on Your Mind*, based on a popular advice column she wrote for the *San Francisco Sun*. It's going to be a fun addition to the show."

After a few smiles and nods in my direction, everyone turned back to Scotty.

"*Plus* she's a lot of fun, especially after a couple drinks, so I'm excited to have her on board and know you will all love her just as much as I do."

More smiles and nods in my direction. I'd never been in a work environment that so blatantly blurred the lines between professional relationships and personal ones, so I was a little thrown by how familiar he was being and wondered how every-one *really* felt about me—especially now that they knew I'd been out boozing with the boss.

I kept waiting for Wendy Davenport to stroll into the room, but she never did.

Where is she?

The meeting seemed to go smoothly, at least what I could understand of it. I quickly learned that TV people use a lot of jargon and acronyms, many of which went sailing right over my head. I was able to decipher some of it through context, but I was tempted more than once to raise my hand and ask for a trans-lation. Not wanting to look like I was in *too* far over my head, however, I feigned understanding while furtively jotting down a long list of questions. I'd get Scotty to explain it all to me later.

The intern played with his phone throughout the entire meeting.

• • •

"So where was Wendy?" Scotty and I were across the street at Argot Tea. I stirred brown sugar into my latte.

"Wendy? She doesn't come to staff meetings all that much."

"Really? But isn't this, well, *her show*?" I was secretly thrilled at this news.

"Yes, but it's in her contract that she doesn't *have* to attend every meeting, especially the regular ones where, as you just saw, we basically go over a checklist of what everyone needs to take care of throughout the week. She comes now and then, especially if we're going to be kicking around ideas for the show, but overall she thinks meetings are a waste of her time."

"You're joking."

He shook his head and smiled. "Welcome to TV, my love. It's unlike any industry you've ever seen, one in which moderately talented people get paid enormous amounts of money to act like spoiled children."

"I would have thought Wendy would be all over *every* meeting. She seemed like the type, you know?"

"People aren't always what they appear to be. Especially that one. You'll see."

"I can't say I'm exactly looking forward to that."

He put his hand over mine. "Please. You'll be fine. So tell me about *you*. You're settling in OK? So far, so good?"

"So far, so good. I'm surprised at how smoothly it's gone, to be honest."

"How are you liking Brooklyn Heights? I think it's one of the prettiest areas in all of New York City. A hidden gem, if you ask me."

I could feel my eyes brighten. "I'm *loving* Brooklyn Heights. It's hard to explain, but in a strange way, I feel like the neighborhood was made for me, Scotty. I just feel so comfortable there. They should have called it *Waverly Heights*."

He smiled. "Glad to hear you're fitting in. I knew you would. So when are you coming up to my roof deck for a drink? Given how much I've been talking about you since you took the job, I think Tad's convinced I'm going to go straight and make a move on you."

I coughed. "Yeah, right. I'd love to come by and meet him for more than two minutes this time. I'm curious about the man who captured the heart of the elusive Mr. Scotty Ryan. I've got to say, I never thought I'd see the day."

"You and me both, princess." Scotty and I had both met Tad at a wedding nearly two years earlier, but the only thing I remembered from my brief encounter with him that night was thinking it wasn't fair that his eyelashes were longer than mine. Scotty, on the other hand, had since moved from Dallas to New York to live with him.

"So when are you free?" Scotty asked.

I held my hands up. "My schedule is wide open–except for having to figure out my new *job*, that is. I hope you won't regret hiring me."

"Kitten, I know a natural when I see one, and you're going to be fine. This is *not* rocket science, so trust me, OK? Do you trust me?" He sipped his tea.

I nodded. "I do. I've learned that doubting you is a losing strategy."

"There you go."

"Well, hello, Scott. And is that you…Waverly?" The sound of a woman's voice made us both look up.

Standing next to our table was Wendy Davenport, holding a cup of coffee to go.

Good lord, her blonde helmet has expanded. How is that even possible?

"Hi, Wendy." I stood up and held out my hand. "It's nice to see you again." I tried not to stare at her hair, but it was seriously hard to look away. I was mesmerized.

She accepted my hand, but just as she'd done when we'd met on the *Today* show set, she didn't grasp it back. Instead, she just held hers there, limp, before we both let go. How is it possible for *anyone* not to realize how creepy that is?

"Welcome to New York." Despite the weak handshake, her smile was magnetic.

"Thanks."

"I see you two are getting reacquainted," she said to Scotty in a tone that I couldn't help but notice was a bit…cold.

"We missed you at the production meeting," Scotty said in a voice that wasn't cold but definitely wasn't gushing with enthusiasm either. It made me wonder what was going on between them.

She waved her hand in front of her. "Oh please, y'all don't need me to take care of those pesky details."

"Of course not," Scotty said. I wasn't entirely sure, but I think he may have rolled his eyes.

She looked back at me and flashed another bright smile. "So are you excited to join my show? It's a smash hit, you know. Some are even calling it a sensation. We're thrilled to have you on board."

I nodded and smiled too. "I'm really looking forward to it. Thanks so much for this opportunity, Wendy. I really appreciate it."

"Oh don't thank me, thank your boyfriend here." She gestured to Scotty. "If it were up to *me*, we would have gone with someone a bit more, shall we say, *seasoned*. No offense, of course."

Before I could respond, she turned on her heel and breezily headed toward the door. "Enjoy this lovely weather. See you at the office," she said over her shoulder.

I looked at Scotty. "Did that really just happen? How could she be so nice and…so *mean* at the same time? She *was* being nice and mean at the same time, right?"

"Indeed she was." He nodded.

"How did she manage to do that?"

He shrugged. "Maybe she's more talented than I thought."

I turned my head toward the exit and watched Wendy cross the street. "And was I imagining it, or does she dislike you even more than she dislikes me?"

"She dislikes us both, but you're straight, so she probably dislikes you less."

My jaw dropped. "She doesn't like you because you're *gay?*"

He nodded.

I reached over and squeezed his hand. "I'm sorry, Scotty."

"Oh don't worry about me, my dear. I've got a thick hide. It's not worth getting upset over."

I narrowed my eyes. "Are you sure? I get upset when anyone doesn't like me."

He laughed. "Really, Waverly, it's not a big deal. She's probably going to be meaner to you than to me anyway—you have nicer skin than she does."

Great.

● ● ●

"I think it's a brilliant idea. How did you come up with it?" Tad refilled my wine glass and set the bottle back in the ice bucket. It was a few evenings later, and we were on the roof deck of the posh building where Scotty and Tad, a sports agent, owned a spacious loft. They lived right by Madison Square Park in the Flatiron District, home to the famous building of the same name.

I took a sip of my wine. "I got the idea from a reader awhile back, actually. I could never quite figure out what to do with it for the *column*, but I thought it could be a fun segment for TV."

"I love it for TV," Scotty said as he sat down next to Tad. "Our viewers will love it too. In fact, if I weren't producing *Love, Wendy*, I might be tempted to use it myself for the *Today* show."

I pointed at him. "Hey now, don't go stealing my ideas. You've already made me paranoid enough about these horrible TV people."

He laughed. "They're not *all* bad. It's just that some of their egos outsize their talent, and that can get a little irritating."

I thought back to the days when I used to work in sports PR. At least there was no doubt that the prima donna athletes I had to deal with back then excelled at their chosen sport. I could only imagine how annoying it would have been to have to coddle them if they weren't even *good*.

My phone buzzed with a text message. "Hey, Kristina's here. Can we let her in?"

Tad stood up and headed toward the stairwell. "I'm on it." Tad already knew Kristina because one of his coworkers represented her husband, the Knicks star Shane Kennedy. Shane was the face for the basketball shoes of a former client of mine from my days when I worked at a big marketing firm, but he was far from a prima donna. He had a degree from Duke, perfect grammar, and not a single tattoo. He and Jake had been roommates in college, and he had introduced us at a trade show. For that act alone, I would forever be grateful to him.

As soon as Tad was out of earshot, I leaned toward Scotty. "I like him, Scotty. He's not at all what I expected, but I really like him."

He leaned toward me. "What did you expect?"

"I don't know exactly, but not *that*. I would hang on to *that* if I were you."

He kissed my cheek. "Look at you, giving *me* relationship advice. You're taking this *Honey on Your Mind* thing quite seriously."

"Apparently I am. But I'm off the clock right now. That was a freebie, my friend, just for you."

He laughed. "Well in that case, let me pay you back by pouring you some more wine. He stood up to retrieve the bottle, and I admired the sprawling roof deck.

"I can't believe you live here, Scotty. This place is unbelievable."

"I'm not complaining."

As he refilled my glass, I looked up at the sky. "You know, I have to say that I can't believe I'm wearing a tank top and shorts at seven thirty. Can we just take a moment to acknowledge how amazing that is?"

"It's the end of summer, Waverly. It's like this every night."

"I know, but I'd *totally* be wearing a ski jacket in San Francisco right now, maybe even gloves and a hat."

He held up his glass in a toast. "This is New York, my princess. As I've learned myself, there's a reason people never leave. But just wait until the day comes when you're literally sweating off your skin. You might change your tune then."

I jumped up when I saw Tad and Kristina walking toward us.

"Kristina! How are you? It's so great to see you." I gave her a big hug and led her by the hand to the table. "You know Scotty Ryan, right?"

She nodded. "Yes, of course, it's nice to see you again."

Scotty handed her a glass of wine. "Most people call me Scott, but I'm sure you probably figured that, given that I'm in my forties."

Kristina laughed. "I *did* figure that. I've gotten used to Waverly's nicknames."

I took a sip of my wine. "Hey now, don't be hating on the nicknames."

Kristina sat down next to me. "So how are you? I can't believe you're living in New York now. This is so exciting."

My eyes got big. "I know, isn't it? I have a brand new life! It may be the wine talking, plus the fact that it's eighty degrees out, but I think I may grow to love this place as much as San Francisco."

"Wait until winter," Scotty said. "Then we'll talk."

Tad put his hand on Scotty's knee. "You really need to get over the weather thing, babe."

"*I* reserve the right to complain about the weather, *you* reserve the right to wear those awful skinny jeans," Scotty said. "That's the deal."

Tad laughed and turned toward Kristina. "Shane's in Boston and Minnesota this week, right? Word on the street is they've got a phenomenal squad this season."

She sipped her wine and half-smiled. "They say that every year, don't they?"

"Only the die-hard fans," Tad said. "And the ticket sales department at Madison Square Garden, of course."

She laughed. "Of course. Actually, Shane *is* optimistic about some of the younger guys they brought over in that big trade in the off-season. He doesn't want to retire until he gets his ring, but I just hope he's not forty-five by the time that happens."

"Isn't it crazy how retiring at forty-five is considered incredibly late in professional sports, while it's unthinkable in pretty much everything else?" Tad said.

I raised my glass. "Don't forget Internet gazillionaires. Some of those guys can retire before they're old enough to rent a car."

"Ah, good point," Tad said, laughing.

"And child actors. Can't forget them," I added.

Kristina put her hand on my arm. "So Waverly, tell me more about your new gig. I'm excited to watch you on TV."

I leaned toward her but didn't lower my voice. "I can't get into any details because my, um, *boss* is in the immediate vicinity, but I'm hoping you'll find it entertaining. My first segment is going to air next week."

"Next week? Already?"

I nodded. "We begin taping on Friday."

"Wow, that was fast. Are you ready?"

"Ready as I'll ever be, and I can reshoot any mistakes until I get it right." I looked at Scotty. "Right?"

He nodded. "That's the beauty of prerecorded television."

I looked back at Kristina. "How much can I screw *that* up? Plus Scotty's going to be directing the crew, so he'll make sure I don't muck it all up."

She smiled and put her hand on my shoulder. "I love your new attitude. When I first met you, I guarantee you'd have been a basket case worrying about what could go wrong. It's great to see you so relaxed and confident."

I took a sip of my wine. "Thanks. I do feel relaxed, although I'd say *confident* is a stretch. But we'll see how relaxed I am when I have to appear on live TV."

"When will that be?"

"Next week. After we get the first segment wrapped, Wendy's going to bring me on as a guest to introduce *Honey on Your Mind* to the world. God knows how that's going to go. She's not exactly a fan of mine."

"You might want to tuck a can of mace in your purse that day," Scotty said as he got up to check the barbecue.

As soon as he walked away, Kristina leaned in and lowered her voice. "Are you carrying this new positive attitude over to your relationship with Jake?" Kristina was quite familiar with my unfortunate tendency to freak-out at inopportune moments, which had nearly ruined Jake and me more than once.

I nodded and smiled. "So far, so good." Then I quietly knocked my fist on the teak table. "Just to be safe, you know."

"That's my girl." She put her hand on my shoulder and squeezed.

On the way home later, inspired by the warm glow of both the moonlight and a couple of goblets of sauvignon blanc, I left Jake a voice mail:

"Hey you, it's me. I'm missing you lots tonight and just wanted to say hi. Here's a little something to make you miss me too."

I paused.

"What did the grape say when it got stepped on?"

I paused again.

"It let out a little whine."

chapter four

I must have woken up five hundred times the night before the taping. When my alarm finally went off at seven, I wondered how many total minutes I'd actually slept. I rushed through a shower, downed some coffee, and jumped onto the subway, mentally walking through the day ahead.

The plan was to meet Scotty and the camera crew at Bryant Park, nicknamed the town square of Manhattan. I'd heard it was a popular—and extremely scenic—spot tucked behind the New York Public Library in Midtown. And I'd heard right. As soon as I surfaced out of the subway station, I was taken aback by how pretty it was. The lush green grass formed a square in the middle of the park and was flanked by tall trees on two sides, all smack in the middle of Manhattan. Bars and cafes lined the northern and southern ends, and there were dozens of white chairs and tables for people to sit and enjoy it all.

"There…she…is…Miss…A…mer…ic…a…" Scotty sang as I approached.

"Am I late?" It looked like everyone else had arrived before me.

"Not at all, you're right on time." He pointed to what looked like a director's chair. "Why don't you jump in that so our makeup wizard Tanya can pretty you up for the cameras, and then we'll get started in a few minutes, OK?" He nodded his head toward a petite, pretty brunette standing next to the chair.

Scotty saw me glance at the enormous chest of makeup sitting on the ground near her feet, then spoke again before I could utter a word. "I know what you're probably thinking, but don't be offended. We *all* need to wear a truckload of makeup to look pretty on TV." He looked at Tanya. "Am I right?"

She smiled and nodded. "You're right."

He looked back at me. "See? There you have it from a professional. So are you ready for your debut?"

"I think so. I took your suggestion to practice my questions in front of the mirror. I felt a little ridiculous doing it, but I think it helped."

"Wonderful. Just relax and have fun, and you'll do great."

• • •

"So what did you think?" It was a few hours later, and the camera crew was putting away its equipment. I felt like we'd gathered enough footage for two feature films, even though my segment would be edited down to approximately four minutes.

"You're a natural, I told you," Scotty said.

I clasped my hands together. "Really?"

"Yep. I can't wait to see the final product, but I already know it will be great."

"So we turn it over to the editing team now?"

He nodded. "Exactly. They're magicians in that little room and will turn it into exactly what you hoped it would be. When that's done, they'll give you a shout to come in and tape the voice-over, but otherwise, you can start thinking about your next segment."

"Wow, this really does move fast."

"Yep, that's why it's not worth stressing over any particular segment, because another one is always coming down the tracks right at you."

"Thanks so much for your help, Scotty, I really appreciate it."

"Hey it's my job, sweetheart, or at least one of them." He looked at his watch. "That reminds me, I need to jet, or I'm going to be late for an interview I have to do for the *Today* show."

"Now? You're amazing. I can't believe you're producing *Love, Wendy* and reporting for the *Today* show too. You're like the Anderson Cooper of entertainment TV."

"Perhaps, but he's not as good looking as I am."

I laughed. "No one is."

• • •

"So how did it go?"

"It went well, or at least I think it did. I wasn't as nervous as I thought I'd be. Knowing we could do as many takes as we needed to get it right took the pressure off a little." I was walking down Montague Street a few blocks from my apartment later that afternoon, chatting with Andie on my cell phone.

"How many people did you interview?"

"You know, that's a good question. I honestly have no idea. It seemed like dozens. It's all kind of a blur, to be honest."

"So what happens now?"

"Editing. They'll take all the footage and turn it into something pretty. From what I've learned so far, it's like writing an entire book, and then cutting it down to one chapter."

"That sounds like a lot of wasted work to me."

I laughed. "I fear you may be right. But I'm sure I'll eventually learn how to be more efficient."

"So did you trip or fall or anything? Knock anyone over?"

"Andie!"

"I'm just asking. You know your track record."

"OK, you have a point. But for the record, *no*, I did not trip or fall, nor did I knock anyone over."

"It's early. You have time."

"Thank you for that. I really needed to hear that right now."

She laughed. "When can I watch it on TV?"

"Next week sometime. Wendy's having me appear live on her show to introduce the segment."

"Live? As in *en vivo*?"

"Live, as in *en vivo*."

"How do you feel about that?"

"How do you *think* I feel about that?"

"Knowing you, I'm guessing you're planning not to eat twenty-four hours ahead of time because you're afraid you might toss your cookies all over the stage."

I laughed. "It's scary how well you know me."

"Hey listen, I'd love to keep chatting, but I need to run. I'm getting a wart removed."

"Thanks for that visual."

"Anytime. See ya."

I was about to toss my phone into my purse when I noticed a new text from Jake:

About to get on plane but wanted to congratulate you on your first day in front of the bright lights. I bet you nailed it.

Even in the midst of NBA madness, Jake hadn't forgotten that I was hitting the streets today for the first time. I had to hand it to the guy. He knew how to make a girl smitten.

• • •

The week flew by in a flurry of shopping trips, subway rides, and people watching, which sometimes bordered on outright gawking because I couldn't always bring myself to look away. So much of life played out on the city streets here, and I was absolutely fascinated. I was doing my best not to get lost on foot *or* enter a train headed in the wrong direction, but so far I was failing on some front at least once a day.

Finally, it was time for my big debut. I was standing, hidden from view, on the edge of the *Love, Wendy* stage, trying not to shake. In a few minutes, Wendy would introduce me to the studio audience for the live show being broadcast in front of millions of people. She was in the middle of interviewing the latest YouTube sensation, some farmer from Arkansas who had trained his cat to ride one of his pigs, with a little saddle and everything. The cat, currently perched on the man's *head*, even wore a tiny cowboy hat. At least he hadn't brought the pig with him.

"Come on, come on," I said under my breath, afraid I would lose what little nerve I had if I had to wait any longer. After the way Wendy had ambushed me the last time we'd been on live TV together, I could only imagine what she had in store for me now. I pulled my phone out of my purse and looked at a text Jake had sent me the night before, after the basketball game. Because of our schedules, it had been a couple of days since we'd been able to connect on the phone, but he knew today was *the* day:

I have no doubt you're freaking out, but don't worry, you'll be great. You always are. Love you.

I smiled into the little screen. *I love you too.*

When I came out of my mini daydream, Wendy was thanking the cat guy. Then she cut to a commercial break.

The director looked at me. "OK, Waverly, you're up next."

I set my purse down and tried to smile, but my lips felt frozen, so I'm not sure how successful I was. "Thanks," I eked out weakly.

A few minutes later, the director cued the audience to applaud. Then he looked at me again and gestured for me to approach the side of the stage.

I nodded and took a step. Then out of the blue, I felt dizzy, and my stomach started lurching all over the place.

I froze, praying I wouldn't faint.

Or throw up.

Or both.

Holy freaking frick.

I took a deep breath and willed my legs to keep moving.

You can do this, Waverly.

As I neared the stage entrance, Wendy looked at the camera and flashed her beauty pageant smile. I froze again, waiting for my final cue.

"Ladies and gentleman, I'm delighted to introduce a *faaabulous* new addition to our show, a fun segment called *Honey on Your Mind*, hosted by a *faaabulous* woman named Waverly Bryson from San Francisco. I had the pleasure of meeting Waverly back in February when we appeared on the *Today* show together, and she recently agreed to move across the country just to join the *Love, Wendy* family! So let's give her a warm round of applause, shall we?"

She stood up and clapped, and the audience cheered along with her. I stood in my tracks until I heard the director say *Go.* Thank God, my legs obeyed.

Don't freak out. Don't freak out!

Hoping it wasn't obvious how rattled I was, I smiled and waved at the audience as I walked gingerly across the stage toward Wendy. She was still standing up in front of her plush couch, and when I reached her she air kissed me on both cheeks, something she'd never done before. I sat down next to her and smoothed my dress, then exhaled and interlaced my hands on my lap.

She smiled brightly, and for the first time ever, she actually looked interested in me.

"Waverly, I can't tell you how *thrilled* I am that you decided to join us. I just know our viewers are going to *adooore Honey on Your Mind.*"

I smiled back. "Thanks, Wendy, I'm honored and excited to be a part of the show."

She gestured toward the audience. "Before we unveil your first segment, can you give us a little background on how *Honey on Your Mind* came to be? I think it's such a fun story." I'd never seen her act so friendly, at least to me.

Maybe this won't be so bad. I smiled back at her and shifted in my seat. "Well, it all started with a line of greeting cards I created called *Honey Notes.* They're all-occasion cards for women to send each other, just for fun."

"Can you give us an example?"

I nodded. "Sure. One of my favorites says, THEY SAY LAUGHTER IS THE BEST MEDICINE? on the front, and the inside says, HONEY, TOSS IT IN WITH GIRLFRIENDS AND WINE, AND YOU'VE FOUND THE FOUNTAIN OF YOUTH."

"Oh, that's sweet," Wendy purred to the audience. "Isn't that sweet?" The audience *ahhhd.*

I sat up a bit straighter "But they're not all sentimental."

"They're not?"

I shook my head. "Nope, some of them are funny. For example, a popular one says, SO, HE DUMPED YOU? on the front, and the inside says, HONEY, HE WAS UGLY ANYWAY."

Wendy laughed, and then turned to the audience. "Who hasn't been *there*?" The audience erupted in laughter, and I wasn't sure if they were laughing at the Honey Note or Wendy's comment. But they sure seemed to be having fun, so I didn't care. Laughter was a whole lot better than silence.

Wendy looked at me again, still beaming. "So you started this fun line of greeting cards, and then what happened?"

I cleared my throat. "Well, the Honey Notes sort of took off, and then one day I got a call from the *San Francisco Sun* asking me if I wanted to write an advice column based on the cards. I decided to call it *Honey on Your Mind*, and well, fast-forward, and here we are."

She clapped her hands together. "I love it! What a *faaabulous* story." She looked out at the audience again. "Isn't that just *faaabulous*?" The audience cheered.

I smiled, finally feeling comfortable. "Thanks, Wendy."

She put her hand on my arm and winked, then turned toward the audience once more. "So what do you think, everyone? Are you ready to see what Waverly's done with *Honey on Your Mind* for TV?"

"Yes!" shouted the crowd.

"Are you *sure*?" Wendy said.

"Yes!" the audience shouted even louder.

I had no idea who *this* Wendy was, but there was no doubting that she was good. TV Wendy was very, very good.

"OK then, let's see it!" Wendy twirled her finger in the air and pointed behind her. An enormous flat-screen TV appeared out of nowhere. Suddenly, my smiling face came up on the screen. The first thing I noticed was that I had a huge underground zit on my forehead.

Darn.

I inhaled deeply and hoped for the best.

I also hoped no one noticed the zit. What a way to shatter a girl's confidence.

But then I was distracted by the familiar yet unfamiliar sound of my own voice.

"Hi, everyone, I'm Waverly Bryson, and I'll be hosting a semiregular feature for *Love, Wendy* called *Honey on Your Mind.* Given that I'm brand new to New York, I thought it would be great to kick off my first segment by approaching some real New Yorkers and asking *them* what's on their minds. Want to join me?" I pointed my thumb over my shoulder, and the camera followed me.

I walked about ten feet down the street, then proceeded to accost total strangers and ask them, literally, what was on their minds. I began each interview with this question:

"Hi there, I'm Waverly Bryson from the Love, Wendy *show with a new segment called* Honey on Your Mind. *Would you mind if I asked what's on* your *mind right now?"*

A fun montage of the responses followed, set to a background of Willie Nelson singing "You Were Always on My Mind" as I made my way from the crowded street through the park.

Guy in suit in line for coffee: "I'm wondering why the *bleep* you're in my face with that *bleeping* microphone. Scat."

Woman in dress standing in line behind first guy: "I'm thinking, why are all the good men married? And why are the people who work at Starbucks always so freaking happy?"

Skinny guy sitting on grass: "The *bleep*ing condom broke last night. *BLEEP!*"

Two girls lying on the grass: "We're thinking about how much we're loving this weather. We're supposed to be in class right now."

Another guy in suit on park bench: "Why hasn't she replied to my text?"

Guy in jeans sitting on bench: "What's on my mind? Bacon, dude, always bacon."

Guy selling roses: "Just ten dollars a dozen, special just for you, lady. You interested?"

Obese tourists on street: "Breakfast! We just *love* the food in New York. Do you know where TGIFriday's is? We heard there's a huge one around here."

Disheveled woman exiting subway: "You want to know what's on *my* mind, Whitney or Wanda or whatever you said your name is? Why do idiots shove themselves into the subway car while everyone else is still trying to get off? *That's* what's on my mind. *What the freaking hell is wrong with people?*" She stormed off.

By the time I finished the last interview, the background music had changed to the classic "Super Freak" by Rick James, which got louder as the segment ended. The entire studio audience was laughing, and some of them were even dancing in their seats. The camera panned back to me, and I signed off with the following:

"So there you have it, my new friends, a taste of what's on the minds of some *real New Yorkers*, who are apparently unconcerned with the ramifications of sharing their most intimate thoughts with a national TV audience. I'm already looking forward to our next segment as I continue to get to know this great city. Wendy, back to you!" I smiled and pointed at the camera.

The screen went black, and the crowd erupted in applause. I could feel my cheeks go bright red, but I felt happy and incredibly relieved. *That was actually pretty good.*

Wendy smiled and put her hand on my knee. "Waverly, that was just fabulous." Then she looked out at the audience. "Am I right? Isn't she *faaabulous*?"

"Yes!" shouted the audience.

"Should we bring her back for more?"

"Yes!" they shouted again.

Wendy turned back to me and beamed. "Well, my love, it looks like I'm not your only fan. I can't wait to see what you do for us next."

"Thanks, Wendy." I couldn't help but smile back at her. She seemed so sincere, so genuine.

Did she really like it?

Does she really like me?

Maybe I was wrong about her.

We broke for a commercial, and I glanced down for just a moment to take off my microphone.

When I looked back up, Wendy was gone.

• • •

"Well?" What did you think? Be honest." I could feel myself make an anxious face into the phone.

"It was awesome."

"Really?"

"*Really.* Well done, dearie."

I felt my whole body relax as I walked toward my apartment. "Thanks, Andie. You have no idea how happy you just made me."

"It was great. You made your hometown proud."

"I'm so glad the audience laughed. I was totally afraid that when they ran the tape there'd be nothing but silence in response...a deafening silence that screamed *You suck, Waverly!*"

She laughed. "Please. It was very entertaining, and the music was hilarious. What did that Wendy woman think about it?"

I shrugged. "You saw as much as I did. The second we broke for a commercial, she jetted off to God knows where, so I didn't talk to her before I left. It was sort of weird, actually. I thought she would have said *something*."

"She seemed to love it. She seemed to love *you* as well, which was odd given how she acted on the *Today* show."

"I know. That's why I'm keeping my guard up."

"What did Scotty say about it?"

"He wasn't there, so I'm not sure. I'll see him at the next taping, though, if I don't hear from him before then. It's crazy how busy he is. Actually, it's crazy how busy *everyone* in New York is. It's like nothing I've ever seen. The whole city is in constant motion."

My caller ID beeped. It was Jake.

"Oh man, case in point. I'm sorry, Andie, but I gotta run. Talk to you later?"

"Sure thing. I want to wax my arms before I leave for work anyway."

I laughed. "What did you just say?"

"You heard me. Bye."

I clicked over to Jake. "Hey, you!"

"Hey, TV star, nice work."

I smiled into the phone. "You saw it?"

"Wouldn't miss it."

"And?"

"You were great."

"Really?"

"Really. I laughed several times. I loved that bacon guy. He was my favorite."

"Me too. How can you not love a guy who loves bacon?"

"You looked like a knockout on camera, Waverly. Gorgeous, actually."

I could feel myself blush. "Thanks. I owe it all to the magicians in the makeup department. It's sort of scary what they can do with some pretty raw materials."

"So what happens next?"

"We're still working out all the kinks. They told me to prepare for a taping tomorrow, but it may get bumped if the crew is needed for something else. Eventually, I'll get used to this erratic schedule, but for now I feel like I'm standing on a skateboard." I put one hand out and bobbled back and forth as I walked. "By the way, you can't see me right now, but I'm pretending to stand on a skateboard."

"Nice visual."

I laughed. "Thanks. You can't see me right now, but I'm taking a little bow." I took a little bow.

"So listen, Miss TV star, I just found out that I have next weekend off. Do you think you could come down for a visit?"

I bit my lip. "Oh man, I'd love to, but..."

"But...?"

"But I feel like I should be here in case anything comes up, just because I'm still so new. I hope you understand."

"I do."

"I'm sorry, Jake."

"Don't worry about it. I just miss you. Not that I don't love listening to you tell jokes on my voice mail, but I prefer the real thing."

I stopped walking and put a hand on my hip. "I *knew* you loved my jokes!"

"I love the sound of your *voice*. Let's just leave it at that, OK?"

My call-waiting beeped again. It was McKenna, who, since having a baby, *never* had time to call.

"Hey, Jake, that's Mackie on the other line, and getting her on the phone is like pinning Jell-O to a wall, so I should take this. I'm sorry." I hated that I had to end our call so quickly. It happened too often.

"No worries, I should run too."

Suddenly I missed him desperately. "Maybe you could you come up here this weekend. I could roll out the blow-up mattress like old times."

He laughed. "Let me see about that. I'll look into it and let you know, OK?"

"Sounds good."

I clicked the phone again, still feeling like I was on a treadmill.

chapter five

The following Thursday, I was nearly home from the market when my phone rang. I somehow managed to dig it out of my purse without dropping my groceries. I unlocked the door to my apartment building and started up the stairs, juggling the bags and my purse with one hand. "Paige, hey, what's up?"

"Can you get on a plane to Chicago tonight?"

"What?"

"Chicago. You. A plane. Tonight. Can you do it?"

"Why?"

"A buyer for Jordan Brooke saw you on *Love, Wendy* yesterday and wants a meeting."

"Jordan Brooke? You're kidding." Jordan Brooke was a national department store.

"Not kidding. She wants to meet you, and she has tomorrow morning open. Can you meet me at JFK at six? There's a seven o'clock flight on Delta, we'll get in around nine."

I held my phone away from me to check the time. It was nearly three, and I was drained from shooting my latest segment that morning. I was enjoying *Honey on Your Mind* even more than I thought I would, but I hadn't realized how time-consuming and exhausting it would be. But Jordan Brooke was a big store, and I knew I'd be foolish to turn down a meeting with them.

"So we'll be there for just one night? Jake's coming in tomorrow for the weekend."

"Yep, in and out. You can be back home by dinner, I promise."

"Are the tickets going to be crazy expensive to buy last-min-ute?" I'd be paying for both of us.

"Sort of, but it will be worth it if she places an order. That's just how it is with sales. Everything's an investment."

"Got it."

"So I'll see you at six?"

"OK."

I hung up the phone, put away my groceries, and ran to pack.

• • •

"That didn't really happen."

"Oh yes it did."

"I still can't believe it. And you *paid* to meet him?"

She nodded. "I paid. A lot."

"Good God."

It was approaching eleven o'clock, and Paige and I were hav-ing our second drink at the hotel bar in Chicago. It was packed, and I found myself wondering where the others were from and why they were there.

"So what is this company called?" I leaned forward to hear her over the chatter around us.

"It's called *Just a Drink*, but after this experience I think I'm going to refer to it as *Just a Joke*."

I laughed. "That's good. So they really told you they would set you up with some quality men?"

She nodded and took a sip of her martini. "In my interview they talked about all the successful, professional men out there who are too busy to find love on their own. I think their tag line is some-thing like *YOU focus on your career, let US focus on your love life.*"

"That's catchy."

"I know, isn't it? What a load of crap." She stabbed the olive in her drink with a toothpick.

"They really told you he was a professor…and he turned out to be a *cab driver*?"

She nodded. "Apparently, in the eyes of the genius screeners at *Just a Joke*, teaching two mornings a week at a community college in the middle of nowhere qualifies you as a professor. A professor *in New York City,* they also said."

"Yikes."

"I mean, I want to be open-minded, but I figured they'd match me with someone with a similar professional background. That seems reasonable, right?"

"Definitely. What did they say when you told them he was a cab driver?"

"Nothing."

"Nothing?"

"Absolutely nothing. It's been ten days, and no return phone call or e-mail. Quite a contrast from how attentive they were when I was thinking of becoming a client."

"But that's so unprofessional!"

She waved her hand in front of her face. "They obviously don't care about being professional. They care about my check, which they already cashed."

I laughed. "I can't believe you let him drive you home from the date in his cab. What if he turned out to be a serial killer?"

She shrugged and finished off her drink. "He was nice enough, so I didn't want to be mean. I mean, it's not *his* fault that they set him up with me. And besides, as evidenced by our current circumstances, one never knows when one might need a ride to the airport in a pinch."

"This is true."

She stood up. "OK, Miss Honey Shop, finish that drink. We have an early meeting tomorrow."

I finished the last of my wine and set the empty glass on the bar. "Done."

"Lobby at eight?" she said.

"Lobby at eight."

We were about to walk away when the bartender approached us and set a full glass of wine in front of me. "Excuse me, ma'am, but the ladies at the other end of the bar would like to buy you a drink."

"Me?"

He nodded. "Yes, ma'am."

I looked toward the end of the bar and saw two heavyset women with short, poufy hair smiling and waving at me.

"Do you know them?" Paige asked.

I frowned. "I don't think so." *Do I know anyone in Chicago?*

"Well apparently they know you. Listen, would you mind if I headed up to my room? I'm beat."

"Of course not."

"Don't stay out too late, OK? We have to be at our best tomorrow."

I saluted. "Got it."

I picked up the wine glass and jostled through the crowd toward the other end of the bar. As I approached, the shorter of the two women stood up.

"Is it really you?" she asked.

I had no idea how to respond, so I just said, "Is it really me?"

"Yes, are you Waverly from *Love, Wendy*?"

Ah!

I smiled. "Yes, that's me. So you've seen the show?"

She nodded. "Oh *yes*, we never miss it! I'm Marge, and this is Evelyn." She held out her hand, and as I shook it, I couldn't help but notice her square, pink, acrylic fingernails. Then I shook Evelyn's hand. She wore her frizzy hair in a banana clip, and her square, pink, acrylic fingernails were even brighter than Marge's. The kindness in their faces struck me more than their appearance, however, and I immediately liked them both.

"I'm Waverly Bryson. It's nice to meet you."

"We're just tickled to meet *you*," Evelyn said. "We live in a small town called Chippewa Falls, way up in northern Wisconsin, so being in Chicago is exciting enough for us. But running into a *real celebrity*? This is just too exciting."

I laughed and put my hand on my chest. "A celebrity? Me?" *Ha.*

"Oh yes," Marge said, completely serious. "I recognized you right away. I turned straight to Evelyn here and said, 'Gosh darn, Evelyn, if that isn't the girl who does that fun new *Honey on Your Mind* segment for *Love, Wendy*.'"

Evelyn nodded. "We're both tickled to death to meet you. I *loved* the segment where you asked people what desserts were on their mind. But I couldn't believe no one said apple pie. Why didn't anyone say apple pie? That's so *un-American!*" She looked confused, as though I'd just told her Sarah Palin's grasp of English grammar could use a little work.

I pointed at her. "Now *that* is an excellent answer. It's too bad I didn't run into you on the street that day. You would have made a great interview subject."

She crossed her hands over her heart. "Me in New York City? Oh my, I don't think I could handle that." She looked at Marge. "Could you imagine? Me in New York City?"

"I loved the segment where you asked people what regrets were on their mind," Marge said to me. "It was just so...*honest.*"

She turned to Evelyn. "Didn't you just about cry when that woman said she regretted not telling her dad how much she loved him before he died?"

Evelyn nodded. "I cried. Then I called my dad. Right there from the couch."

Marge laughed. "So did I!" She put her hand on my arm and squeezed, then became very serious again. "You've got something really special on that show, Waverly."

I felt myself blush and had no idea what to say. I often thought of my segment as pure entertainment fluff, but these women were sincere...*fans*. And I was sincerely touched by their enthusiasm.

Maybe I do *have something special*, I thought.

Thankfully, Marge broke the silence. "What's it like working with Wendy Davenport? Is she as beautiful in real life? We think she's just wonderful."

I took a sip of my drink and nodded. I knew that if I said anything I was really thinking I'd completely burst their bubble *and* sound like a bitch, so I decided to change the subject. "She's great. So what brings you ladies to Chicago?"

"Oh, we're here for the big scrapbooking convention," Marge said.

"The big scrapbooking convention?"

Evelyn nodded. "You don't know it?"

I shook my head. *Huh?*

"No way. For real? But it's such a big show," Marge said. She looked incredulous.

I took another sip of my wine. "What is scrapbooking? Is that like putting together a photo album?"

They looked at each other as though I'd asked them who the president was.

Marge patted my arm and smiled. "My dear, comparing a scrapbook to a photo album is like comparing pastrami hash to corned beef hash. Can you imagine?"

Huh?

I feigned understanding because it was clear we were never going to be in the same book, much less on the same page. "Oh wow, I had no idea. I'm sorry. I hope I didn't offend you."

Evelyn laughed. "No offense taken, my dear. We wouldn't expect you New Yorkers to have the same hobbies that we do in the Midwest. You're all so fancy."

Me? A New Yorker? Am I a New Yorker now?

I started thinking about how much my life had changed— and all in a matter of weeks. New career, new city, new life.

It had all happened so fast.

"Waverly?"

I blinked. "I'm sorry, what did you say?"

Evelyn smiled. "So what about you? What brings you to Chicago?"

"Oh, I'm here for a meeting tomorrow morning with a buyer for a line of products tied into *Honey on Your Mind*." As soon as I said the words, I realized how late it was getting. If I was going to be sharp for the meeting, I really needed to get to bed.

Marge's eyes opened wide. "You have a line of products tied into *Honey on Your Mind*?"

I nodded. "It's called Waverly's Honey Shop. It's just online right now, but I'm working on expanding into regular stores. The meeting tomorrow is with Jordan Brooke."

Evelyn clapped her hands together. "Jordan Brooke? I love that store! I shop there all the time. I want to buy something from Waverly's Honey Shop."

"Me too," Marge said. "Our friends back in Chippewa Falls are going to be so jealous we met you. Do you have a card?"

I fished around in my purse and handed them each a card. Then I gestured toward the elevators. "I hate to drink and run, but I need my beauty rest if I'm going to be fresh for that meeting tomorrow morning. Would you mind if I said good night?" *Beauty rest? Did I really just say that?*

"Only if you take a picture with us first!" Marge pulled out a camera from her enormous purse, and I proceeded to pose for a few pictures.

For their scrapbooks, of course. Not their photo albums.

They hugged me good-bye and wished me well.

Then I hit the hay, Midwestern-style.

• • •

Lobby at eight meant *wake-up call at seven*, which came much too early for me, even with the time difference in my favor. I bolted upright and grabbed the receiver to stop the piercing ringing.

"Thanks," I said groggily to the automated voice, not sure why I was talking to a recording.

I hung up the phone and collapsed back on the pillow, wishing I hadn't had that extra glass of wine. It had been fun to meet real "fans" in Evelyn and Marge, but I needed to be sharp for the meeting, and I was feeling quite dull at the moment.

A steaming hot shower and two cups of coffee later, I felt much better as the elevator doors opened to the lobby. I exited and looked around for Paige. She was sitting in a plush chair near the bar area, scrolling through her phone.

"Hi, Paige, did you sleep OK?"

She shrugged as I approached, still looking at her phone. "Not great. Listen, I have some bad news."

"Uh oh, I don't like the sound of that."

She tossed her phone in her purse. "The buyer just canceled on us."

"What? Are you joking?"

"Not joking. Something came up, and she had to fly to Indianapolis last night."

I sat down in a chair next to her. "Last night? And they just told you now?"

She nodded. "Her assistant just e-mailed me."

"So we came all the way here for nothing?"

"Not necessarily. The buyer's scheduled to return this afternoon, so they're asking to move the meeting to four o'clock."

"Four o'clock?"

"Yep."

Frick.

Jake was flying into New York at seven.

Paige looked hopefully at me. "Can you stay? If we get on the seven o'clock flight, we'll be back in New York a little after ten."

"Do I have a choice?"

She smiled. "It's your company, but if I were you, I'd stay."

I knew she was right. But still, *ugh.*

I nodded. "OK, let's do it."

• • •

Several hours later, we were in a cab on the way to the meeting when Paige's phone rang. As she fished it out of her purse, I gazed out the window and admired the beauty of the crisp fall Chicago afternoon. The leaves were changing colors and swirling in the air all around us.

"Hello? Oh, hi, Amber, we're on our way to your office right now. What's up?"

Pause.

"Oh no, really?"

I snapped my neck around. *Oh no,* what?

Paige nodded. "I see."

I see what?

"Uh-huh, I understand."

"You understand *what*?" I whispered to Paige. She swatted me away.

"Let me check with Waverly." Paige covered the phone with her hand and looked at me. "The buyer isn't getting back from Indianapolis until late tonight now. She wants to meet us for brunch tomorrow."

"And her assistant is just telling us this *now*?"

Paige whispered, "I get the feeling she's not about to be promoted anytime soon," and pointed to the phone. "So what do you want to do? I know this is screwing up your weekend with Jake. I'm so sorry."

I slouched in my seat. "I can't believe this." Jake was having dinner with Shane and Kristina in Manhattan, but he was expecting to meet me at my apartment at eleven. I already felt terrible for making him wait a few hours.

"I know, and I'm really sorry, Waverly, but unfortunately this is how the business works. We're selling a product, which means we're at the mercy of the buyers, and they know it."

I sighed. "OK, fine."

"Fine?"

I nodded.

"You sure?"

I nodded again. "Yeah, it's OK. Let's meet her tomorrow. I have a ton more work e-mails to deal with today anyway." Maybe I could even take a nap before dinner. I couldn't remember the last time I'd taken a nap.

She smiled and squeezed my knee as she put the phone back to her ear. "Amber, are you still there? OK yes, brunch tomorrow will work."

I leaned toward the cab driver as Paige coordinated our plans for the next day with Amber. "Can you take us back to the hotel, please?"

• • •

"This is like *Groundhog Day*." I took a sip of my wine and set it on the bar. Paige and I were back at the crowded hotel a couple hours later, having a drink, and trying to stay positive.

She laughed. "At least the hotel didn't give away our rooms. It would *not* be fun wandering around Chicago looking for a place to stay on a Friday night. Can you imagine if we ended up at a scary Motel 6 in the middle of nowhere?"

I pointed at her and nodded. "True. I wonder if those scrapbooking ladies will find me again."

"You mean your *fans*?"

I laughed. "I admit it was a bit surreal, but they were super nice, despite the fact that they don't seem to realize it's not the eighties anymore."

"Yeah, it must be a trip to have total strangers recognize you like that."

"It was. It was like they felt they really knew me, even though they'd never even met me. It was strange. Can you imagine how *real* celebrities must feel?"

She sipped her drink. "It seems like a lot of people are watching *Love, Wendy*, so you're probably going to have to get used to it."

"I don't know if I could ever get used to it, to be honest."

"So things are cool with Jake?" I'd noticed that Paige asked me about him quite a bit, which always made me feel a little bad for her. It was obvious she really wanted to be in a relationship, so I didn't want to talk too much about how great mine was.

"Yeah, but I feel awful that he's in New York right now and I'm still here. He knows it's not my fault, but I could tell he was disappointed." At least I'd been able to reach him with my latest change in plans before he boarded his flight. "He's going to stay with friends tonight, and he and I will meet up tomorrow for dinner. It's not ideal, but at least I'll still get to see him."

"He sounds like a good one, Waverly."

I smiled and nodded. "Yeah, he's great."

"I think I'm done with trying to find the right guy for me. Dating is just too painful." She took another sip of her drink and sighed.

I put my hand on her shoulder. "Hey now, don't think that way. You sound exactly like me, before I met Jake."

"I do?"

"Just ask your cousin. Remember those crazy dating stories I told you when we first met?"

She nodded.

"Those are just a few of like…a billion. I was *convinced* I'd be alone forever. So trust me, there are good guys out there. If *I* could find one, anyone can."

She sighed again. "I'm just sick of it, you know? Every time I get my hopes up, I'm inevitably disappointed, or I get hurt, or both. Here I am in my midthirties, and I'm still dealing with awkward first dates. I just never thought I'd still be alone at this age."

I looked at her and remembered how many times I'd said something similar, if not those exact words, to Andie and McKenna. With so many people in the world, why was finding just *one* to love who will love you back so hard?

Suddenly I wanted to talk to Jake. I also felt like giving Paige a hug but decided otherwise. I didn't want her to think I felt sorry for her or that there was anything wrong with being single, or with her not *wanting* to be single. She was smart and kind and funny. She would find someone who deserved her eventually, wouldn't she?

I wished I knew for sure.

I stood up from the barstool. "I'll be right back, OK?"

She nodded, and I walked to a quiet part of the lobby. I pulled out my phone and called Jake's number. It went straight to voice mail.

"Hey, Jake, uh, I know you're still on the plane, but I just wanted to say...I love you. I...I love you lots. Uh, OK, I guess that's it. Oh, this is Waverly. Bye."

I hung up and cringed slightly, wondering if I'd ever get any better at leaving voice mails.

When I got back to the bar, Paige was chatting with a tall man with sandy brown hair and broad shoulders.

"Hi," I said as I approached.

The man turned around, and I was struck by how attractive he was. He was rugged and chiseled and looked like an Abercrombie & Fitch model, or, rather, like the father of an Abercrombie & Fitch model, most of whom looked about sixteen.

"Well hello there, I'm Gary." He held out his hand for a firm shake. "I'm in town from Nashville."

"I'm Waverly. It's nice to meet you."

I quickly peeked at the ring finger on his left hand, which was bare. Then I looked at Paige, who had seen me do it and smiled knowingly as she handed me a full glass of wine. "Gary just ordered us another round. Wasn't that nice of him?"

I took the glass and smiled back. "Thank you, yes, that was very nice of you."

Gary held his glass up to ours for a toast. "Here's to new friends in new places."

We clinked our glasses against his. "So what brings you to Chicago?" I asked.

"Business meetings. I'm in sales, nothing too exciting. I was just telling Paige that I'd love to take her to dinner tonight, but she said she couldn't leave her friend. So what do you say? There's a world-class steak house just a couple doors down from the hotel, and I'd be honored to treat you both." He spoke with a Southern drawl that was slight enough to be charming yet not distracting. He reminded me of Blake Shelton.

I stole a quick glance at Paige, who nodded quickly. Then I regained eye contact with Gary. "Um, sure, why not? We don't have any pressing plans tonight, do we, Paige?"

"I don't think so." She said the words casually, but there was a spark in her eye I'd never seen.

Gary tapped his palm on the bar. "Well then, it's settled. Tonight Nashville is taking New York out on the town in Chicago."

"Sounds like a plan," Paige said.

I sensed I had a long night ahead.

• • •

By the time dessert came, I was a little buzzed and a lot exhausted. I took a bite of flourless chocolate cake and wished I were up in my room. I felt like we'd been at the restaurant for hours, but Paige was clearly having a ball. Gary was super charming, not to mention super attractive, so I was determined to hang in there and be a good wingman for as long as she needed me.

Until then.

Gary held up his wine glass. "So, are you ladies up for a drink back at the hotel? Maybe some dancing?"

I looked up from my plate and tried not to laugh. "Did you just say *dancing*?" There was *no way* I was going dancing.

Paige nodded. "A drink back at the hotel sounds like fun. Count me in. As for the dancing, we'll have to see."

"Atta girl." Gary said to her, and then looked at me. "What about you, Waverly, are you in for another round at the hotel?"

I shook my head. "Thanks, but I'm beat. I think I'm going to head up to my room and crash."

"Are you sure? It's still so early." Paige gave me a look feigning disappointment, but I knew she didn't care. And why would she? Gary was, well, *hot*. I had a boyfriend I loved dearly, but Gary was still hot.

It was definitely time to cut the wingman loose.

I yawned and thought about all the e-mails I still needed to deal with in the morning for *Honey on Your Mind*. "I know it's early, but I'm exhausted and have a lot of work to do. If I want to make a decent impression at brunch tomorrow, I need to go to bed."

Paige laughed. "Andie told me you need your fourteen hours of sleep."

I nodded. "That girl knows me well."

Gary paid the bill, and the three of us walked back to the hotel. I said good-bye in the lobby and proceeded to follow my own instructions: I went upstairs and crashed.

• • •

I slept like a corpse, and by the time I met Paige in the lobby at ten thirty, I'd already showered, scanned the paper, answered a bunch of reader e-mails, and spoken to Jake on the phone. I was quite proud of myself for being so productive on a Saturday.

Paige, on the other hand, didn't look so perky when she arrived.

"Ouch, you don't look so good."

She nodded. "I'll take that. I slept two hours."

"Two hours! Are you serious?"

"Shhh, not so loud." She took off her sunglasses and sat down in a chair next to me.

I lowered my voice. "What happened?"

She smiled.

"Well?"

"We ended up having a couple of more drinks at the bar, and then we went dancing at some club downtown, and then..." her voice trailed off.

"And then what?"

She smiled again.

"You hooked up with him?"

She nodded. "Nothing too serious, though. He was a complete gentleman."

"Nice! He's super dreamy."

She kept nodding. "Isn't he?"

"Is he still here?"

She shook her head. "He left early this morning for the airport. *But*, he's coming to New York next week for work, so we're going to meet up then."

"That's great, Paige. He seems like a nice guy. I love his Southern manners." I was so excited for her. If anyone needed a nice guy with manners, it was Paige.

She put her sunglasses back on. "I do too. Maybe that's been my problem all along. I've been casting my rod for New York men, when apparently I should have gone fishing in the South all along. They're like a different species, you know?"

Jake was from Florida. I knew.

We gathered our things and headed out for our brunch, which I half-expected would be canceled en route.

• • •

Finally, the meeting happened.

From our seats at the table, Paige and I watched a woman enter the restaurant and approach us.

She was fifteen minutes late.

Rebecca Clark was a senior buyer at Jordan Brooke. From what Paige had told me about her, she was powerful, had great instincts, and was highly regarded within the industry.

In other words, she was a big shot.

She also wasn't anything like I expected.

Disheveled and out of breath, she rushed to the table and sat down.

"Ladies, I'm so sorry to be late, and I'm *so sorry* for being so hard to pin down. I hate when people cancel on me, and I can't apologize enough for doing it to you twice. And in the same day! Goodness me." She shook each of our hands, then immediately

reached for a croissant and began to butter it. "It's just so unprofessional, and I'm mortified. Just mortified. And as for my tardi-
ness this morning, let's just say my kids are going to get an earful
when I get back to the house. Again, I apologize." She took a bite
of croissant and sighed. I tried not to laugh.

This *is the senior buyer who had me so nervous?*

"Don't worry, we completely understand," Paige said. "These
things happen."

I nodded. "Of course. It's completely fine. It's so nice to meet
you, Rebecca."

"Oh please, call me Becca." She smiled, and I couldn't help
but notice that a flake of croissant was clinging to her lip. She
looked at me. "I'm so glad you could stick around for an extra
day. I'm a huge fan of *Love, Wendy,* and when I saw you wearing that adorable T-shirt during your segment, I just knew it was
something our customers at Jordan Brooke would really like."

"Which one was I wearing?"

"It was pink, and it said I KNOW NOTHING, BUT AT LEAST I
KNOW THAT. Delightful!"

I laughed. "Ah, yes, I like that one too." *And it's true. If I
learned anything each day of my life, it was that I pretty much
knew nothing.*

After the waiter took our order, Paige leaned down and
pulled out her huge binder. She removed a laminated sales sheet
with photos of all my Honey Tees and handed it to Becca, who
wiped her hand on her napkin before taking it. The flake of croissant still lingered on her lip.

Becca nodded as she looked over the sales sheets. "I love it.
These are great."

Paige proceeded to pull out sales sheets for the other Honey
products, and as Becca looked over them, I stared at the flaky

chunk, just dangling there like a child's loose tooth. It was a good distraction for me, because I honestly wasn't sure what else I should do. The two of them were engrossed in conversation, chatting in retail jargon that sailed right over my head. Paige may have been running on fumes, and Becca was hardly a model of panache, but both of them clearly knew their stuff. I was impressed.

After defying gravity for several minutes, the remaining croissant finally fell off, and shortly thereafter, the waiter returned with our meals. As Becca cut up her French toast, she looked at me, and then Paige, and then back to me. She didn't speak but looked like she was about to, so we remained silent.

Finally, she took an enormous bite, so I did the same with my omelet. The moment my mouth was full, she spoke.

"Waverly, to be frank, dare I say you've got something special here."

I swallowed as fast as I could and drank some water. "You think so?"

"I do indeed." She took another enormous bite of French toast and nodded. A tiny droplet of maple syrup attached itself to her chin.

I glanced at Paige, who nodded quickly and winked.

Then Rebecca "Becca" Clark, respected senior buyer at Jordan Brooke, made clear her intention to place my first official retail order.

A significant order to begin in the new calendar year.

Waverly's Honey Shop was officially open for business.

• • •

On the way home from the airport later that day, my phone rang. It was Scotty.

"Hi, Scotty, what's up?"

"Hey, sugar, listen, I need you to tape a segment tomorrow. I just found out they're having a jam and marmalade street fair on the Upper East Side, and I think it would be good to have our resident Honey expert there. Apparently, several local honey makers have booths."

"There's an entire street fair dedicated to *jam and marmalade*? Are you joking?"

"This is New York, my dear. We have street fairs dedicated to people who have rabbits as pets."

I laughed. "OK, fine. What time do I need to be there?"

"Can you do eight? Jeff will meet you there with a camera."

"Eight in the *morning*? What kind of street fair starts at eight in the morning?"

"Jam and marmalade people are early risers. They make breakfast food, you know."

I did the math in my head. Getting to the Upper East Side by eight meant I'd have to wake up by six, if not earlier, to shower and get camera-ready.

Ugh.

"OK, I'm in."

"Beautiful, beautiful. Thanks."

I hung up, closed my eyes, and leaned back into the seat of the taxi.

Things were definitely moving forward in a good way, but I was exhausted.

● ● ●

By the time I finally met up with Jake that evening, it was nearly time for me to go to bed again.

"A jam and marmalade street fair? For real?" Jake finished the last bite of his steak. We were at Jack the Horse Tavern, a popular restaurant on Hicks Street not too far from my apartment. I'd wanted to celebrate my first real "account" with a fancy dinner, but I was fighting just to stay awake. And I was already stressed about having to get up again at the crack of dawn.

"For real. I've given up asking questions. Now I just go where I'm told." In the two months since I'd arrived, I'd shot footage for *Honey on Your Mind* at a tiny dog show, a cupcake bakery, a brewery, and a store that sold items made only out of licorice. Some we never used, but much of it had been well received. Scotty and the production crew clearly knew what they were doing, so I'd quickly learned to just go with it.

"Should I come with you?" Jake asked.

I looked up from my plate. "You want to come with me?"

"Yeah, why not? It'll be fun to see you in action. Plus you know what they say, a real man can never have enough marmalade in his pantry."

I laughed. "But what if I choke?"

"You won't choke."

"But what if I get all nervous and flustered because I know you're watching?" I pointed at him. "You know my unfortunate history of getting nervous and flustered around you."

He smiled and put his hands up. "OK, OK, I won't go."

Suddenly, visions of my earlier standoffish behavior toward him, back when we were first getting to know each other, flashed before my eyes. I didn't want to make that mistake again.

"You know it's not that I don't want to spend time with you, right?" I said quickly.

"Of course I do."

"Because I totally want to spend time with you, I really do."

He motioned for the check. "It's OK, really, I know. Don't worry, I'll find something else to do. Maybe I'll play tourist and check out Times Square or the Empire State Building."

I did the math in my head. If I was gone all morning that would mean I'd cut our "weekend" together down to one dinner at which I'd been half-asleep.

Suck it up, Waverly.

"How about you come, but maybe you could promise to stay...like a hundred blocks away during the taping?" I smiled weakly and awaited his reply.

He laughed and scratched his eyebrow. "Did you just say *a hundred blocks away?*"

I held up two fingers. "Or how about we agree on *two* blocks away? Two blocks should provide me with a freak-out-free buffer zone."

"Make it one and you have a deal."

I paused for a moment, then reached across the table and shook his hand. "Done."

"You drive a hard bargain, Miss Bryson."

"I could say the same thing about you, Mr. McIntyre."

He held on to my hand and smiled at me, and when I looked into his blue eyes, I stopped thinking about marmalade. I also stopped being tired.

I pulled his hand to one side of the table without letting go. "You ready to get out of here?"

"I thought you'd never ask."

• • •

When my alarm went off at six the next morning, I knew exactly how Paige had felt the day before. Hooking up with a hot guy until the wee hours is awesome…until the sun comes up and it's time to face real life.

I sat straight up in bed and reached to turn off the alarm, and then put my face in my hands.

Good lord, I'm exhausted.

My face is going to look puffy on camera.

Holy frick, I'm tired.

Jake put his hand on my lower back. "You doing OK?" His voice was soft and warm.

My face was still in my hands. "I'm so tired, Jake," I whispered. "How do people survive on so little sleep?"

"You'll get used to it. You're playing in the big leagues now."

I kept my face in my hands. "I don't think people who need nine hours of sleep last very long in the big leagues."

I would have gladly ironed everything in my closet to be able to sleep for three more hours, but I knew the show must go on, literally, so I dragged myself out of bed. Jake, who was apparently immune to sleep deprivation, made us coffee and went downstairs to retrieve the paper while I showered. I'd grown to love reading the Sunday *New York Times* on the couch in my pajamas, but that clearly wasn't going to happen today.

We were out the door by seven.

chapter six

Scotty's street fair idea was a hit with the loyal viewers of *Love, Wendy,* who flooded us with thanks for giving them a fresh slice of life in New York City. Unfortunately, however, that success meant that suddenly I was working every weekend, when most street fairs take place. Before I knew it, I'd covered the Puerto Rican Day Parade, Oktoberfest, the Great Third Avenue Fair, the Times Square Autumn Carnival, the Brooklyn Flea, and the Union Square Autumn Fair. And that was just on weekends. During the week we'd also continued our man-on-the-street interviews at the hockey rink at Chelsea Piers, the zoo in Central Park, Coney Island, the new World Trade Center site, and Governor's Island.

It was fun, but with everything going on with both *Honey on Your Mind* and Waverly's Honey Shop, I felt like I was living on a conveyor belt. The days flew by, and before I knew it, I'd gone nearly a month without speaking to Andie or McKenna. New-mom McKenna probably didn't even notice, but Andie had left me at least two voice mails, maybe even three. Between tapings, meetings, managing online product orders, schlepping them to the post office, and dealing with reader e-mails, it was all I could manage to try to speak to Jake each night before collapsing into bed, and sometimes I wasn't even able to do that. Throw in the three-hour difference between New York and San Francisco, and I could never find the right time, much less the energy, to call anyone back. I couldn't even remember the last time I'd spoken to my own dad.

Finally, one unusually quiet Wednesday night, I sat down on the couch, picked up the phone, and called Andie.

"Hello?"

"Hey, it's me."

"I'm sorry, but I think you have the wrong number. I don't know anyone named *me*."

"Andie…"

"Who is this again? I don't have this number programmed into my phone."

"C'mon, Andie. Throw me a bone here."

She laughed. "OK, OK. Bone thrown."

"I'm sorry, I totally suck. I know I suck."

"It's all right. I know you've been crazy busy getting rich and famous. Are you having fun?"

I looked at the boxes of Honey products stacked around my living room. "Hmm. Fun? I'm not sure I'd call it that yet. I could call it *exciting* maybe, but *fun* would be a stretch because I'm stressed out and exhausted, and you're not supposed to be stressed out and exhausted if you're having fun, right? Plus, I think stressed out and fun might be mutually exclusive. Are they mutually exclusive?"

"Good lord, girl. Chill. Deep breaths, deep breaths."

I laughed and leaned back into the couch. "I'm sorry. I think I'm losing it. You know how much sleep I need, and it's just not happening right now."

"How many hours a night are you getting?"

I yawned and scrunched up my face. "Six? Maybe seven on a good day?"

"For real? You can't survive on six hours."

"Tell me about it. I think I'm keeping the local coffee shop in business."

"At least you're contributing to the economy. Look at it that way."

"Ha. Soon I'll be putting their kids through college. So tell me about *you*. I'm sick of me. What's new out there? What's going on with Nick?"

"Nick is good."

"Are you guys good? Is he still the funniest man I've ever met?" Andie was dating my former coworker Nick Prodromou, a quick-witted teddy bear with a huge heart.

"He's good, we're good, and yes, he's still funny. He made Diet Coke come out of my nose the other night."

"Again?"

"Again. He was doing his Chewbacca voice. It gets me every time."

"Awesome. I miss that guy." Andie never exercised but she had told me she was getting a six-pack from laughing so hard all the time.

"He misses you too. He's always asking when you're going to come back to visit the little people who knew you way back when. He thinks you've forgotten us already."

"Yeah, like I could ever forget you guys. I can't believe he makes you laugh so hard that Diet Coke comes out of your nose. Do you know how lucky you are?"

"Tell me about it. *I* can't believe I have a boyfriend. It's so not *me*. You know what I mean?"

"I totally know what you mean. But having a girlfriend is so not *him* either, which is what makes you two perfect for each other."

"I keep thinking I'm going to freak out and run."

"Please don't, Andie. He's great."

"I know he is. But you know me and commitment."

"Stop it. You're *not* going to freak out and run."

"He asked me to move in with him."

I sat up straight. "*What?*"

"Yep."

"When?"

"Last week."

"What did you say?"

"I told him I'd think about it. I mean, agreeing to date exclusively is one kind of commitment, but giving up a rent-controlled apartment is on a whole different level. Am I right?"

I nodded into the phone. "You're totally right. That's practically like getting married!"

"I know! I mean, what if it doesn't work out? What if he starts acting like a vagina and I have to bail?"

I coughed. "What?"

"You heard me. My policy is that there's only room for one vagina in my house, and it belongs to me."

I laughed. "You have a *policy* for that?"

"Yep."

"You kill me."

"I'm just being real. You know my job requires client dinners and evening events several times a week, and Nick can be a little whiny about my schedule sometimes. I don't know if I could deal with that twenty-four/seven. I love him to death, but when he starts acting like a girl, God help me, I want to pop him one."

I laughed again. "I have no idea how to respond to that."

"If he gets too clingy and I have to pull the rip cord, where does that leave me? Without a place to live, that's where."

"Would he consider moving in to your place?"

"No way. My apartment is too small for two people. If a big guy like Nick moved in here, he'd break something within the hour. Then I'd *definitely* kill him."

"So when are you going to decide? This is huge!"

"I'm not sure. I was thinking maybe I'd come visit you for a girls' weekend to help me think about it. Are you around the weekend before Christmas? It would be sweet to celebrate my birthday in New York."

I jumped up from the couch and practically shouted into the phone. "Yes! Come to New York! Come to New York!" I didn't realize until that moment how much I missed her, how much I missed home, how much I missed just hanging out with her and McKenna on a regular basis.

"Down girl. I need to check flights first."

"I wish you could come earlier, before it gets too cold. Actually, what am I saying? It's *already* too cold for my blood." The only good news about the impending seasonal shift was that the colder the weather got, the fewer outdoor events there were for me to cover. Unfortunately, however, the minute a weekend opened up in my schedule, Paige invariably pounced on it and roped me into some apparel tradeshow or industry event. But as far as I knew at that moment, the weekend before Christmas was still open.

• • •

The next evening I had plans to grab a drink with Paige before heading uptown to meet Kristina for dinner. It was purely a social call, which was exactly what I needed. I was so burned out that I thought I might toss my cookies if the word *honey* even came up in the conversation.

I arrived at Harry's a few minutes early and ordered a beer, then sat down at a high table. As I looked around the bar, I realized it didn't feel new to me anymore. The unfamiliarity had faded away, a shift in perception so gradual that I hadn't even noticed until right now. The place had become a somewhat regular hangout for Paige and me, and she had become much more familiar to me—and much more than a sales rep. I'd met many people since moving to New York, but Paige was becoming a true friend.

At seven sharp, I saw her walk through the door.

With Gary from Nashville by her side.

No way.

I knew she'd seen him once after our trip to Chicago, but she hadn't mentioned him since then, so I figured that was it.

Apparently, I was wrong.

"Hi, Waverly, how are you?" she gave me a hug as I stood up. "You remember Gary, right?"

I held out my hand and smiled. "Of course, Gary from Nashville. How could I forget that yummy steak dinner in Chicago? How are you?"

He laughed. "I'm doing great, happy to be in town to see this pretty young thing here." He put his arm around Paige, who was about Andie's height, which, on a good day, was barely five foot two. "Can I get you a drink?" he said.

I held up my nearly full beer and shook my head. "I'm good, thanks."

"OK, I'll be right back." He walked to the bar, and I immediately turned to Paige and lowered my voice.

"So things are good?" I practically mouthed the words so Gary wouldn't hear me.

She grinned and nodded.

"Wow," I whispered.

"I know," she whispered back. "He's super cute, isn't he? What's he doing with *me*?"

I shooed her away. "Please, you're super cute too."

Gary reappeared with beers for himself and Paige, and we quickly switched to a more appropriate topic of conversation.

"So Waverly, Paige tells me she's been quite busy running this product line of yours. From what I hear, it's about to take off."

I took a sip of my beer and smiled. "I guess we'll see. I would be lost without Paige. I don't know how she keeps track of all her clients. I can barely keep track of myself. She's amazing."

He put his hand on her shoulder. "Yes, she is certainly that." His deep voice was undeniably sexy. What is it about that twang that makes a girl go a little weak at the knees?

"So what brings you to town?" I asked.

"A few sales meetings, nothing too exciting. I don't want to bore you with work talk."

Was that what he said when we met him in Chicago? I tried to remember. He'd said something about boring meetings then, but hadn't elaborated on exactly what they were. A tiny warning bell rang in a far corner of my brain. There was no denying his charisma, but he almost seemed too good to be true.

"Waverly? Are you there?" The sound of Paige's voice snapped me back to the present.

I looked at her. "Huh?"

She gave me a funny look back.

"I'm sorry, I spaced. What did you say?" I turned to Gary.

"I asked if you're missing San Francisco. When we met, you mentioned that you're a recent transplant from California."

"Yes and no. It's sort of strange, really. I never thought I'd leave San Francisco, much less California, but now that I live in New York, I realize that you can love living in more than one place, even if they're totally different. I'm not sure how much sense that makes. Does that make sense? I'm sorry, I'm a little spacey tonight."

He laughed. "That makes a great deal of sense. Is your family still out there?" The kind look in his eyes made me feel bad for thinking he might be sketchy. I took another sip of my beer and told myself to get a grip.

"Well, my only real family is my dad, and yes, he's still out there. He lives in Sacramento." The mention of my dad made me realize again how long it had been since I'd talked to him. I made a mental note to give him a call.

"Good for you for being adventurous. I love New York and have always wanted to try living here, but I can't leave Nashville, at least not now."

I looked at Paige. *I can't leave Nashville?*

"Gary's youngest is in high school," she said.

"Oh." I had no idea what to say.

"It's complicated," Gary said.

"Oh," I said again, suddenly feeling awkward. Was he separated? Divorced? How many kids did he have? Would it be appropriate to ask? Call me sheltered, but I'd never really hung out with anyone who'd been separated *or* divorced, much less with kids on top.

Mercifully, Paige changed the subject. "So, Waverly, I know you're swamped these days, but I need you on a plane again." As she spoke, Gary excused himself to use the restroom.

I raised my eyebrows. "Somewhere exciting, I hope." Our last couple of trips had certainly been lacking in the glamour department. Central New Jersey and upstate New York? Enough said.

"How do you feel about Cleveland?"

"Cleveland? As in...*Cleveland*?"

She laughed. "The one and only. I have a buyer for Bella's Boutique who wants to see your line, and she specifically wants to meet you."

"She specifically wants to meet *me*?"

"Yes."

"Why? You know the products as well as I do now."

Paige laughed. "Hello? You're a minor celebrity, Waverly. A lot of women out there watch *Love, Wendy*. Or have you forgotten that?"

I looked at her. "Do *you* watch *Love, Wendy*?"

"Me?"

I nodded.

"No."

I pointed at her. "See? You don't watch it. Andie and McKenna don't watch it. Kristina doesn't watch. Even *I* don't watch it. *That's* my reality, which is why it's so weird for me to hear that yet another complete stranger wants to meet me. I've lived in New York for...how long now?" I held up a hand and counted the months on my fingers. "Three months? And in that time, how many times have I been recognized on the street by someone who lives here?"

"How many?"

I collapsed my fingers around my thumb. "Zero."

"Really? Never?"

I shook my head. "Not once. Anytime I get recognized, it's always a tourist from somewhere like...Cleveland."

She laughed. "So can you go?"

"When would we leave?"

"Can you do Thursday afternoon for a Friday late-morning meeting?"

I pulled my day planner out of my purse and flipped through it. "Yes, I'm not taping on Friday, so that should work."

"Good, because you know what *else* is happening in Cleveland on Friday?"

"In Cleveland? I have absolutely no idea."

"Guess."

"Um, pumpkin festival?"

"Nope."

"Quilt fair?"

She shook her head. "Try again."

I held my hands up. "Hog parade?"

She laughed. "Try the Atlanta Hawks versus the Cleveland Cavaliers."

My eyes opened wide. "No way!"

"Indeed. *Now* how do you feel about a trip to Cleveland?"

I smiled at the thought of seeing Jake...at the thought of spending an entire night with him. "Why Paige Murphy, I *love* the idea of a trip to Cleveland."

"I thought you would. I'm excited to meet this Jake you're always talking about. You think he can hook us up with some tickets?"

"I would think so. Are you a basketball fan?"

"I'm a fan of anything that involves athletic men in shorts."

I laughed and held up my drink. "That sounds like something your cousin would say. Oh my God, that reminds me. She's coming to visit!"

"Really? When?"

"The weekend before Christmas, for her birthday. I'm so excited. I haven't gone this long without seeing her since we were in college. I'm totally going through Andie withdrawal."

She laughed. "Be careful. That girl is a whole lot of trouble in a very small package."

"Oh, believe me, I know. Why do you think I love her so much? Are you around that weekend? You've got to come out with us if you are. I know she'd love to see you."

She lowered her voice and leaned toward me. "I'm not sure yet. Gary and I are planning to spend a weekend up in Vermont sometime in December."

"Really? I've never been to Vermont, but isn't that supposed to be, like, the most romantic place *ever* in December?"

She nodded. "He's incredible, Waverly. I mean I know we've only seen each other a few times, but he's completely different from any other guy I've dated. He just makes me feel so...so...I don't know...*connected*. Does that make sense?"

I loved her choice of word. It was exactly how Jake made me feel. *Connected*.

I smiled. "That makes complete sense, Paige. I'm so happy to hear that."

"Happy to hear what?" We both turned our heads at the sound of Gary's voice.

I coughed. "Oh, nothing, I was just telling Paige about, um, about a nice e-mail I got from, um, a fan the other day."

"A fan?"

Paige nodded. "Waverly's a celebrity."

I laughed. "Hardly."

Gary looked interested. "A celebrity? Really? How did I not learn this in Chicago?"

I shrugged and took a sip of my beer. *Because you and Paige were flirting too much with each other to ask me any questions.*

"Believe me, I'm *not* a celebrity," I said.

"Celebrity." Paige put her hand on my shoulder and nodded. "Just ask the folks in Cleveland."

"Not a celebrity." I shook my head. "So hey, I know this is totally changing the subject, but I have a question for you guys."

"Still a celebrity," Paige said. "So what's the question?"

I leaned toward them. "I was on the subway earlier today and noticed this girl with a huge nose ring, and all I could think was *How in the world does she blow her nose?* I mean, how does that *work?*"

Paige laughed. "You're nuts, Waverly." Then she turned to Gary and put her hand on his arm. "We were just chatting about our next trip for Waverly's Honey Shop. We're off to Cleveland after you ride your white horse back to Nashville." I'd never seen her flirt like this before.

I coughed. "*We're off to Cleveland after you ride your white horse back to Nashville?* That sounds like the name of a bad country song." I closed my eyes for a moment and pretended to play the guitar.

Gary laughed. "I like you, Waverly from San Francisco. You've got spunk."

I smiled and held up my glass to his. "I like you too, Gary from Nashville."

• • •

The next morning, the entire *Love, Wendy* crew had a planning meeting at NBC. Wendy attended it, but arrived a few minutes late, looking a bit disheveled. That woman had never looked disheveled in all the time I'd known her, but today she just looked...*off*. Even her helmet hair was droopy. She sat down next to me at the far end of the conference table. I briefly took in her unusual appearance, and then turned my attention back to Scotty at the front of the room.

"So the powers that be at NBC have chosen December twelfth, at the lovely New York Athletic Club on Central Park South. If you have a conflict, that is unfortunate, because I believe the contract has already been signed, sealed, and delivered. Correct?" He gestured toward the intern, who nodded his confirmation without looking up from his phone. I think that thing was surgically attached to his hand.

"What's he talking about?" Wendy whispered to me.

"Holiday party. It's for all the daytime shows," I whispered back.

"Oh, yes, of course. I knew that." She seemed distracted, even a little dazed. What was that look in her eyes? Despite the typical power play of stating that *of course* she knew the party date ahead of time, she didn't look as, well, as *evil* as usual. I'd long ago abandoned my efforts to figure out what made her tick, but I was still curious.

Scotty kept talking. "Details to be announced, but it's going to be fun and fancy and full of famous people, so start shopping for that perfect outfit now." I adored Scotty, and so did everyone else, except Wendy. How could you not love a male boss who actually cared about what anyone was going to wear to the company holiday party?

"Also, I have another announcement. A big one," Scotty said.

We all looked at him.

"The bosses upstairs have decided to let us participate in the New Year's Eve show."

We all raised our eyebrows.

"You mean the live show?" I said, swallowing. *Live? As in the one with the ball?*

"Yes and no. We'll film it live from Times Square, but it will be aired at our regular time slot the next morning."

"So…still basically live?" I said, feeling hoarse.

He nodded. "Exactly. We expect enormous ratings for this because they're going to promote it on the regular live New Year's Eve show, so this is our chance to really make a name for *Love, Wendy.*"

A wave of energy engulfed the room as everyone began chatting excitedly about the pseudo live broadcast. Amid the mayhem, I glanced up at Scotty, who looked at me and nodded slightly. This opportunity was a big deal for all of us, and I knew the pressure was on.

Yikes.

• • •

After Scotty went over the logistics for the New Year's Eve show, he dove into the normal planning meeting. Soon, Wendy snapped out of her haze and returned to her old self. I flinched when she suggested we do a show on…child beauty pageants.

You can't be serious.

"I mean, I think that would make for a wuuunderful show, don't you agree?" She batted her eyelashes and looked around the room. As usual, no one disagreed…everyone was too afraid of her. Scotty wasn't intimidated like the rest of us were, but he rarely challenged her opinions either. I wondered whether that could be because he really didn't care. After all, he had plenty to think about with the *Today* show, the darling of the network.

Normally, I didn't care all that much either because my contribution to the show was taped separately, but this new idea of Wendy's was too much for me.

I cleared my throat. "Um, don't you think that might be a little offensive to some people?"

She turned and looked at me. "Offensive? Why do you say that?" Her surprise at my objection seemed genuine.

How can you be so clueless? I wanted to say.

I shifted in my chair. "I mean, well, because there are a lot of people out there who think child beauty pageants aren't…aren't a very good idea."

She waved a hand in the air. "That's nonsense, Waverly. Beauty pageants are important for positioning women as strong members of society, and they provide wonderful educational opportunities through scholarships. That's how I put myself through college." The *when I was Miss South Carolina* went unsaid, because we'd all heard her say it a thousand times.

I swallowed. "I totally understand that, but I mean *child* pageants. Adult pageants are one thing, but child pageants seem to be more about the parents than the kids." I quickly scanned the faces around the table for help. I could see support in everyone's eyes, but no one spoke up.

"Well, I disagree," Wendy said. She didn't sound angry, however. Then she completely surprised me. Instead of vetoing my dissenting opinion outright, she looked around the room. "What do y'all think? Do you think Waverly is right?"

I pleaded around the table with my eyes. *Come, on people!*

Finally, a couple of people nodded their heads.

"I think she's right," Scotty finally said. "To be honest, I think child pageants are awful."

The intern raised his hand without looking up from his phone. "I second that."

Wendy's eyes got big. "Really? Do y'all really think that?"

One by one, everyone in the room nodded.

I was afraid Wendy was going to slap me and storm out, but all she did was shrug her shoulders.

"Well, OK, then, I guess we'll scratch that idea. How about we move on to the cutest dog contest? I'm thinking only dogs that fit in purses could apply. Wouldn't that be *faaabulous*?"

And that was that.

• • •

Later that morning, I was chatting with Scotty in the kitchen about the New Year's Eve show when Wendy walked in. Given her moodiness, I'd learned to mirror her behavior and not speak to her before she spoke to me, but for some reason, that day I decided to roll the dice and be friendly. Maybe it was because of her change of heart about the child pageant show, or maybe it was because I knew I'd be on a plane to Cleveland in a couple of days. When I was about to see Jake, nothing could sour my cheeriness, not even crazy Wendy Davenport.

"Hi, Wendy, how's it going?" I said with a smile.

Scotty looked up from his coffee mug at the sound of my voice, clearly surprised to hear it. He knew my strategy for dealing with her because he employed it too: *Don't speak until spoken to.* I think pretty much everyone who worked on the show did the same thing.

She sighed loudly. "Hello, Waverly. Hello, Scott. I'm doing fine, not great." She placed a tea bag into a mug and poured hot water over it.

Now I was the one who was surprised. In all the months I'd known her, Wendy had never been so candid.

I couldn't think of anything to say, so I didn't say anything.

"I just haven't been sleeping well lately," she added, her back still to us.

I looked at Scotty, who raised his hands in an *I have no idea* gesture.

"Um, I'm sorry to hear that," I said.

She turned around and half smiled. "Thanks. To be honest, I'm a bit stressed out about something."

Now I was nearly speechless. *Who are you, and what have you done with Wendy?* I stole a glance at Scotty, who looked equally confused.

We sat there in awkward silence for a moment, and then I finally spoke.

"Um, would you like to have lunch with us? Maybe talk about it? Or get your mind off it? Your call." *Did I just invite Wendy to have lunch with Scotty and me? Who am I, and what have I done with* Waverly?

She smiled. "Really? That would be lovely."

I pulled my phone out of my purse and looked at the time. "We were going to meet with the editing team and then go to lunch around noon. Would that work?"

She smiled again and shook her head. "I'd love to, but I have an appointment." She pointed to her forehead and whispered, "Botox."

I nodded. "Got it. Maybe another time."

"I'd like that. Thanks, Waverly." She picked up her tea and nodded politely to both of us, then walked out of the kitchen.

I looked at Scotty, who again held his hands up in a what-the-hell? gesture.

"Now I feel sort of mean for hating her," I whispered.

"I don't," he whispered back.

• • •

Thursday morning, I got up at the crack of dawn to tape a new segment at a trendy gym in the West Village. (Getting in shape for holiday parties apparently was on many people's minds). Afterward, I stopped by NBC to discuss a few things with Scotty, rushed home to handle a few orders for Waverly's Honey Shop, took them to the post office, and then sprinted back home again to pack for Cleveland. I'd meant to hit the post office the day before, but I'd been at the studio late working on a different segment with the editing team. When I finally got home, I fell asleep on the couch watching an old episode of *Seinfeld*. I woke up at two o'clock with the newspaper stuck to my face, then crawled into my bed, and passed out again until my alarm went off at five.

Late that afternoon, I jumped into a cab and met Paige at the airport, and soon we were on our way to Ohio. I took the window seat and planned to be asleep in approximately seven minutes.

"We did it," she said a few minutes after the plane took off.

I looked up from my magazine. "We did what? We made our flight?"

"*It*. Gary and I. We did it."

I opened my eyes wide. "You hadn't done it yet?"

She shook her head. "I'm Paige, not Andie, remember?"

I laughed. "I'm sorry. I just assumed it was in your shared DNA. So how was it?"

She leaned back in her seat and smiled. "I think…I think I'm in love."

"No way. For real?"

She sat up straight. "OK maybe not *love*, but I'm definitely in like."

I nodded. "In like is good."

"In like is very good. It's all so good. I can't believe how good it is."

I tucked my magazine into the seat pocket. "So what about his kids, his ex, the whole Nashville thing. Doesn't that scare you a little bit?"

She shrugged. "It's not ideal, but what is ideal anymore? I'm thirty-four years old, and until recently I've been dating guys who are my age—if not *older*—who still act like they're in college. They don't call or even text when they say they will, they expect you to hop in the sack on the first date, and they're usually dating half of Manhattan along the way. New York is filled with playboys, and I'm just sick of that whole scene. I'd rather date a divorcé who lives in another state than deal with another asshole."

I'd never heard her speak with such conviction. It made me smile.

I thought about what she said before replying.

"I hadn't thought about it until now, but having a boyfriend has definitely made my move to New York easier. Trying to deal with dating on top of everything I've got going on would be too much. At least with Jake, the only issues we're dealing with are geography and our crazy schedules." Those issues were beginning to concern me, however, and I was really looking forward to seeing him in person.

"See what I mean? Dating is really hard here," she said.

I nodded. "I don't think I could take the anxiety of wondering if or even when he was going to ask me out again." It hadn't been very long since I'd been in that exact position and I never wanted to go back there.

She stuck out her tongue. "I *hate* the dating scene here. It's too competitive for me. On Monday, the night before Gary came into town, I had another date through that dating service I told you about."

"The one you hate? What did you say it was called? *Just Joking Around*?"

She laughed. "*Just a Drink*, but I call them *Just a Joke*, because they suck."

"If they suck so much, why do you keep using them?"

"Because I paid them up front for a set number of dates. That's why they don't care about setting me up with losers—they already have my money. A lot of it."

"Yikes."

"Yeah, like I said, they suck. Anyhow, they set me up with this man they said owned his own business, so I figured he had to be interesting, right?"

I narrowed my eyes. "I don't know if I want to hear where this is going. Am I going to need a drink to hear where this is going?" I pretended to flag down a flight attendant.

She laughed. "They also told me he was funny, and that he liked wine."

I held up three fingers. "Owns own business. Funny. Likes wine. I *would* say 'How can you go wrong?' but something clearly went wrong."

She nodded. "So the guy walks in and sits down at the bar, then proceeds to order a glass of tap water because he doesn't drink."

"He ordered tap water at a *bar*?"

"Oh yes. Plain, *free*, tap water. Nothing else."

I scrunched up my face. "Not good."

"Definitely not good. So then, we start chatting, and despite what the agency people have told me about him, he is not funny. He is the opposite of funny. He is Eeyore."

I laughed. "Eeyore? From *Winnie the Pooh*?"

She nodded. "He could make Debbie Downer look like the life of the party."

"I could never understand why Eeyore was so sad all the time. Why was he so bummed out? I mean, Winnie the Pooh and Piglet and even Christopher Robin seemed fun to hang out with, right?"

She put her hand on my arm. "Focus, Waverly."

"Oops, sorry." I blinked and shook my head. "OK, I'm focusing. So he doesn't drink, and he's clinically depressed. What happened next?"

"So I'm sitting there drinking my *wine* while he drinks his *tap water*, and we get on the topic of our jobs." She gestured to me and then back to herself. "I told him about Waverly's Honey Shop and my other accounts."

"OK…"

"So then he starts to tell me about his *company*, and it turns out that it has just one employee, which is of course…him."

I nodded. "Ah, yes, a company of one. I know that scenario well."

"Yes, but you don't go around saying you own your own company, do you?"

I laughed. "Hardly."

"So you want to know what his real *job* is?"

"I'm not sure I do."

She put a hand on her heart and tried not to laugh. "He is, *I kid you not*, a magician."

"A *magician*?" Several people seated near us turned their heads.

"Shhh, you're screaming."

"A *magician*?" I whispered. "You're joking."

She shook her head. "Totally not joking. Birthday parties, corporate events, hourly fee or flat rate, all prices negotiable." She checked the services off on her fingers.

"You mean pulling rabbits out of a hat, cutting women in half, the real deal?"

She nodded. "I paid two hundred dollars to go on a date with a depressed magician who doesn't drink."

"You paid *two hundred dollars*?" My voice went back up a few decibels.

She put her hand over my mouth and lowered her voice. "Waverly, seriously, keep it down."

"I'm sorry," I whispered. "But two hundred dollars for one date? With a magician? That company *is* a joke."

She nodded. "Totally."

"You weren't kidding about the dating scene in New York. I can see why you're not so worried about Nashville or the kids."

"Yep. I'd rather deal with kids in Nashville than a serial killer clown."

I tilted my head to the side. "A serial killer clown?"

"Yes. I figure a depressed magician isn't that far away from a serial killer clown, right? They're definitely in the same family."

"Good point. So is the trip to Vermont happening?"

She smiled. "Yep, the weekend before Christmas. Is that still when Andie's coming?"

"I think so. Bummer."

"Tell her not to get you into too much trouble. If even one photo of you dancing on a bar in your underwear turns up on Facebook, your Midwestern fans might turn on *you*, and that would be a disaster for Waverly's Honey Shop."

I saluted. "Yes, ma'am. I'll try to remember that."

• • •

The next day we had our meeting with the buyer at Bella's Boutique. It went well, and like the woman from Jordan Brooke, she placed a big order to begin the first of January. Her favorite product was the Honey tote bag that said JUST SMILE. After she and Paige worked through the details, she asked me to pose for a photo with her, which once again, weirded me out. I was still struggling to figure out how to manage my new celebrity, however minor. On the one hand, I wanted to laugh at it because I found it so absurd, but I didn't want to hurt the feelings of the complete strangers who seemed genuinely thrilled to meet me in person. So I followed my own advice and *just smiled.*

It was exciting to have all this new business lined up for January and beyond, but at the rate the new orders were coming in, when it came time to fulfill them I was going to have to hire a full-time product manager—or ask Paige to become my first real employee. I knew how much she loved the flexibility of working for multiple product lines, however, so I didn't know how she'd feel about it. Plus, so far I felt like she'd been working *with* me as a consultant, not *for* me as an employee, and I was wary of disrupting the professional/personal relationship we'd developed. The more time I spent with her, the more the personal side of that relationship meant to me, and I didn't want to screw it up by becoming her "boss."

As usual, so much was happening, and so fast.

• • •

Jake got us center-court seats for the Hawks-Cavaliers game just a few rows above the bench. I, of course, wanted his team to win, but Paige and I didn't really care that much about the game itself. It was fun having VIP seats though, and we had a great view of the players in their shorts, so we weren't about to complain.

After it was over, Paige took a cab back to the hotel to do some paperwork, and I waited by the locker rooms for Jake. As I stood against the wall and watched the media, arena employees, team staff, and various hangers-on come and go, I thought about how much had happened since the last time I'd seen him in person. I'd made tremendous strides since the early days of our relationship, when I'd been afraid to open up and really share with him what I was thinking, much less what I was *feeling*. I'd nearly lost him because of that, and now I made a concerted effort to keep him updated on everything that was going on in my life and my head, the good *and* the bad. But the distance and our jobs certainly didn't make it easy. And it wasn't just my relationship with Jake that had suffered from the crazy new life I was living. At least he and I were in regular contact, while I'd barely spoken to McKenna and Andie. I wondered if they had any idea how much I missed them. There just never seemed to be enough time to call.

And I never seemed to get enough sleep.

And I hadn't worked out in weeks.

And I still hadn't called my dad.

You suck, Waverly. Call Dad!

I thought about what Paige had said about how Gary made her feel.

Connected.

I was living a life that so many people would call a dream come true, and I was enjoying it, I really was. But as the hallway slowly emptied out, I realized I felt a bit disconnected too.

• • •

"Are you sure you're not too tired for dinner? You seem tired."

I smiled and leaned my head against Jake's shoulder as we walked into the hotel. "I'm fine, and dinner sounds great." We'd just exited the team bus, which had been a dark and quiet ride, as nearly everyone on board was listening to headphones or dozing. The Hawks had lost, so the energy level was subdued. "I'm so happy just to be here with you. And Paige really wants to meet you."

He put his arm around me and pulled me tight. "I'm glad you're here too. It's been too long."

"Mmm," I said softly, nodding my head.

We took the elevator up to his room, and as he opened the door, he said, "Just give me two minutes to change, OK?"

I saluted. "Two minutes it is. Are you going commando right now?"

He leaned down and kissed me on the forehead. "You'll have to wait and see."

I walked over to the bed. "I'm going to rest my eyes just for a minute." I kicked off my shoes and curled up on top of the covers.

He dropped his athletic bag on the floor and disappeared into the bathroom. "I can't wait to hear everything that's been going on and actually see your face when you're telling it to me. I've missed that pretty face of yours."

I touched my hands to my puffy, sleep-deprived cheeks. "You are way too kind. My face is far from pretty these days."

"Your face is always pretty to me." I heard him turn on the faucet, and I felt my eyes closing.

"I've missed you, Jake," I whispered to the pillow.

Then I promptly fell asleep.

• • •

I woke up in the middle of the night, sweating.

Where am I?

I sat up in bed. I was still fully dressed, still on top of the bedspread. I looked to my right. Jake was sleeping in the adjacent queen bed.

My throat was killing me, as was my head. I stood up and walked to the dresser to open a bottle of water. I tried to be quiet as I gulped it down, but Jake woke up.

"You OK?" he mumbled.

"I don't feel well, Jake." I walked over to his bed and sat down. "I'm so hot, and my throat hurts."

He sat up and put his hand on my forehead. "You're burning up."

I looked at the clock between the beds. It was four in the morning.

"I fell asleep on you, didn't I?"

He nodded. "You crashed a couple minutes after we got up here. You looked so tired that I couldn't bring myself to wake you up."

"I'm so sorry, Jake."

He scratched the back of his head. "It's OK. I grabbed dinner with some of the guys. I texted you and left you a note on the sink in case you wanted to come meet us, but when I came back you hadn't moved."

I pressed my palms against my cheeks. "I'm so hot. Did I already say that?" Everything seemed so fuzzy. I lay down on the bed next to him. "I'm so tired."

He put his hand on my forehead again. "You definitely have a fever. Do you want to change out of your dress?"

Before I could answer him, I was asleep again.

• • •

I didn't wake up until nearly one o'clock the next afternoon. I was drenched with sweat, and my throat was still killing me.

Jake wasn't in the room. I sat up and held my head in my hands. It hurt to swallow. I stood up and wobbled into the bathroom, where Jake had left another note:

Hey, sick girl, I'm going to work out in the gym and grab the newspaper. Call or text when you get up, and I'll bring you breakfast.

P. S. I turned your phone on silent so it wouldn't wake you.

I held the paper to my heart. *What did I do to deserve this guy?*

I stripped off my dress, splashed cold water on my face, and brushed my teeth. I wrapped a towel around my shoulders and walked over to my purse to check my phone. The display said I had eight voice mails.

Eight voice mails?

I sat on the bed in my bra and underwear and listened to my messages:

10:32 p.m.: *"Hey there, it's Paige. I'm at the hotel dying to meet this Jake of yours. Are you back yet? Call me."*

10:58 p.m.: *"Hey, it's Paige again. Where are you? I'm at the hotel bar feeling sort of like a loser sitting here by myself. OK, bye."*

11:17 p.m.: *"Hi again, I have to get out of here because way too many creepy old men are hitting on me. I really hope you're OK! Call me in the morning. Promise? Bye."*

9:12 a.m.: *"Hi, Waverly, it's me again. I'm at the airport. Are you OK? What happened to you last night? I'm a little worried, so please call me as soon as you can. Plus, we need to go over the order from Bella's Boutique, which is so exciting! Enjoy the rest of your weekend with Jake. I really hope you're OK."*

I couldn't believe how nice Paige always was. I had totally blown her off, and she wasn't even upset. Andie would have had my head if I'd stood her up like that.

I kept listening to the messages:

9:19 a.m.: *"Kitten, it's Scotty. Please call me as soon as you get this. Thanks."*

10:11 a.m.: *"Hey, Waverly, it's Kristina. Want to come over for dinner tonight? Give a shout. Hope you're well."*

10:46 a.m.: *"Hi, Waverly, it's, um, it's Dad calling. Can you please give me a call when you can? I have some news. Thanks."*

12:42 p.m. from Andie: *"Hey, woman, it's me. We're on for the weekend of the nineteenth. Be scared. Bye!"*

After I finished listening to all the messages, I put the phone down on the bed and followed with my head on the pillow.

Then I fell asleep again.

When I woke up it was dark outside. I was still in my bra and underwear, the towel half covering me. I sat up and held my head in my hands for a moment, then looked at the clock. It said 7:09 p.m.

Seven o'clock? Good lord. What is wrong with me?

Just then, Jake walked out of the bathroom. "Hey, sleepy-head, how are you feeling?"

I blinked a few times. "I can't believe I've been out all day. I'm so sorry." We both had morning flights to catch, so once again I'd cut our time together short.

He sat down on the bed and put his hand on my forehead, then my neck. "Your fever broke. How's your throat?"

"Sore, but much better. My whole body is stiff. And I'm starving too."

"I can only imagine. You've been asleep for nearly twenty-four hours."

"I still can't believe it's already seven. I wanted to spend the day checking out Cleveland with you. Did you have fun? What did you do?"

"I sat here and watched you sleep, of course."

I narrowed my eyes. "No you didn't."

He laughed. "OK, you're right. I just chilled out at the hotel, mostly. After I worked out I showered at the gym so I wouldn't wake you, and then took a cab downtown for lunch with a couple of the players who hadn't left town yet."

"How is downtown Cleveland? Is it fun?" Our hotel was about two miles away from anything resembling a "downtown."

"It's a huge party, actually. I'm drunk right now. Can you tell?"

I laughed. "Shut up. What else did you do?"

"After the guys took off for the airport I found a cushy chair in the lobby and finally finished reading that JFK biography, so all in all, it was a good day."

"Haven't you been reading that book for like four months?"

He nodded. "Yes, so thank you for getting deathly ill, which forced me to sit down and finish it." He rumpled my hair, which probably had enough oil in it to power the kitchen of a small restaurant.

"I'm so sorry for ruining our day, Jake. I think my body is trying to tell me something."

"I think you're right. Are you up for a shower and dinner? Or do you want to stay up here and order in? I'm perfectly happy to sit and watch you, as long as you stay in your underwear. Or better yet, out of your underwear."

I laughed, then stood up slowly and wobbled over to my suitcase. "Shower, yes. Dinner, let's see how I feel after the shower. Deal?"

"Deal. But I still like the idea of you out of your underwear."

• • •

"What did your dad have to say?" Jake refilled my water glass and set the pitcher down on the table between us. The hotel restaurant was about as far as I could manage to go, but at least I was finally out of the room.

"I haven't called him back yet. I haven't called anyone back yet." I sighed into my pasta. "I know if I'd called Scotty, I'd probably already be on a plane back to New York to cover some random event tomorrow morning, so I couldn't bring myself to do it."

"Will he be upset?"

I nodded. "Maybe. Probably. But I was just too tired to deal." I tried to smile. "I'm feeling a bit overwhelmed right now, in case you couldn't tell."

"That's not surprising. You've been burning the candle at both ends for months now."

"I know, I know, but despite my complaining, I thought I could handle it. Now I'm not so sure. I mean, my body basically gave out on me last night. That's sort of scary, Jake."

"You just need to set some boundaries. You're clearly being pulled in too many directions."

I looked at him. "But *how* do I set boundaries? I mean, I've only been at *Love, Wendy* for a few months, and Waverly's Honey Shop is just getting off the ground. I feel like I can't say no to either, so what am I supposed to do?"

"Can you ask for help?"

"Help how?"

He scratched his eyebrow. "Help with Waverly's Honey Shop, for example. It seems like you're spending so much time on it, but aren't there things you could have someone else do for you?"

I nodded. "I was thinking about that just yesterday, actually. In fact, I planned to talk to you about that last night. I totally forgot." I pressed my hand against my forehead. "I think I'm really losing it."

He laughed. "You're not losing it. You just have too much on your plate right now. You'll sort it out."

I looked down at the nearly empty dish in front of me. "Speaking of plates, would you stop loving me if I ordered another of this yummy pasta? I'm still starving."

"I might love you even more."

I smiled and gestured toward our waiter.

● ● ●

I called my dad on the cab ride home from the airport the next afternoon.

"Hello?" My dad apparently still hadn't figured out caller ID.

"Hi, Dad, it's me. How are you?"

"Well, hello there, Waverly. It's great to hear your voice all the way from the Big Apple." I smiled into the phone and wondered if *the Big Apple* was as grating to New Yorkers as *Frisco* and *San Fran* were to me. I made a mental note to do a segment about that for the show.

"I'm sorry I didn't call you back yesterday. I'm sorry I haven't called you in a while, actually."

"Oh, don't apologize, baby. I know you're quite busy these days. Betty is just over the moon to see you on TV all the time. Did you know that *Love, Wendy* is now her favorite show?"

I closed my eyes and thanked the universe for bringing my dad Betty, his girlfriend of nearly a year. As far as I knew, she was the only woman he had dated since my mom died when I was just a toddler. It sounded so cliché, but since he'd met Betty, he was like a new person, someone I'd gone my whole childhood not knowing. Now his newfound happiness was on display for me and the world to see, and I was so grateful not to feel like I was the only person in his life who truly cared about him. That's a lot of weight for an only child to carry.

"I didn't know that, Dad. Please tell her I said hi. How is she?"

"Actually, she's why I called you."

My heart dropped. *Oh my God. She broke up with him. She's hurt. She's dying.*

"What's wrong?" I took a huge breath and held it.

"Oh, nothing's wrong, baby. In fact…it's the opposite. We're getting married."

I exhaled and smiled…a huge smile. "You're getting *married*?" A few tears swelled in the corner of my eyes.

"Yes, can you believe it? I asked her, and she said yes. *I* really can't believe it." I sensed something in his voice I'd never heard before.

It was pure…joy.

"That's wonderful, Dad. I'm so happy for you!"

"I'm just thrilled, baby. I'm still amazed she said yes."

"Come on, you know she loves you."

He chuckled. "I know, I know. I'm just so incredibly lucky to have met her. I never thought I'd find someone who would love me as much as your mother did."

As soon as he said that, I started crying. They were small tears, but it was hard to speak normally, so I didn't reply. *What is wrong with me?*

"Are you OK, baby?" He sounded nervous. I don't think I'd ever cried in front of my dad.

"I'm fine, Dad. I'm just happy for you, that's all."

"It took awhile, but I found her, Waverly. Your old man found her."

I wiped a few tears from my eyes and looked at the cab driver, who smiled at me in the rearview mirror. I smiled back at him. "So when's the wedding?"

"We're thinking Valentine's Day. Will that work for you?"

Valentine's Day? I swallowed a laugh. *Ah, Dad.* "Can you give me a day to check that I don't have to work?" I hated myself for having to say that. Who has to check to see if she can attend her own father's wedding?

"Of course, of course. I know that TV show isn't going to stop for me, so you do what you have to do. Were you planning to come home for Christmas?"

"Christmas is sort of the same deal. I'm sorry, Dad. I just need to check with the producer before making any decisions around holidays. As I'm rapidly learning, that's sort of the way it goes with TV." After the year I'd spent freelancing for the *San Francisco Sun*, not being in charge of my own schedule was starting to get to me. I thought I would probably have Christmas free but knew for a fact I was going to have to work on New Year's Eve, given how New Year's resolutions are on practically *everyone's* mind that day.

"It's fine, baby, really. I understand. You just let me know, OK?"

"I will, I promise. Congratulations, Dad. I'm so happy for both of you."

I looked at the cab driver again and wondered what he was thinking of me now.

chapter seven

Before I knew it, December had arrived, and the holiday party was just days away. After my minor breakdown in Cleveland, I tried to put the brakes on a bit, but it wasn't easy. To my relief, Paige agreed to manage all sales and operations for Waverly's Honey Shop, officially beginning in January. She would work without a salary in exchange for a significant commission. Knowing she'd soon be on board full-time reduced my stress—no more trade shows on weekends or regular trips to the post office!—but any time that was freed up in my schedule was quickly swallowed up by the growing popularity of *Love, Wendy,* which meant more work for all of us.

"So does everyone have a date?" Scotty looked around the room. "I know several eligible bachelors and bachelorettes if anyone wants to get set up."

I looked up from my notebook. "You know people who are willing to be set up for a complete stranger's *company holiday party*? Who does that?"

"Waverly, have you ever been to the penthouse of the New York Athletic Club?" Scotty asked.

"The penthouse? No." I'd met Kristina there once for coffee before I moved to New York, but had never gotten past the lobby.

"Well, believe me, it's *worth* pimping yourself out for the night for the view alone."

Wendy patted her hair and nodded. "I know I rarely agree with Scott's taste, but he's right. The view of Central Park is absolutely incredible." Since her sudden softening in the kitchen several weeks ago, she had settled into a haphazard routine of teetering between "sort of mean" on some days and "sort of nice" on others, never quite fully tipping one way or the other. I'd come to the conclusion that she wasn't a *complete* bitch and had given up taking her jabs personally. Plus, by now I was comfortable with the crew and the routine of producing my segment, so she didn't scare me as much.

"Sounds gorgeous," I said, excited at the prospect of having Jake on my arm. Jake looked great in a suit. Actually, he looked good in anything. Or nothing.

Wendy lowered her voice and leaned toward me. "I can give you the names of a few people if you want some help."

I raised my eyebrows. "Help?"

She looked me up and down and smiled. "Hair, makeup, you know what I mean. We both know your appearance isn't your strong point, right?"

I sighed and fake smiled back at her, and then turned my head back toward Scotty at the front of the room.

Blech.

"So, Waverly, do you have anything to share with us today?" Scotty asked.

I looked up at him. "Excuse me?"

"E-mails. Got any good ones lately?"

As the ratings for *Love, Wendy* grew, so did the collective fan mail. People often wrote me to say they enjoyed *Honey on Your Mind*, but they also loved sharing what was on *their* minds. And some shared a bit too much. Reading the wackiest e-mails aloud to the staff had become a highlight of our weekly meetings.

I smiled. "Actually, I do have some good ones. Want to hear?"
Everyone in the room nodded.

I pulled out a sheet of paper from my notebook. "OK, here goes:

"Hi, Waverly, being alone forever is what's on my mind. I've been single for a while now, so last night I decided to try the online dating thing. Get this: shortly after I posted my profile, I got messages from three men. One of them was holding a cat in his photo. A cat. Another was sitting on a donkey. I'm not joking, a donkey. The third guy looked normal. His message, however, said he'd love to meet me but asked if I'd be willing to strip on a webcam first. There's really not much more I can say."

"Dear Waverly: You know what's on my mind? Idiots who misuse basic words. I have a coworker who every single Monday sends around an e-mail raving about the movies she watched over the weekend on her paper view. P-A-P-E-R V-I-E-W. Yes, you read that right. Or is it you R-E-D that W-R-I-T-E...?"

Laughter from the room.

"Waverly, why do people insist on sharing every boring and/ or gruesome detail of their lives in their mass holiday letters? Your daughter had a baby? Wonderful! Your son graduated from college? Good for him! But do I want to hear about Aunt Louise's gastric bypass surgery? Not so much. And is it really necessary to explain how you waffled for months between getting a Kindle or a Nook? Definitely not. And do I really care about your bacterial infection?"

More laughter.

"Hi, Waverly, you know what I've been thinking about lately? Massages. Why do people pay for them? I mean, why give money to a complete stranger to rub his hands all over me for an hour when I can put on a slutty outfit, walk into any bar in America and have ten guys volunteer to do it for free? I'm just sayin'…"

More laughter.

"What up, Waverly, this is all I have to say: Tiny nylon running shorts + any man who isn't in the Olympics = GROSS. Bye."

More laughter.

I looked around the room and held up the sheet. "And the last one on my list just came in this morning. Perfect timing, given that we're talking about escorts for the holiday party:

"Dear Waverly: I have a good dating story for you. This guy from my volleyball league recently asked me to brunch, so I figured why not? He's cute and seemed nice enough. We're both in our late twenties and work in downtown Philadelphia. So anyhow, we're at the restaurant about to order, and he looks around the place, then leans across the table to me and says with a proud grin, 'My friends and I used to run out on the bill here all the time.' Uh, what?"

Everyone cracked up, even Wendy.
I took a seated bow.

• • •

The day before the holiday party, Paige and I met for an afternoon catch-up meeting at Connecticut Muffin on picturesque Montague Street, the "Main Street" of Brooklyn Heights. Jake was flying in a few hours later.

"So you're off to Vermont next weekend?"

She nodded. "I haven't gone away for the weekend with a guy in six years."

"Six years? Really?"

She held up six fingers. "Six years. I plan to spend the entire weekend naked."

I laughed. "So you're meeting him there?"

She nodded. "Late Friday night. His son has a basketball game that afternoon, so he can't get here in time to drive up with me, which would have been so nice. But it will be great anyway."

"How old are they?"

"The kids?"

I nodded.

"Seventeen, nineteen, and twenty. Two girls and a boy."

"Wow, three kids. That doesn't freak you out at all?"

"A little, but like I said, it's worth it. So hey, are you ready?"

"Ready for what?" I picked at my sticky bun.

She spread her hands on the table. "We need an office."

I looked up at her. "An office?"

"Yes. Once those big accounts kick in, it's time for us to up the ante."

"But wouldn't that be crazy expensive?" So far, we'd managed to run Waverly's Honey Shop out of our apartments, plus a variety of bars and coffee shops. I'd lost track of how many sticky buns I'd eaten at the Connecticut Muffin.

She shook her head. "I found a great space in Dumbo that would be perfect for us, and it's available at the beginning of

January." Dumbo, an acronym for "Down under the Manhattan Bridge overpass," was a trendy neighborhood within walking distance of my apartment and just one subway stop from Paige's place in lower Manhattan.

I didn't respond immediately, and Paige followed up with, "It's right across the street from a super cute coffee house/bakery place, *and* next door to a chocolate shop."

My ears perked up. "Chocolate shop?"

She laughed. "I knew that would get your attention."

I smiled. "OK, I'm listening..."

"We also need employees."

"We need employees?"

She nodded. "Nothing major, but we definitely need a couple of minions to manage the orders and deal with production and inventory so that I can focus on running the accounts, not to mention opening new ones, and so you can focus on client relations and promotion, not to mention expanding the product line."

My head was spinning. "OK..."

"We also need an accountant."

"An accountant?"

"Yes, just part-time for basic bookkeeping, but yes."

"You think we're ready for all that?"

She didn't hesitate. "Yes, and eventually we're going to have to hire a marketing manager too."

"Can I afford all that?" I'd already incurred a ton of expenses flying us around the country to meet with potential buyers, not to mention the cost of manufacturing and new product designs, and the small revenue stream from the online orders hardly covered what I was putting out. I'd been able to pay for everything so far from my TV salary, but if the whole Honey operation blew up in my face, I'd soon be dipping into my nest egg, which was really more of an egg*let* and wouldn't go very far if I had to pay a whole staff New York salaries.

She nodded. "I've run some numbers, and with the large orders we have lined up for January, we can lower our manufacturing costs through production volume discounts, and switch to a distribution center that handles bigger clients. That will bring our cost of goods sold way down, streamline shipping, and more than cover the cost of our additional overhead. We'll also be able to accommodate future growth without disrupting our existing accounts."

I blinked. "That was a lot of business-school speak you just rattled off. I don't speak that language."

She smiled and tapped a finger against her temple. "Trust me."

A vision of me in bankruptcy court flashed before my eyes. Boxes of T-shirts and tote bags in my apartment and a sales rep who worked entirely on commission was one thing. An office and hourly employees was another. Was I getting in over my head? I began to shred my napkin into little bits.

Sensing my anxiety, Paige reached across the table and gently squeezed my arm. "It's taking off, Waverly. You should be excited. This is *exciting*."

"It is? I should? It is?"

She nodded and smiled. "*Yes.* It's really happening."

I looked down at the remainder of my sticky bun sitting among the napkin pieces. "Then why do I feel sort of sick?"

"You mean aside from the fact that you just ate an enormous ball of sugar?"

I nodded. "Good point. But seriously, Paige, just last year Waverly's Honey Shop existed only in my imagination, and now I'm going to have an *office*? And *employees*? I can't believe it."

"Why not? You came up with a fantastic idea, and you've worked extremely hard to turn it into a real product. That's a lot easier said than done."

I didn't reply.

"You should be *proud* of yourself, Waverly. *I* am."

I stared at the table. *She's right, Waverly. You* should *be proud of yourself.*

I still didn't reply.

"Waverly?"

Finally, I looked up at her, still in a daze. "Thanks, Paige. I…I'm so grateful for all your help. None of this would have happened without you."

She smiled. "It's been a pleasure. So you want to walk over and check out the space?" She gestured toward the exit.

I tossed the remaining chunk of sticky bun into my mouth and nodded. "Let's do it."

• • •

"Want me to call a cab? Or should we take the subway?" I yelled from my bedroom. It was nearly seven the following evening, and I was digging through my jewelry box to find a necklace to wear with my new dress. *Why didn't I think about accessories before?*

"Your call, I'm easy," Jake called from the living room, where he was watching the Hawks game on TV. He'd been granted a quick hall pass to take me to the NBC holiday party and was flying to meet the team in Salt Lake City the next day.

I pulled out a small diamond pendant and clasped it behind my neck. "You *do* realize that when you say 'I'm easy' on the way out to a party, it makes you sound like a paid escort," I said at a normal decibel as I walked into the living room.

"Does it? Then I guess we'll have to figure out a payment plan after the party." He looked up at me and smiled. "Wow, you look gorgeous."

I curtsied. "Why, thank you." I'd spent half a day shopping for the "perfect" holiday party dress, something red, sparkly, and amazing…but I hadn't found it. The red dress I *did* find, however—pretty, strapless, and just above the knee—wasn't bad. And I didn't really mind. I'd learned that I was never going to stand out as a fashionista in New York City, and it felt good not to wrap my self-esteem up in something as superficial as a dress. It made me feel…grown up.

Jake stood up and gestured toward me. "Come here."

I stepped toward him, and he put his arms around my lower back. "You're stunning," he whispered into my hair.

I closed my eyes and smiled.

• • •

We splurged for a cab and were soon standing at the entrance to the New York Athletic Club, a majestic building located on Central Park South, directly across from the park itself. We made our way through the lobby, and as the elevator doors closed behind us, I clenched my hands into fists against my chest.

"You OK?" Jake asked.

I nodded. "Just a little nervous. I'll be fine."

The doors opened onto a room full of people I didn't recognize. The women were all wearing floor-length gowns, some with fur coats draped over one arm. And I was sure they were *real* fur coats. I tried not to stare, but I was not used to hanging around with people who wore real fur. Or floor-length gowns.

"I didn't expect to be so nervous," I whispered to Jake, not sure what to do with the nervous energy I felt pulsing through my veins.

"Let's get a drink," he whispered back.

Floor-to-ceiling windows overlooked Central Park on one side and Seventh Avenue on the other. Guests were milling about and socializing, the music not yet loud enough to drown out the cocktail chatter. After checking our coats, Jake took my hand and led me toward the bar.

"Hey, there's Scotty and Tad." I gestured to the opposite end of the room.

"Meet you there in a second with drinks?" Jake said.

I smiled at him. "Have I told you lately how wonderful you are?"

"Perhaps, but a man can never hear that enough. What's your poison going to be tonight?"

I thought for a moment. Given my history, beer or wine was the best choice. I tended to get "emotional" if I drank hard alcohol, "emotional" being a euphemism for "plastered." And plastered was the last thing I wanted to be at a work party. I'd done that once before and ended up getting super sick—in a public restroom, no less. It was not one of my finer moments.

"I think I'll have a glass of red wine," I said, cringing at the memory.

"I'm on it." He continued toward the bar, and I went in search of Scotty and Tad. The room was filling up quickly, and I could no longer see them. I did, however, see Wendy. She had her back to me, but it was impossible to miss that bright yellow thimble she called "hair."

Blech.

Should I say hello now?

Get it over with?

I decided to bite the bullet and at least *act* professional and pleasant, despite my inner angst. I walked over and tapped her on the shoulder. "Hi, Wendy."

She turned around and flashed her megawatt smile. "Waverly, hello! It's so luuuvely to see you!"

She was clearly in "sort of nice" mode tonight. *Thank God.* Maybe it wouldn't be that painful to chat with her.

She reached for the arm of the tall man standing next to her, whose back was to me. "Waverly, you must meet my huuusband," she purred.

The man turned around and smiled.

If I'd been holding a drink, I would have dropped it on the floor.

"Waverly Bryson, this is my huuusband, Gary Davenport."

Oh my God.

It was Paige's Gary.

I held out my hand and tried to mask the look of horror on my face. He looked equally shocked.

"Um, hi, Gary, it's…it's nice to meet you."

He shook my hand and squeezed it—hard. "The pleasure is all mine."

I had no idea what to say.

Holy crap holy crap holy crap.

"Waverly works on my show," Wendy said, oblivious to the tension between us.

"Oh really?" Gary said. I think his forehead may have started to bead with sweat, but I couldn't bring myself to look at him to confirm or deny it. I just stared at Wendy.

Wendy nodded. "She does a cute little segment a few days a week, a *man on the street* sort of thing, isn't that right, Waverly?"

I nodded and swallowed. "Um, yes, it's called…*Honey on Your Mind*."

"*Honey* on Your Mind?" Gary asked with a nod, putting the pieces together.

"It's fun," Wendy said. "She also has an adorable line of products around the *Honey* concept. T-shirts, tote bags, that sort of thing. I love them."

I looked at her. *Did she just pay me a compliment?*

Just then Jake appeared, thank God. He handed me a glass of wine, which I was tempted to knock back in one gulp.

"Jake, um, this is Wendy Davenport from *Love, Wendy,* and her husband, Gary. Wendy and Gary, this is my boyfriend, Jake McIntyre."

Jake shook their hands. "It's great to meet you both. Wendy, I like your show."

Wendy pushed me in the shoulder, a bit harder than necessary or appropriate. "Why loooook at you, I didn't know you had a boyfriend." The gesture didn't seem overtly malicious, however, and I wondered how much she'd had to drink.

I nodded and took a huge sip of my wine. There was a good reason Wendy didn't know about Jake. After our initial meeting back on the *Today* show, I'd never talked to her about my personal life. *Ever.*

"And all this time I thought you were a single girl, flirting your way around town with the camera crew in tow." She took another sip of whatever she was drinking. A big sip.

I shook my head, my face still half in my wine, which part of me now wanted to toss in her face. How was I supposed to respond to that comment with Jake standing right next to me?

Wendy put her hand on Gary's arm. I could tell he was staring at me, even though I hadn't made eye contact since Wendy had introduced us. "When I met Waverly on the *Today* show, she was single, and my, oh my, did she have her share of dating stories." She laughed a bit too loudly.

I looked up from my drink. *Did she just say that right in front of Jake?* I was tempted to elbow him but didn't want to be obvious. I'd told him all about crazy Wendy, but he was finally getting to see for himself.

Gary was still staring at me.

I finished my wine and looked at Jake. Professional etiquette be damned, I had to get the hell out of there. "I think I'm going to get another drink and look for Scotty. You ready?"

He nodded, and then held out his hand to Gary and Wendy again. "It was a pleasure meeting you both."

As we walked away, I could feel Gary's eyes burning into my back.

"Oh my God, oh my God, oh my God," I whispered.

"Are you OK?" Jake said.

"Wine isn't cutting it tonight. I need a stiff drink." I pulled him by the arm toward the bar. Screw my fear of getting hammered at a work event.

He laughed. "Come on, she wasn't *that* bad. I expected her to be much worse, to be honest."

I looked at him, and the second we made eye contact he could tell something was wrong.

"Waverly, what's going on?"

I glanced over his shoulder at Wendy and Gary, who were now chatting with some people I recognized from the *Today* show.

"Waverly?"

I looked back at Jake and pulled him deeper into the crowd. "It's Gary."

"Gary? What about him?"

"He's—"

Before I could finish the sentence, I felt an arm around my shoulders.

"There's my princess. I was wondering when you were going to arrive at the ball."

I looked to my right and saw Scotty and Tad standing there, both dressed to the nines.

"Hi, Scotty." I kissed him on the cheek, and then did the same to Tad. "You guys remember Jake?"

Scotty smiled. "Of course. How could we forget *Jake*?" Scotty and Tad had been instrumental in finally getting Jake and me together after a year of mishaps, or, perhaps more accurately, a year of my acting like a total lunatic every time I saw him.

Jake shook both their hands. "Scott, Tad, it's good to see you. This is quite a party." He looked around the room, which was becoming more packed by the minute. "NBC knows how to celebrate the holidays, that's for sure."

Tad raised his hand. "I'm getting a round. Who wants a drink?" We all put in our orders, including mine for a vodka tonic.

Jake looked at me. "Vodka tonic? You sure about that?"

I nodded. "Believe me, I need it."

Scotty gave me a strange look. "Everything OK, kitten?"

I smiled and nodded. What could I say? I certainly couldn't go around telling everyone that Wendy's husband was cheating on her—especially her executive producer, even though he *was* a good friend. What do they say—never mix business with pleasure? Apparently "they" are right, whoever "they" are. *Damn them.*

Jake gave me a strange look too, clearly wondering what was going on.

For the time being, I figured my best option was to change the subject.

I adjusted my necklace and looked at Scotty. "So I was thinking we should get the whole gang together sometime. You and Tad, me and Jake, and Shane and Kristina. What do you think?" I had barely seen Kristina since I'd moved to town, and I hadn't seen Shane at all.

"That sounds lovely, my dear, but it will have to be after the holidays. Tad and I are running ourselves ragged with all the parties on our calendar."

"Hey, that reminds me, what are the plans for the show over the holidays? I know we're doing a big show for New Year's Eve, but do I need to be around for Christmas or Christmas Eve?"

He took a sip of his drink and shook his head. "I don't think so. You planning to head out West to see your dad?"

"Maybe. But I looked at flights yesterday, and I wouldn't be able to come back until the day before New Year's Eve without breaking the bank. I've been so busy lately that I forgot to book a ticket earlier."

"Oh, sweetheart, you'd have to be back way before then. I'm sorry."

I shrugged. "That's OK. I sort of figured the timing wasn't going to work out this year, anyway."

Just then, Tad reappeared with our drinks. As he handed me mine I saw Gary several feet behind him, his back to me. I took a huge gulp of vodka tonic and stood as close to Jake as I could without stepping on his feet.

"What did I miss?" Tad said. "Is it time to do shots yet? Are we going to get jiggy tonight?" He did a little dance.

Scotty laughed. "We were just talking about the busy holiday party train on which you and I have once again embarked."

"Oh yes we have," Tad said with a wink. "I love December in New York."

Scotty held his drink up for a toast. "Cheers, everyone. Here's to people who watch daytime television, or better put, here's to the bloated advertising budgets of corporate America."

We all laughed and clinked our glasses together, although my laughter was mostly of the nervous kind. I stole a glance at Gary as I took another sip of my drink, then huddled next to Jake.

"Are you OK?" he whispered. "You're acting really weird."

"Sorry, I know," I whispered back. "Would you mind if we got out of here?"

Before he could respond, Scotty picked up the conversation again. "So, Waverly, how *is* your dad doing? I haven't heard you talk about him much lately."

I smiled. "Actually...he's getting married."

Jake looked at me. "Your dad's getting married?"

I winced. I'd been so busy that I'd completely forgotten to tell him. "I'm sorry, I just found out a few days ago. He's getting married on Valentine's Day."

Scotty, the consummate diplomat, immediately diverted attention away from my faux pas. "Valentine's Day will, of course, be a big day for *Honey on Your Mind*, but you can't miss your dad's wedding. We'll work around it."

I smiled at him. "Really?"

He nodded. "Of course. Don't worry about it."

"Thanks, Scotty. That means a lot to me." One less thing to worry about.

He put his hand on my shoulder. "Waverly, you're an important part of the show now. At this point *Love, Wendy* needs you almost as much as you need *Love, Wendy*, so don't be so timid, OK? Try to believe in yourself a little more."

I nodded and eked out a smile. "OK."

"I've been telling her that for months, but she still doesn't believe me," Jake said, putting his arm around my shoulders. "What's your secret to getting her to listen to you?"

Scotty laughed. "I sign her paycheck."

I laughed as well and pointed at them. "Hey now, don't you two gang up on me."

Tad sidled up on the other side of me and put his arm around my waist. "I'm next in line for this girl, so you two be careful, now."

I rested my head on Tad's shoulder, the alcohol finally calming my nerves. "Yeah, you two be careful, or I may run off with Mr. Blondie, here."

Scotty excused himself to use the restroom, and shortly thereafter, Tad disappeared into the crowd to mingle. As soon as they were gone, Jake set his drink on a table and put both hands on my arms.

"Are you doing OK now? You still want to leave?"

"I need to tell you something," I whispered. "I'm sort of freaking out."

"About your dad?"

I shook my head.

He scratched his eyebrow, and then gestured toward the enormous terrace. "Want to talk outside?"

I nodded. "I've heard the view is amazing, but before I go *anywhere* I need to empty the canteen."

"Empty the canteen?"

"Work with me, Jake. I need to pee."

He laughed. "You're nuts, did you know that?"

"Believe me, I'm well aware."

"How about I get our coats and meet you by the door leading to the terrace? It's cold out there."

I saluted. "Sounds good."

I hurried to the restroom. As I washed my hands, I kept one eye on the door, afraid Wendy would walk in at any moment. Next to Gary, she was the last person on earth I wanted to see right then. I looked in the mirror and saw the confusion written all over my face.

Paige's boyfriend is Wendy's husband? What? How can that be?

When I emerged from the restroom, I spotted Wendy in a far corner, chatting with a few people I recognized from promotional posters lining the hallways of NBC. I didn't see Gary. I headed toward the terrace, scanning the crowd for Jake. I was about halfway there when I felt a pull on my arm.

I looked up and saw Gary standing there.

Frick.

"Can I talk to you for a minute?" he asked.

I tried to pull my arm away, but he kept a firm grip on it. "I'm sort of busy right now."

"Just let me explain, OK?"

I put my free hand on my hip. "*Explain*?"

"I told you, it's complicated." He glanced around the room.

"I've heard your wife talk about you, Gary. It certainly doesn't sound *complicated* to me." I remembered how Wendy had bragged about marrying her high school sweetheart back when I'd first met her on the *Today* show. Her picture-perfect marriage was the ticket that had taken *Love, Wendy* from a hit relationship-advice column to a hit TV show, but now it turned out that her picture-perfect husband was sleeping with my friend.

"You don't understand," he said, still holding my arm.

I yanked my arm away from him. "I don't think I *want* to understand, Gary. Now please let *go* of me."

As I turned to go, I saw Wendy approaching us.

Oh, God help me.

"Darling, is everything OK? You two seem to be in quite a tiff over here." She put her hand on Gary's arm.

I opened my mouth but couldn't think of anything to say.

"It's fine," Gary said.

"We're fine," I said, nodding.

Wendy gave me an icy look. "You sure about that? Several people across the room seem to think otherwise."

I could feel my face turn the color of my dress.

"Really, it's nothing. Listen, Jake's waiting for me outside, so I really need to go, I'm sorry. Wendy, I'll see you next week, OK?" I turned to Gary and nodded. "It was nice meeting you."

Before they could respond, I bolted. I walked as fast as I could toward the terrace, looking desperately for Jake. When I finally spotted him, I nearly broke into a trot.

"Whoa, slow down, girl, what's the rush?" He held out my coat as I approached.

"We need to get out of here. Now."

"Waverly, what is going *on* with you tonight?"

"Can we please talk about it later? I just want to go home."

"OK, OK, we're going." He helped me put my coat on, and we made our way through the crowd back to the elevator. I kept my head down until the doors closed behind us.

I didn't even say good-bye to Scotty.

• • •

"Wow, that's quite a story. No wonder you were acting so crazy in there," Jake said.

I pointed my spoon at him. "See? Sometimes I have a good reason." We were sitting in a booth at Shake Shack, a popular diner on the corner of Eighth Avenue and Forty-Fourth, eating hot fudge sundaes.

"Only sometimes."

I shrugged. "I'll take that. I think Paige is *in love* with him, Jake. She talks about him all the time, and they're even spending next weekend in Vermont together. This is going to crush her."

"So you're going to tell her?"

I sighed. "I don't know. I guess I should, right? I mean, wouldn't *you* want to know? I would."

He didn't say anything.

"Well?"

He set his spoon down. "I don't know, Waverly. His wife is a celebrity. You never know what's going on inside a marriage like that. I see some crazy arrangements with NBA players."

"Arrangements?"

He nodded. "A lot of the guys are definitely cheating, but I think an equal number have tacit approval from their wives. For some women, it comes with the territory of being married to someone so high profile."

I ate another spoonful of my sundae and thought of how many times Wendy had talked about her *huuusband*. She was so proud of having landed the quarterback of the high school football team, the prom king, the best-looking guy in school, all rolled into one.

"I don't know, Jake. Wendy sure doesn't talk about her marriage like it's an *arrangement*. I mean, her entire career revolves around her successful relationship."

"Exactly."

"Exactly?"

"Yes, exactly. Think about it. If her own relationship *weren't* so successful…what would that do to her credibility?"

I nodded. "Maybe you're right. So you think maybe they have some sort of deal where he runs around on her, and she looks the other way, all in the name of fame and fortune?"

He put his hands up. "I don't know. It's not my style, but I'm just saying it's possible, that's all. She may be running around on him too."

"But even if that's true, it still makes him a sleaze, because Paige is going to be crushed when she finds out."

He nodded. "Probably."

I pressed a hand against my forehead. "I promised myself I wouldn't meddle in my friends' love lives anymore."

"You did?"

"Yeah, I tried doing that with two coworkers back in San Francisco, and it was a total fiasco."

"You really think Paige is in love with him?"

I nodded. "Head over heels."

"Then you may have a big decision to make."

I took another bite of my sundae. "Why does life have to be so complicated? Why can't we just eat ice cream and have fun, like when we were kids?"

"Welcome to adulthood, Miss Bryson."

I sighed. "Being a kid was so much easier."

He reached over and touched my nose. "Now *that* sounds like something you should put on one of your Honey Tees."

I reached to swat his hand away, but he caught mine and held it.

"So listen…I was wondering…" he began, suddenly sounding serious.

I looked at him.

"Since you're not going to go out to see your dad for Christmas, would…would you like to come with me to Boston?"

"Boston?"

He nodded. "My sister's having the whole family over this year."

"Your whole…family?" I swallowed as I eked out the words.

He smiled. "The whole McIntyre clan. What do you think?"

I felt a tear form in the corner of my eye. "You…you want me to meet your whole *family*?"

"Sure, why not?" He squeezed my hand.

"Would I be the first girl you bring home to meet your family since…you and Holly broke up?" From the little Jake had told me, his entire family, and especially his mom, were huge fans of Holly. She had been a childhood friend in Florida, conveniently now lived in Atlanta, and, as far as I knew, still carried a bit of a torch for him. So, while I tried not to be insecure about the situation, of course I was, at least little bit. Plus, I'd seen her once, all tan and super-modelish, which certainly didn't boost my fragile ego.

He squeezed my hand again. "That's in the past, Waverly."

I smiled weakly. "I know."

"Come on, they'll love you."

"They will?"

"I know they will. How could they not?"

I smiled and squeezed his hand back. "OK then, I'd love to."

chapter eight

I was dreading the week ahead. I didn't want to see Paige, and I certainly didn't want to see Wendy.

But it was not to be. Paige called first thing on Monday. She wanted me to meet her and the leasing agent later that morning to sign papers for the new office. I tried to get out of it by saying I wasn't feeling well, which was technically true. I wasn't sick in the literal sense, but I certainly *was* feeling ill about the whole situation.

I did my best to resist, but she was persistent.

"Come on, Waverly, this is important. Can't you rally for just a few minutes? We'll meet you in Dumbo."

Frick. I was already at the NBC office, where I probably wouldn't be if I were actually sick. The NBC office was hardly near Dumbo.

"My throat is killing me, Paige. Can't it wait a few days?" *A few years, maybe?*

"If you want the space, you need to sign the lease. Today. This is important."

I looked at the ceiling and sighed. "OK, fine. But can we do it later, like after lunch maybe?" At least that would give me time to get back to my apartment first and put on some jeans.

"That should work. Let me call the broker."

Ugh. What am I going to say to her?

Later that afternoon, I set out on the mile-long walk from Brooklyn Heights to Dumbo. As I cut through Cadman Plaza Park, I pulled my hat down over my ears and wrapped my coat around me. It had yet to snow, but it was already way colder than it ever got in San Francisco. I didn't mind it, though, at least not yet. While I'd spent a fair amount of time up in Lake Tahoe over the years, I'd never experienced a traditional "winter," and I found myself looking forward to the first snowfall.

I exited the park, descended East Cadman Plaza Street under the entrance to the Brooklyn Bridge pedestrian walkway, followed it down as it turned into Washington Street, and then made a left on Water Street. In spite of my mood, the roar of the subway train rolling over the Manhattan Bridge made me look up and smile. Taking the rickety subway over the East River was one of my favorite things about living in Brooklyn. Most of the subway trains in New York ran underground, but crossing that open-air stretch across the bridge felt like living in another era, or even a fantasy one. It was almost as though Batman himself might swoop down onto the train and guide it safely into Gotham City.

Paige was standing outside the building as I approached, chatting with the leasing agent.

She looked the same as she always did, pleasant and in a good mood. Despite the cold weather, I broke into a sweat the moment I saw her.

She saw me and smiled. "Hey, Waverly, how are you feeling?"

Rattled, I wrapped my coat around me and searched her eyes for a clue. What did she know? What had Gary told her? I hoped for a sign, but I couldn't detect anything other than normal, friendly, ever-professional Paige.

When I didn't answer, she gestured to the man standing next to her. "Waverly, this is Eric, our broker."

"Hi, it's nice to meet you." I extended my hand.

"Likewise," he said, shaking it.

Paige pointed to the storefront across the street. "I know you're not feeling well, Waverly, so we can wrap this up quickly. Should we duck into Almondine for a coffee?" She looked from me to Eric, who nodded.

"Sure, that sounds good," I said, although what I really felt like doing was sprinting into the chocolate shop next door to hide from the situation, maybe even in a big vat of chocolate. Now *that* would be a good place to hang out for a while.

The three of us walked into the bakery and took off our coats. We ordered drinks, and after some quick chitchat, Eric pulled out the lease and went over the basics.

A few minutes later, I signed it.

And that was that.

As of January 1, the worldwide headquarters of Waverly's Honey Shop would officially move from my living room to a real office.

Wow.

Eric stood up and shook our hands again, preparing to leave. I wanted to go with him so I wouldn't have to be alone with Paige, but I couldn't think of a way to get out of there without being rude.

Don't leave, Eric! I willed him to stay, but my telepathic powers failed.

As I wistfully watched him walk out the door, Paige put her hand on my arm and gave it a light squeeze.

"So hey, I have some news."

I looked at her and raised my eyebrows. "News?"

She smiled. "So you know Gary and I are going to Vermont this weekend, right?"

I nodded. *How could I possibly forget?*

"Well, he called me last night and said he has something important he wants to tell me."

I sat up a little straighter. "Something important?"

"Yes." She smiled and took a sip of her hot chocolate. "So I'm thinking it has to be one of two things. Either he's going to say he wants me to meet his kids...or..."

"Or...?"

"Or...he's going to say he loves me."

I caught my breath but didn't speak.

"What do you think?" She looked so happy, and my heart broke for her a little bit.

I nodded. "Um, yeah, both of those make sense." I tried to sound more enthusiastic than I felt. I sipped my hot chocolate and stared at the table. What was I supposed to say?

She reached over and put her hand on my arm. "You weren't kidding about not feeling well, Waverly. You don't look good at all."

I nodded. "I'm sorry. I'm just not myself today." *If you only knew why.*

She stood up and put her coat on. "Let's get out of here so you can get back to bed. You don't want to be sick for the holidays. Hey, speaking of which, how was the NBC party?"

I put my hat on and forced a smile. "It was fun. Nothing too crazy."

"I bet it was a blast. I love the holidays in New York. There's just so much energy everywhere you go, it's like electricity in the air. Andie is going to love it. I'm so sorry to miss her. When does she get in?"

I buttoned my coat. "Friday afternoon."

"Please tell her I said hi, OK?"

"Will do."

She held open the door, and as we were about to part ways, she turned to face me. "Congratulations on the lease. Today is a big day for you, for me, and for Waverly's Honey Shop. Thanks so much for allowing me to be a part of it." She gave me a hug, and suddenly I felt like I was going to cry.

"Are you OK?" she asked.

I nodded. "I will be. I just need...to rest."

"You take care of yourself, OK?"

I smiled. "I'll try to."

He doesn't deserve you, I thought.

As I walked away from the bakery, I pulled the lease out of my purse and stared at it. By signing it, I'd officially marked a new beginning for both Paige and myself. I just hoped the heartbreak she was in for wouldn't ruin it.

chapter nine

While I was able to escape my encounter with Paige relatively unscathed, I wasn't so sure I'd be able to do the same with Wendy at that week's planning meeting, assuming she showed up. Why had I let her see me arguing with Gary at the party? While I didn't regret what I'd said to him, I *did* regret how and where it happened. I had no idea what he'd told her afterward, and I had no desire to know.

Blech.

I walked into the conference room a few minutes early and sat down with a fresh cup of coffee. I pulled out my notebook and started jotting down ideas for future *Honey on Your Mind* segments. I'd also printed out a few funny e-mails to read to the group:

"Dear Waverly: You know what's on my mind? 😷 *EMOTICONS! Great for little kids, beyond annoying for adults. The guy I'm currently dating e-mails and texts like a fourteen-year-old girl, with stupid smiley faces* 😀😊😉 *everywhere, not to mention LOLs and TTYLs and OMGs. I can't take it anymore! I am SO dumping him.* 😶*"*

"Dear Waverly: I just got back from swimsuit shopping. Good lord. I ended up so depressed that the only thing I bought was a bottle of wine to drink when I got home. Just thought I'd share. Gotta go pop a cork now. Bye."

"Hi, Waverly, thought you'd enjoy this: I've been out a few times with a guy who not only sends me meeting requests for DATES via Microsoft Outlook, but who also makes suggestions for possible dates over e-mail and signs them, 'Please advise.' My girlfriends have 'advised' me to send him a fake auto-reply message that says, 'I regret to inform you that Karen no longer dates corporate robots. If in the future you feel better qualified for this position, please resubmit your resume. Until then, good luck getting that stick out of your ass. Respectfully yours, the management.'"

I'd already read the e-mails several times, but reading them again made me chuckle. Nothing like comic relief to reduce your stress level.

"Whatcha got there?"

I looked up and saw Ben, the intern, sitting down across the table from me. I think that was the first time I'd ever heard him speak.

"Oh, just some viewer e-mails I wanted to share with…"

Before I could finish the sentence, he was playing with his phone.

I bet he's president of NBC some day, I thought.

"Good morning, Waverly." The sound of Wendy's voice made the hair on the back of my neck stand up.

I slowly looked to my right. "Hi, Wendy, how are you?" *Damn it.*

She nodded politely, her hair as blonde and stiff as ever. A few staff members trailed in behind her, followed by Scotty, who was carrying a big pink box and a pile of napkins.

"Are those what I think they are?" I quickly stood up.

"If you think they're granola bars, then the answer would be no." He set the box in the middle of the conference table and opened it. We all pounced and grabbed doughnuts; some people grabbed two. I snagged an old fashioned glazed, my favorite.

"So did everyone have fun at the party?" Scotty said. "Anyone still hung over?"

I looked up at him. "Still hung over? It's *Wednesday*."

"This is *New York*, Waverly. When are you going to realize that you live in *New York*?"

"Touché." I laughed and took a bite of my doughnut.

"Those aren't going to help your figure," Wendy said under her breath.

At least she was back to normal.

• • •

Wendy didn't mention my encounter with Gary during the meeting, and she left as soon as it was over. I relaxed in my chair for a few minutes, glad it was over, at least for now. I looked at my notepad in front of me, full of new ideas for *Honey on Your Mind*. I had a ton, but I still hadn't come up with one for the New Year's Eve show, which I knew had to outshine the rest.

I closed my eyes for a moment and thought of everything I had on *my* mind: Meeting Jake's family at Christmas, Andie's visit in a couple days, my dad's wedding, Paige and Gary, Wendy and Gary, the New Year's Eve show, the growth of Waverly's Honey Shop, and everything that came with it, including a fear that it would all explode in my face.

Then, of course, toss in regular sleep deprivation and the stress of having a boyfriend who lived in another state and traveled for work even more than I did.

I took a deep breath.

Could I handle it all?

I didn't feel like I had any choice.

• • •

Late that afternoon I called Jake, even though I knew the chances he'd be able to chat were slimmer than a teenage runway model. I hung up when I got his voice mail. I needed to talk to someone though, so I decided to try McKenna on the off chance she would answer her phone.

Again, no luck.

Sigh.

I really had to talk to someone.

Andie was coming to town in two days. What was I going to do? Should I tell her that her favorite cousin's sweetheart of a new boyfriend was, in fact, married to my psycho boss? I never kept secrets from Andie, and I knew she wasn't *super* close to Paige, but still, who was I to get involved? The same went for Scotty. Since he worked with Wendy, he was off-limits too. I had to stay professional, no matter how freaked out I was.

In a last-ditch effort to find someone to confide in, I called Kristina, whose busy schedule rivaled that of all my other friends. Surprisingly, she answered on the second ring.

"Waverly! How are you?"

"Hey, Kristina! Actually, I'm in semi-crisis mode."

"Uh-oh, that doesn't sound good."

I sighed. "I really need your level head right now. Any chance you're free to lend me an ear?"

"I'm at the hospital now but get off at eight. Would that work?"

"Yes! I'll come to you. Just tell me where."

We made plans to meet at a coffee shop called Daisy's Café on the Upper East Side. A couple of hours later, I was sitting at a table across from her, a huge brownie on a plate in front of me. I'd just finished telling her all about Paige and Gary, hoping she could help me figure out what to do.

"So that's the story." I picked up the brownie and lifted it to my mouth. "As you can see from the thousands of calories I'm about to inhale, it has me a little stressed out."

She laughed. "That's definitely intense."

"I know. I hate being in the middle like this. What do you think I should do? Should I tell Paige?"

"You want my honest opinion?"

"Yes! You know way more about the celebrity world than I do." It had been several years since Kristina had won her Olympic silver medal in figure skating, but she still got looks of curious recognition nearly everywhere she went. And being married to Shane Kennedy? I couldn't even imagine what it was like when they were together.

"Honestly, I think you should say nothing, do nothing," she said.

"Really?"

"Really. The thing is, you have no idea what's going on in that marriage. She may know all about his cheating and want to stay with him anyway, even if he *is* a total scumbag."

I nodded. "That's what Jake said. But if she *does* know, it just sounds so...so...*seedy*. Who could live like that?"

"You'd be surprised. Shane and I see it all the time. People put up with a *lot* to live the lifestyle of the rich and famous."

"I just feel so bad for Paige, and for Wendy too. I mean, don't get me wrong, I still sort of hate Wendy, but it must be awful to know your husband is out there cheating on you. And Paige is such a kind person. She deserves better."

"I can't imagine what that must feel like, for any of them." Kristina and Shane had met years before they became famous, which she often credited for the success of their marriage.

I broke off a chunk of brownie. "And even if Wendy *doesn't* know, I still feel bad, because *I* know."

"Maybe she's cheating too."

I shook my head. "That's what Jake said, but I doubt it. The way she talks about her *huuusband* is so over the top. I don't see how you could fake that."

"Maybe there's a reason it's over the top."

I raised my eyebrows. "I never thought about it that way. So you think she knows?"

"I have no idea. I've never met her. But people have their reasons, and you never know what's going on behind the scenes."

I took a sip of water. "So you think I should just keep quiet?"

"It's your call, but I would."

"And Andie?"

"I wouldn't say anything to her either because it's her cousin. Getting involved, even if you mean well, could get dicey."

I pressed my palm against my forehead. "Andie can always tell when I'm hiding something. She's superhuman that way. And you know my tendency to blurt things out of my big fat mouth."

Kristina smiled. "Well, you're going to have to try to keep it shut, aren't you?"

I nodded. "Apparently so."

chapter ten

On Friday, I rose as usual at the crack of dawn, this time to interview a married couple in their nineties who had lived in the same Upper West Side apartment for more than seventy years. My body was slowly getting used to the early mornings, although I still hated starting my day when it was dark outside. This morning, though, I had a spring in my step because Andie would be in town soon! She was coming straight to my apartment from the airport early that evening, and after a brief tour of my neighborhood, I planned to take her to the trendy Meatpacking District for dinner. With Paige off in Vermont, I had a rare weekend respite from my Honey line, and unless Scotty called with a last-minute assignment, I was also free from *Honey on Your Mind*. I couldn't remember the last time I hadn't worked for at least a few hours on either Saturday or Sunday—or both.

The buzzer in my apartment rang a few minutes after seven. I jumped up from the couch and practically sprinted to the intercom.

"*Hola*?"

"We're here!"

I paused for a moment.

"Did you say *we*?"

"Yes, *we*! Now buzz us in, it's freezing out here."

Huh?

"OK, I'm on the fourth floor." I pressed the button and cracked open my front door, then walked back to the living room and sat on the couch. *Huh?* Had Andie brought her boyfriend with her? I loved Nick, but I'd been so excited for a girls' weekend. How could we talk about boys over drinks if one of the boys we'd be talking about was drinking right there with us?"

A couple of minutes later, I heard the elevator door open, then footsteps, followed by the sound of Andie's voice. "Hey, TV star, I brought you a present," she yelled from down the hall.

I stood up and ran to the front door. I was expecting to greet Nick, but I jumped up and down in excitement when I saw the tall blonde standing next to Andie.

"Mackie! Oh my God!" I wrapped my arms around her.

"Hello? Am I invisible?" Andie put her hands on her hips.

I laughed and hugged her too, then looked back at McKenna. "What are you doing here?"

"I'm visiting my famous friend in New York. What does it look like I'm doing?"

"I can't believe you're really here! How did you get away?" I took her suitcase and wheeled it into my apartment.

"My parents flew down from Oregon to help Hunter. I pumped enough breast milk to feed a small village, and then jumped on a plane with Andie. And here we are."

I looked at Andie. "I can't believe you didn't tell me about this."

She lightly pounded her chest with her tiny fist. "Hey now, you know I'm a champion at keeping secrets."

As soon as the words were out of her mouth, I thought of Paige. *I hope I can be a champion at keeping secrets too.*

• • •

Three hours later, we were contemplating dessert at Spice Market, a trendy Asian fusion place in the Meatpacking District. For the latter part of dinner, McKenna had been sharing stories of how much her life had changed in the six months since Elizabeth was born. Diapers, breastfeeding, crying, more diapers, more breastfeeding, more crying, very little sleep. She'd gone from a high-paying banking job to an endless cycle of caring for a helpless blob whose only form of compensation was a heart-melting smile. Despite it all, she was obviously head over heels in love.

"Thanks for the birth control, I mean the updates," Andie said, signaling to the waiter to bring us another bottle of wine. "Sounds just like the life I've always dreamed of...if by 'dreams' you mean 'nightmares.'"

McKenna laughed. "I *do* love it, and I *do* love her, but good *God*, it's a lot of work, and the amount of work is inversely related to the amount of sleep I get. I'm spending a small fortune on concealer to hide the bags under my eyes."

"Put Benadryl in her bottle," Andie said. "That would knock the little crier out."

"Andie!" I covered my mouth, trying not to laugh.

She put her hands up. "Hey now, I'm just trying to help."

"I think I might end up in jail if I did that, but thanks for the suggestion," McKenna said, also trying not to laugh.

Andie shrugged as the waiter opened a new bottle for us. "It's only illegal if they catch you, you know."

McKenna put a hand on Andie's shoulder and squeezed. "I'm going to have to start writing your little sayings down." Then she looked at me. "So let's talk about *you*, Wave. Are you loving your new job?"

I nodded. "Yes, I really am. When I first started, I had literally no idea what I was doing. I mean *no* idea. But it gets easier every day."

"Do you like seeing yourself on TV?" Andie asked. "I don't think I'd like that. High-definition is not a friend of the thirty-something complexion."

I put a hand on my cheek. "Tell me about it. Thank God for the makeup artists. They're like Photoshop for real life."

She sipped her wine. "Are you getting more comfortable in front of the camera?"

"I don't know if I'll ever be *entirely* comfortable, but I'm getting used to it. Sort of like how I feel about wearing a thong."

"What about the unpredictable schedule?" McKenna said. "I know how much you hate getting up early."

"I still do. I'm getting used to the erratic hours, but I'll *never* get used to rising before the sun does."

"Are you getting any exercise?" McKenna asked.

I slouched in my seat. "Not really. I went to a yoga studio down the street once, but the teacher was a total yoga Nazi, so I never went back."

"A yoga Nazi?" McKenna said. "How so?"

I played with my earring. "It was advertised as just a regular *vinyasa* class, but it was super hot in there, and I was dying. I mean *dying*. At one point I literally thought I might sweat to death."

"Gross," Andie said. "Sweat is yet one more reason not to exercise."

"So I asked the teacher to open a window. That's a reasonable request, right?" They both nodded.

I tapped my palms on the table. "Well, by the look on her face, you would have thought I'd asked her to throw her newborn baby out the window while she was at it, and maybe a couple puppies too. She gave me the evil eye, then walked away, window still closed."

"Skinny yoga bitch," Andie said.

"So that was the end of me and yoga. *Namaste.*" I pressed my palms together and did a little bow.

"What about running?" McKenna took a sip of her wine. "Have you found any good routes around your neighborhood?" Back in San Francisco I'd never been in great shape, but I'd run more or less regularly, or at least enough to make up for my more or less regular ice cream consumption.

I frowned. "I know I should get into some sort of a routine, but I just can't seem to make myself. I've gone for a run a handful of times, but that's about it. I suck."

Andie picked up her wine glass and waved her free hand dismissively. "I still don't know why you would want to do that anyway."

I looked at her. "You mean run?"

She nodded. "It's just so, I don't know, *unnatural.*"

McKenna laughed. "Unnatural? What do you mean?"

Andie set her wine glass down and cupped her cheeks with her hands. "I mean just *think* what all that jarring up and down is doing to your skin, which is already in a losing battle with gravity. I like to think that by *not* running, I'm preserving the structural integrity of my face."

I laughed. "Did you just say you're *preserving the structural integrity of your face?*"

McKenna pretended to look for a pen. "I'm writing that one down too."

Andie nodded. "My mom used to say that all the time when I was little. Now that I think about it, it may be the one thing she and I actually agree on."

I laughed again. "You're nuts. Did you know that?"

"We'll see who's nuts when we're fifty." She shrugged and took a sip of her wine.

I tapped my palms on the table. "So hey, we haven't talked about Nick yet. Are you going to move in with him?"

"Oooh yes, do tell," McKenna said. "Now that I'm married with a baby, I need to live vicariously through you two."

Andie shook her head. "I don't want to talk about that tonight, my friends."

I narrowed my eyes. "You don't? Is everything OK?"

She nodded. "Everything's fine. I just don't want to talk about it."

"You sure everything's OK?" McKenna asked.

She nodded again. "I'm sure. I just need a night off from thinking about my future, all right? I'm *sick* of thinking about my future. Tonight I just want to celebrate my birthday with my best girlfriends and live in the moment."

I knew how *that* felt.

"OK, birthday girl, we'll table that discussion for later." I turned back to McKenna and refilled her wine glass. "So when are you going back to work?"

"I'm hoping next month."

"Are you looking forward to it?"

She sighed. "To be honest, yes *and* no. I mean, on the one hand, I'm dying for more intellectual stimulation, because taking care of a baby can be mind-numbingly boring."

"Now there's a shocking piece of information," Andie said.

"But on the other hand..." McKenna's voice trailed off.

"On the other hand *what*?" I said.

Suddenly, McKenna began to cry.

"Mackie are you OK?" I put my hand on her shoulder.

She nodded and wiped a tear from her eyes. "I'm fine."

"You sure aren't *acting* fine," Andie said. "What's going on? Are you still all hormonal? Do I need to give you a shot in the butt or something?"

McKenna laughed. "No, really, I'm fine, I swear. It's just that, while I'm eager to get back to work, the thought of leaving Elizabeth…it's just…*hard*."

I kept my hand on her shoulder. "You really love her, don't you?"

She smiled. "Wave, you have no idea. It's indescribable."

"You know what *I* love?" Andie said, standing up to use the restroom.

We both looked at her.

"Uninterrupted sleep. And sex whenever I want. And spit-up-free clothes."

McKenna laughed again and wiped her tears away with a napkin. "Stop it."

"And of course I love *you* as well." Andie blew McKenna a kiss as she walked away. As soon as she was gone, I flagged the waiter and told him it was Andie's birthday. He nodded politely and quickly disappeared.

"So when will you know for sure when you're going back?" I picked up my wine glass and turned back to McKenna.

"We just need to find the right nanny, which is a lot harder than I thought it would be. Now that Elizabeth is an actual *person* and not just the idea of one, the thought of leaving her with a stranger all day every day is scary."

Andie reappeared and sat back down. "What's scary?"

"The thought of leaving Elizabeth with a stranger," McKenna said.

Andie shook her head and lowered her voice. "I can only imagine. I get nervous when I let a stranger wax my privates."

"And there's another one for the list," McKenna said.

I laughed. "Oh, how I've missed you, Andie Barnett."

"And oh, how Andie Barnett has missed you back." She rubbed her hands together. "So let's get this party started. I heard there are great places to go dancing in the Meatpacking District. What do you ladies think?"

"Dancing?" McKenna and I said at the same time.

Andie stretched her tiny arms over her head and nodded.

"Are you serious?" McKenna said.

"Yeah, why not?"

McKenna looked at me. "Do you go dancing very often?"

I laughed. "Is that a rhetorical question?"

"How many times have you been dancing since you moved to New York?" Andie asked.

I held up a fist to start counting on my fingers. "That would be…zero." I kept my hand in a fist.

McKenna looked at Andie. "We're in our *thirties*, now, Andie. I have a *child*. I think dancing in the Meatpacking District is in the rearview mirror." She pointed her thumb over her shoulder.

"On the contrary." Andie shook her head. "That pathetic, fat egg Waverly just showed us is exactly why we should go dancing. Come on, ladies, we're in *New York*! It's Friday night, and it's my *birthday*, and now you want to, what, just go *home*?"

McKenna and I exchanged glances.

"Yes?" I said.

"Wrong answer." Andie pounded her hand lightly against the table. "I'm the *birthday girl*, so you two have to do what I say. And I say that we are *not* going home."

"We're not?" I said.

She shook her head. "Definitely not."

"I don't like the sound of this," McKenna said.

"Have you ever noticed that you're sort of bossy?" I said to Andie.

"Why, thank you," Andie said.

Just then, the waiter appeared with a slice of cake, a big candle on top.

Andie grinned and put her hand on her heart. "For *moi*?"

I grinned back. "Of course! Nothing but the best for the birthday girl."

She pushed her hair behind her ears and leaned toward us. "Nice. Now ladies, before I blow out this candle, I want you to remember something."

We looked at her.

She held up three fingers with each hand. "I'm thirty-three, and this weekend it's all about *me*. You got that? Thirty-*three*, and it's all about *me*."

McKenna laughed. "Noted."

We sang happy birthday, and as Andie blew out the candle, I scooted next to her and put my arm around her. "Did I mention how much I've missed you?"

• • •

"*How* much?"

"Sixty-six."

"Sixty-six dollars for *three drinks*?"

The bartender gave me a curt nod. "Would you like to open a tab?"

"Um, I guess so." I reached into my purse, but just then, Andie appeared and shooed me away.

"Move aside, amateur." She handed the bartender her credit card. "Can you add three tequila shots to that order? Top shelf, please."

The bartender smiled at her. "Coming right up."

As I stepped back, I looked to my right and saw two younger women aggressively jostling for bar space next to Andie. They looked just out of high school and were dressed in spandex, ultra-short minidresses that barely covered their behinds, not to mention their water-balloonish cleavage.

I turned the other way and lowered my voice to McKenna. "Holy underage prostitution ring, do you *see* the outfits on the other side of me? Those girls look like they're about fourteen. Did *you* dress like that when you were fourteen?"

"I wore a headgear when I was fourteen."

I laughed, then leaned toward the bar and poked my head over Andie's shoulder. "By the way, did you just say *shots*?"

She grinned and nodded. "Oh yes, I did."

"I can't remember the last time I did a shot," McKenna said.

"It's got to be hard to do a shot with a headgear on." I looked behind her at the crowd, which was filled with girls in outrageous outfits that were equally—if not *more*—slutty than those of the two at the bar. Who *were* these people?

Andie handed each of us a tiny glass. "I remember the last time you did a shot, McKenna."

"You do? When was it?"

Andie grinned. "About five seconds from now."

McKenna laughed. "Thanks for remembering."

"Anytime. Ready, girls? Here's to a night full of birthday memories so fun we won't even remember them."

I laughed. "What?"

"You heard me. Now *drink*, TV girl. I'm thirty-three, and it's all about me, remember?"

I looked at McKenna, who was preparing to take her shot. "You're really doing it?"

She shrugged "When in Rome. Or the Meatpacking District, I guess."

"Down it," Andie said to me.

"OK, OK. Thank God your birthday doesn't come around every day."

We held up our shots, and then threw them back like old times. Despite my best effort to appear poised and dignified, I made a face as the tequila stung my throat. I set my empty glass on the bar and sucked on a lime. "That was disgusting."

"You're welcome." Andie gestured toward the bar. "Fresh cocktails are waiting for you both right there. Now if you'll excuse me, I need to pee."

She took off for the restroom, leaving McKenna and me to observe the scene around us. The place was getting more crowded by the minute.

"Can you believe we're in a *club*? And in *Manhattan*?" I reached for the drinks.

"I can't believe I'm up past eleven."

I laughed and handed her a glass. "I still can't believe I live here. How did that happen?"

Before she could reply, two dorky looking guys approached us. I know that sounds mean, but dorky is by far the most accurate word in the English language to describe them. One had short hair with girl bangs. The other was wearing a yellow turtleneck.

"How are you two doing tonight?" Girl-Bangs Guy said.

I smiled. "Not bad. We're here celebrating a friend's birthday."

"The big twenty-one?" Turtleneck Guy elbowed me, and I flinched.

"Not quite." I shot McKenna an *Are you kidding me?* look.

"Are you from here?" Girl-Bangs Guy said.

McKenna pointed to herself and then to me. "She lives in Brooklyn, and I'm visiting from San Francisco."

"Frisco? That's so cool! I've never been to Cali," Turtleneck Guy nodded enthusiastically.

I cringed at the double offense of Frisco and Cali in the same sentence. It took all my will power not to kick McKenna.

"We live on Staten Island," Girl-Bangs Guy said. "We were in the city for a conference today."

"A conference?" I wondered what kind of event would attract this pair. Maybe a comic book expo? Video games? Computing hacking?

Turtleneck Guy nodded. "Yeah, it was an all-day thing."

McKenna took a sip of her drink. "What was it for?"

"It was a self-help conference," Girl-Bangs Guy said with a smile.

I nearly spat out my drink. *Oh God, I'm the one who needs help right now.*

"It was really good," Turtleneck Guy said. "Look at us now, talking to you two gorgeous women." I couldn't stop staring at his upper lip, which now glistened with beer.

McKenna smiled brightly. "Excellent. Good for you." Then she held up her left hand. "But unfortunately I'm married, so it's probably best if you guys chat with women who are available. Good luck to you both."

Before they could reply, she grabbed my arm and pulled me away.

"Nice escape," I said when we were out of earshot. "That was almost Andie-ish in its execution."

She laughed and finished off her drink. "Let's just say my tolerance for alcohol isn't the only thing that has gone down since I had a baby." I think she might have been slurring her words a bit, or maybe my ears weren't functioning properly. However you wanted to slice it, the wine, the shots, and the mixed drinks had clearly begun to kick in.

And were about to kick our butts.

Just then, Andie reappeared. She held her arms open when she saw us. "Ladies! Ladies! Looks like you could both use another drink. Am I right? Am I right?"

McKenna and I exchanged glances and started giggling.

"Did I miss something?" Andie said.

"Nope. Just glad to see you," I gave her a hug, and McKenna followed.

"Have I told you guys lately how much I mean to you?" McKenna slurred.

Andie laughed. "How much *you* mean to *us*?"

I hiccupped. "You know what she means."

"This is going to be ugly," Andie said. "You guys are way out of practice."

I nodded and poked her shoulder with my finger. "Have I told *you* lately how smart you are?"

• • •

"Chop chop, ladies, time to get a move on." Andie stood at the foot of my bed and clapped her hands.

I didn't open my eyes. "What time is it?"

"Eleven."

"What time did we go to sleep?"

"Four."

"Can you come back in three hours?" I cracked open an eye. McKenna was lying comatose next to me. "I'm sure my couch is missing you."

Andie sat on the foot of the bed. "No can do. We have a lot on the agenda today. I'm calling the shots this weekend, remember?"

I finally opened my eyes all the way and looked at the ceiling fan. "Can you please never, *ever,* say that word again?"

"Oh my God, I feel disgusting." McKenna pulled a pillow over her head.

"Ditto. Now will you please go away?" I weakly waved an arm in the direction of Andie's voice.

Andie stood up and put her hands on her hips. "OK, fine. I'm taking a shower, and when I get *out,* you two are getting *up.* Do you hear me?"

"I hate you right now," McKenna said. "And I hate your stupid birthday powers too."

"You two are embarrassing yourselves." Andie stomped her feet as she walked out of my bedroom.

"I want to die," McKenna said, her head still under the pillow. "I haven't drunk that much since…since way before I was pregnant. Actually, have I *ever* drunk that much?"

I slowly sat up and held my head in my hands. "I'm dying too. I haven't gone out on the town like that the whole time I've lived here." I turned to look at her. "Did I just dream it, or did we dance on the top of a table at some point last night?"

She removed the pillow from her face and started laughing. "Oh my God. I think that really happened."

I winced. "I didn't make out with anyone, did I? You know my history of making out with randoms after a few drinks."

"I don't think so, although you *were* chatting up that guy in the purple vest."

I squinted at her. "Did you just say I was chatting up a guy in a *purple vest*?"

"You were."

"*Why*, exactly?"

"God knows. I remember chatting with some guy for a while too, but then, for some reason, I think I starting talking about breastfeeding. He bolted shortly thereafter."

I laughed. "You brought up breastfeeding at a *bar*?"

She covered her face with the pillow again. "I'm never drinking again."

I swung my legs to the floor. "Don't tell Andie that. It will just fire her up for tonight."

"I really hate that girl sometimes."

I laughed. "Me too. She's the best."

• • •

An hour and a half later, we were finally showered, out of the apartment, and reluctantly accompanying Andie on her quest to eat at the world-famous Katz's Delicatessen on the Lower East Side. Still dragging, McKenna and I were each nursing a huge cup of coffee from Connecticut Muffin as we emerged from the subway and entered the cavernous restaurant.

After ordering at the counter, we found an empty table and sat down to wait for our food. McKenna put her hand on her forehead and groaned. "I haven't been this hungover since the last time I was in New York."

"You mean when the three of us came here right before your wedding?" I said.

She nodded. "You two are bad news."

"Hey now, it wasn't me." I pointed to Andie. "*She's* the one who kept buying all those drinks."

Andie pretended to hand me a platter. "Do you want some cheese with that whine? You grandmas really need to suck it up."

She unzipped her hoodie to reveal a blue Honey Tee that said BEER GOGGLES ARE THE LONELY GIRL'S CUPID.

"Did you steal that from my living room?" I asked.

She shrugged. "I was just helping reduce the clutter. You have like fifty boxes of Honey crap in there."

"Not for long, thanks to Paige. Soon it'll be like a real business." I clapped my hands like a little kid.

McKenna narrowed her eyes at Andie. "How is it possible that you feel so good right now? Were you secretly drinking less than we were?"

She shook her head. "I'm dating Nick Prodromou, remember? My alcohol tolerance is at an all-time high."

I nodded. "Ah, yes, I forgot. Nick can drink like no one's business." I'd gone out for drinks with Nick a few times when we were coworkers at the *San Francisco Sun,* and I'd always paid dearly for it the next morning. It was a good thing he was such a blast. It was the only thing that made the day-after suffering worth it.

Our number came up, and the workers behind the ancient counter handed us our pastrami sandwiches, which could more accurately be described as towering piles of meat held together by a couple of slices of plain, un-toasted bread.

"Tell me again why we're here?" I stared at my plate.

"This place is *legendary.* I can't believe you've never eaten here," Andie said. "It's been here for more than a hundred years. Just look around." She gestured toward the walls, which were covered with photos, old and new, of people, famous and not so famous, all tucking into towering piles of meat held together by a couple of slices of plain, un-toasted bread.

I looked back down at my plate. "This is more food than I normally eat in a week."

"I'm going to barf." McKenna put her face in her hands.

"You look terrible," I said to her. "You're really pale."

Andie sat up straight and pushed her hair behind her ears. "Focus on what's in front of you and eat, ladies. I promise it will make you feel better. By the way, did you know this is where they filmed that famous scene from *When Harry Met Sally*?"

My ears perked up. "You mean the one where Meg Ryan fakes the orgasm?"

Several people turned around, and McKenna laughed and put her hand over my mouth. "Shhh, Waverly, you're totally yelling."

I lowered my voice. "Oops, sorry. I'm still talking in my drunk voice."

Andie shook her head. "You two are totally JV now. It's really quite disappointing."

• • •

After lunch, we debated what to do next as we strolled through the Lower East Side. Given that it was the weekend before Christmas, we'd already decided to avoid the shopping zoos of SoHo and Times Square.

"I don't think my stomach can handle a ferry right now," McKenna said in response to my halfhearted suggestion of a river tour.

"Actually, I have a bit of a stomachache too," Andie said.

I poked her shoulder with my finger. "It's no wonder. Why did you insist on eating your entire sandwich? That thing probably weighed more than you do." McKenna and I had barely made it through half of ours before giving up.

Andie looked at me. "I couldn't just *leave* it there. That would be like walking off the field in the eighty-fifth minute of the World Cup final, with the score tied."

McKenna laughed. "You're insane."

"I'm a *champion*," Andie said. "And wasn't I right? Were those sandwiches not totally amazing?"

McKenna and I both nodded.

"You were right," I said. "Very tasty."

"Like amnesia on bread," McKenna said. "For a few moments there, I forgot all about how sick I feel."

Andie put a hand on her heart and took a little bow. "Of course I was right. You don't question the master."

I lifted my arms and one leg in *Karate Kid* fashion. "Got it, Mr. Miyagi."

"I'm going to pretend I didn't see that." She approached a card table on the sidewalk that was covered with T-shirts. "Hold up for a minute, ladies. I need to buy Nick one of these." Nick's trademark was his collection of T-shirts with witty sayings. The first one I ever saw him wear said Even Awesome Needs to Sleep. He'd been wearing it *at the office* and proudly called it "a crowd favorite."

The three of us started plowing through the pile, looking for shirts that were funny but not offensive—or at least not *too* offensive. It's a fine line.

"How about this?" I held one up that said I'd rather be quilting.

Andie gestured for me to give it to her. "I like it, hand it over."

"Check out this one." McKenna held up It's not a beer belly, it's a gas tank for the sex machine.

"He already has that one," Andie said.

I looked at her. "You're joking."

She looked back at me. "Have you *met* Nick?"

"Good point."

McKenna tried again. "How about this?" It said REAL MEN DON'T MANSCAPE.

Andie grabbed it out of McKenna's hands. "I love it! I'm buying him that one too."

The day was clear and crisp, but not nearly as cold as I'd feared. We kept walking and soon started popping in and out of funky little stores. I was grateful not to be swimming through a sea of frantic holiday shoppers. Navigating crowds of tourists was painful enough when I wasn't hungover.

"So speaking of the T-shirt man, Andie, what *is* the latest?" I held open a door to a vintage clothing boutique. "You were evasive last night."

She pushed past me into the store. "I know, I know."

McKenna and I followed her. "Are you going to move in with him?" I asked.

She didn't say anything.

"Well?" McKenna said.

"Well?" I echoed.

Finally Andie spoke. "Ladies…"

"*Yes?*"

"I think…I think I'm going to take the plunge."

"Wow!" McKenna said. "That's huge!"

"For real? You're going to give up your apartment?" I said.

Andie shrugged. "I know, I know. It's a total leap of faith, which is unlike me, but it just *feels* right, you know what I mean?"

McKenna, who had been with Hunter since before we could legally rent a car, smiled. "I know *exactly* what you mean. I'm so happy for you."

I sifted through a rack of dresses. "I can't believe it. I never thought I'd see the day."

"Me neither," Andie said. "After so many years of being emotional Teflon, I didn't think I'd ever find someone who would actually *stick*."

McKenna rolled her eyes. "Please, you're hardly emotional Teflon. You're just…picky. That's not a bad thing."

Andie held up a hand. "You don't have to sugarcoat it. I know I'm a handful. But, despite my…for lack of a better word, *bitchiness,* Nick makes me feel so, I don't know, *accepted,* no matter how mean I am. I'm not sure what the right word is. But whatever it is, he does it."

I walked over and hugged her. "You're going to make me cry. And I agree with Mackie. You're not emotional Teflon, and you're not mean. You're spunky and dynamic and interesting and *wonderful*, and I hope you know how lucky he is to have you."

She hugged me back for a moment, and then pushed me away. "OK, enough about my stunted emotional development. So what about *you*? What's going on with Jake? We haven't talked about that yet either."

I smiled. "I'm happy to report that Jake is great. *Wonderful*, in fact. He could probably even play a prince in a Disney movie."

"I'm going to pretend you didn't just say that." Andie fake-choked herself.

I laughed and started looking through the dresses again. "The only problem is that I don't get to see him that often. Our schedules are both so busy."

"Have you freaked out on him lately?" McKenna said.

I slowly put my hands on my hips. "You will both be proud to hear that *no*, I have not. I've made a huge effort to talk to him nearly every day, and you know how bad I am about talking on the phone."

"Yeah, you really suck at that," Andie said.

"I'm not one to cast stones," McKenna said. "These days I don't even know where my phone is half the time."

"You have a baby, that doesn't count," Andie said to her.

I adjusted my ponytail. "So anyhow, I've been making a big effort to include him in everything that's been going on with me, the good *and* the bad. And guess what? I've even shared a big secret with him."

As soon as I said that last part, I wanted to cover my mouth. *Shut up, Waverly!*

Andie's ears perked up. "A big secret? Do tell."

I hesitated.

"Well?" she said.

"I…I really shouldn't, I'm sorry," I said.

What is wrong with you, Waverly?

"You're keeping a secret from *us*? For real?" Andie looked from me to McKenna, who put her hands up as if to say *I don't want to get involved.*

I shook my head. "I'm sorry, Andie. I can't. I shouldn't have mentioned it."

She looked a bit hurt, which surprised me. Didn't she have any secrets that were just between her and Nick?

I decided to change the subject. "Anyhow, speaking of Jake, I have some big news."

Their eyes immediately darted to my left hand.

I laughed. "Not *that*."

"Well, what then?" McKenna said.

"He invited me to spend Christmas with his family."

"No way!" Andie pushed my arm. "That's huge."

"I know. Can you believe it? I'm totally nervous."

"Congratulations. That's a major milestone in the relation-ship department," McKenna said.

I bit my lip. "Tell me about it. Like I don't already have enough on my mind right now."

"What do you mean?" Andie said.

Before I could reply, I felt a light tap on my shoulder.

"Excuse me, are you Waverly from *Love, Wendy*?"

I turned and saw two women in their early twenties smiling at me. One wore a baseball hat, the other a high bun. I smiled back and hoped they hadn't overheard our conversation.

"Hi, um, yes, that's me."

"We love that show!" Hat Girl playfully clapped her hands as High-Bun Girl whipped out her phone.

"Can we take a picture with you?" High-Bun Girl asked.

"Um, sure," *Ugh.* I wish I'd bothered to put on makeup, because I knew that picture was totally going on Facebook for the whole world to see. Where was Tanya and her magic toolbox when I needed her?

"I'll take it!" Andie put out her hand. "So you like watching *Love, Wendy*?"

"We love it," Hat Girl said as she handed over the phone. "We watch it all the time at our sorority house. We go to Rutgers."

"What house are you in?" I asked.

"Delta Gamma," High-Bun Girl said.

"*Waverly* was a Delta Gamma," Andie said. "Did you know that?"

Both girls looked at me. "You were?" they asked in unison.

I nodded. "At Cal Berkeley. She was too." I pointed to McKenna.

"That's so cool!" Hat Girl said.

"So speaking of *Honey on Your Mind*, can you tell that Waverly has a Delta Gamma-style hangover on *her* mind right now?" Andie said.

"Andie!" I gasped as McKenna covered her mouth and cracked up.

Hat Girl laughed too. "We're totally hurting too. We had our holiday formal last night."

High-Bun Girl nodded. "It was intense. On the way home, my date threw up out the window of the bus."

"That happened to me once," McKenna said. "KA spring fling. Jason Parker. Off the balcony."

"I think it happens to everyone at least once," Andie said, nodding.

I thought of my sorority days from way back when. It was hard to wrap my head around how many years had passed since then. The two women standing here seemed so young, which of course made me think about how old we must seem to them. *Are we really that old now?*

As I posed for a photo with my "fans," I glanced at McKenna and thought of her husband and baby at home, then took a quick look at Andie and thought of the big move that awaited her back in San Francisco.

There was no getting around it. No matter how immature we acted on occasion, we were grown up now. We were hardly *old*, but no one would consider us kids anymore.

• • •

"So how long do you think you'll stay in New York?" McKenna finished her water and set the glass on the table. She had insisted on an alcohol-free dinner that evening, at least for herself. Meanwhile, Andie, more determined than ever to remain childless after seeing how far McKenna had fallen from her glory days of barhopping the night away, had ordered a bottle of pinot noir that she and I would split.

"I'm really not sure. At first, I had it in my head that I'd stay for a couple years, but after living here a few months, I can see how two years could easily stretch into like...*ten*. There's just so much to *do*, and I haven't even scratched the surface."

She shook her head. "Don't stay away *too* long. Elizabeth's early education won't be complete without witnessing a few Waverly moments. It's just not the same hearing about them over the phone."

"Thank you, Mackie. That's what I'll think the next time I slip on a patch of ice or a pigeon drops a load on my head: I wish little Elizabeth had seen that."

Andie refilled my wine glass. "I hate pigeons. They're like flying rats. So how's it been working with Paige?"

I felt the blood in my veins go cold. So far, I'd managed to avoid the topic of Paige and had been hoping to get through the rest of the weekend without having to talk about her at all. Knowing me and my big mouth, I knew the chances were excellent that I'd inadvertently blurt out something inappropriate.

"Paige?"

"Yeah, how's that going?"

I had to say *something*, but I didn't want to lie. I was a horrible liar, and Andie was perceptive, so I needed to be careful.

I decided to tell the truth and exercise selective omission.

"She's great. Amazing, actually. She's lined up some big retail accounts for Waverly's Honey Shop, and in January she's coming on board full-time."

"Full-time, for real?" Andie said. "You'll be paying her a salary?"

I shook my head. "Commission, but a really good commission. And did I tell you guys I'm opening an office for Waverly's Honey Shop? I feel like I didn't tell you that."

"I think I need to subscribe to your blog to keep up with your life," McKenna said.

"Please, like I would *ever* in a million years have a blog."

"And thank God for that," Andie said.

I nodded. "I *hate* personal blogs. Why people feel the need to share the minutia of their lives with the whole world is beyond me. Why on earth would I want anyone to know about my bunions? Or what type of shampoo I use? It's madness!"

"I feel the same about people who Tweet," Andie said.

I pointed at her. "Exactly. And don't even get me started on Facebook."

"You two want to get off your social-media soapbox so Waverly can tell us more about her office?" McKenna said.

I smiled. "I'm sorry. I just get a little fired up about stuff like that. Anyhow, the Honey products really seem to be taking off, and while I'm exhausted from running around at Paige's beck and call, none of it would have happened without her. She's really good at her job."

"She's crazy smart," Andie said. "I remember when we were kids, she knew all the answers on *Jeopardy*. She was a brainiac, even back then."

I took a sip of wine and thought about how I could change the subject. Before I could say anything, Andie spoke again.

"So is Paige seeing anyone these days?"

Damn.

Don't lie, don't lie, don't lie.

"Um, I think so," I said, burying my nose in my glass.

"Really? I'm glad to hear that," Andie said. "That girl has been through the dating ringer."

McKenna looked at her. "More than Waverly?"

I coughed. "Thanks for that. It's nice to know I'm a barometer by which to measure romantic failure."

"Hey now, she's just telling it like it is. Don't be afraid to own it," Andie said. "And yes, Paige's list of dating horror stories rivals Waverly's. At every family reunion she seems to have a new one that tops the one before it."

"Really?" McKenna said.

"Oh yes. Has she told you about Wait-for-a-Taxi Guy?"

I looked at her. "*Wait-for-a-Taxi Guy*?"

"Yeah, it was when she lived in Baltimore. That story is *unbelievable*."

"Well?" McKenna said. "Are you going to leave us just hanging?"

Andie leaned toward us for a moment, and then sat up straight. "Are you sure you want to hear this? It's gross, and we're eating."

McKenna waved a hand in front of her. "Please. You don't know gross until you give birth."

Andie nodded. "True. It doesn't get much grosser than pushing a fully formed human being out of your vagina."

"Andie!" I said, laughing.

"*She* brought it up," Andie said with a shrug.

McKenna rubbed her hands together. "OK, lay it on us."

Andie leaned in again and lowered her voice. "OK, so listen to *this*. When she lived in Baltimore, Paige went on a blind date with some guy who worked with a friend of hers or something."

"OK…" I said.

"So the date went fine. Not amazing or anything, but not awful, either. Just *fine*. They went to dinner at some restaurant in her neighborhood, nothing fancy."

She paused to take a sip of her wine. We waited for her to continue.

"Apparently Paige was living in an area where there aren't a lot of cabs cruising around on a Thursday night. So after dinner, her date suggested that he call a cab and wait for it at her apartment after walking her home. She was like, OK, whatever. But just so you know, I have an early flight tomorrow morning, so I need to pack."

I rolled my eyes. "Lie."

"No. Totally true. And she was going to be gone for like ten days, so she really *did* need to pack."

McKenna gestured for her to continue. "OK…"

"Paige told him this, but he still wanted to come up, so they walked to her building and went upstairs, and he called a cab. She showed him around the living room and handed him the TV remote, then started packing. For like five minutes she was in and out of the bedroom and the bathroom getting her things together…until she heard some weird noises coming from the living room."

I raised my eyebrows.

"At first she thought it was the TV, but the noises kept getting louder, so she decided to see what was going on…"

"And?" McKenna and I said at the same time.

"And…I kid you not…"

"And *what*?" we said.

Andie lowered her voice even further. "And…the guy was… well…he was…having a little party on her couch."

"A little party?" McKenna said.

Andie made a squeamish face. "Yeah, you know…like a party for one? Like…in his pants?"

I laughed aloud. "You're joking."

"Totally not joking."

"No way," McKenna said.

Andie held her palms in front of her. "Paige *swears* it's true. Why the hell would she make up a crazy story like that?"

"So what happened then?" I asked.

"Well, she was like, Um, what are you doing, you perv? And apparently he jumped up, zipped up, and took off. And that was it."

"Wow, that guy had some balls," McKenna said.

I looked at her and laughed. "Yeah, literally."

"At least she didn't *like* that one." Andie gestured to herself and then to me. "Both Waverly and I have had our dating nightmares, but most of them were more funny than sad. Poor Paige has dated some serious assholes. She puts on a good face, but she's been hurt a lot."

"Yeah, I've sort of figured that out," I said.

Andie nodded at me. "It's not fair. She's so nice, you know?"

"Yeah, it's not fair." *If you only knew.*

The ring of McKenna's cell phone saved me from having to say anything more.

"I'm sorry, ladies, that's Hunter. I should get this." She stood up to take her phone outside.

"I'll get up too," I said. "I need to use the restroom."

"That means more wine for me," Andie said, refilling her glass.

Crisis averted.

• • •

"So your dad's getting married?"

I took a sip of my coffee and smiled. "Can you believe it? I never thought I'd see the day, but he's like a new man since he met Betty."

Andie nodded. "Scary how that works. I keep hoping some guy will come along to make a new woman of my mom, but apparently my dad isn't going anywhere, so she's still a huge bitch."

I laughed. "Come on, she's not *that* bad."

"Oh no, she's a nightmare. But it's OK. I've come to accept it."

We were finishing up brunch the next morning and trying to figure out how to spend our last hours together before Andie and McKenna left for the airport. I was so sad the weekend was already coming to a close. McKenna still wasn't feeling great after our big night out Friday, so we'd again abandoned the idea of a nausea-enhancing ferry ride.

"How about we take one of those tours at the Tenement Museum on the Lower East Side? I hear they're cool," I said.

Andie shook her head. "Too depressing. I'm already depressed enough that we're leaving."

McKenna took a bite of her French toast. "Can you imagine sharing one or two bathrooms with like twenty other families?"

"I can't even imagine having a roommate," I said, suddenly feeling guilty at all the food I was leaving on my plate.

After brunch, we finally made a decision to walk the High Line, an abandoned elevated subway track that had been turned into a charming park covering a mile-long stretch on the west side of Manhattan. After strolling the length of it, we finished off the afternoon with a hot chocolate up in Bryant Park, and then took the subway back to Brooklyn Heights.

We got home later than we should have, so Andie and McKenna ended up packing in a mad rush. I grew sad as I watched them throw their bags together.

"I can't believe the weekend is already over. That went way too fast."

"I know. I didn't even eat a cheap hot dog on the street," Andie said. "Nick is going to be so disappointed in me."

"You know what? I'm sad to leave, but I'm also excited to get home to Elizabeth," McKenna said. "I can't believe how much I miss that adorable, toothless grin of hers. I even miss her little baby smell."

"You'd *better* not be talking about the smell that most people associate with babies," Andie said. "If so, you've totally lost it."

"And you miss Hunter too, of course," I said.

McKenna laughed. "Of course. Hunter smells good too."

The buzz of the doorbell alerted us to the arrival of the taxi. Out of nowhere, tears started welling up in my eyes. My tiny elevator wasn't big enough for all of us with their luggage, so I held the gate open for the two of them before descending the stairs alone.

I met them at the elevator, which was so rickety and slow that I beat them there.

"I think I just suffocated to death." Andie jumped out of the tiny cage into the fresh air of the lobby. "I think I may be dead right now."

"Good lord, you're so high-maintenance," McKenna said. "Does Nick know you're so high-maintenance?"

Andie tilted her head to one side. "Does Hunter know you were dancing on a table two nights ago?"

"Touché," McKenna said, laughing.

Andie nodded. "Don't poke the bear."

Once we were on the sidewalk outside my building, they took turns hugging me good-bye.

"Good luck meeting Jake's parents," McKenna said.

Suddenly I was nervous. "Thanks. I may need it."

"No you won't, that was just an expression. They're going to love you. How could they not?"

Andie nodded. "You *are* quite loveable. Now, don't be a stranger. I don't want to have to tune into *Love, Wendy* to make sure you don't cut your bangs too short again."

I laughed. "I promise to be better about keeping in touch."

McKenna put her arm around me. "So I guess we'll see you at your dad's wedding?"

I felt the tears welling up again. "You're really going to come?"

She nodded. "Wouldn't miss it."

"Ditto," Andie said. "What better way to celebrate Valentine's Day?"

I smiled. "You two are the best. I don't know what I'd do without you. What *would* I do without you?"

"Apparently, you'd be turning into a TV star in the Big Apple," Andie said. She made scissors with her fingers. "Remember, don't cut those bangs."

I saluted. "I promise."

I hugged them each once more, and then let out a sigh as I watched their cab drive away. *I wish you both lived here.*

After the taxi turned the corner, I unlocked the front door of my building and slowly climbed the stairs back to my apartment. Now feeling gloomy, all I wanted to do was curl up with a blanket and watch a sappy movie on Lifetime. I also wanted to call Jake and fill him in on all the fun details of the weekend. I needed to hear his soothing voice.

Before I even sat down, however, my phone rang. It was Scotty, asking me to cover a free concert in Prospect Park that had just been announced for that evening. I glanced at my watch to check the time. If I was going to make it, I'd need to leave my apartment in twenty minutes.

So much for my break from reality.

chapter eleven

The following week was more hectic than I'd thought possible. Because so many of us were going to be gone around Christmas, we all had to prepare a lot of material ahead of time. Wendy was doing two shows a day in front of a live studio audience, and as a result, my team was shooting at least one if not two features each day. A couple of times, I actually had to change clothes to make it look like a separate day. I found this absurd, given that it was winter and in every outdoor segment I was wearing a huge black coat that covered most of what I had on underneath. But that was the protocol at *Love, Wendy*, so I kept my mouth shut. Although we had a long list of features to shoot, I still hadn't come up with a good idea for the New Year's Eve show.

Late Wednesday afternoon, I squeezed in an hour between shoots to meet Paige for coffee. She wanted to catch up on work stuff before she took off to visit her parents for the holidays. We'd only texted, so I still had no idea what had happened during her weekend with Gary. As I pushed open the door to The Coffee Bean & Tea Leaf, a wave of dread swept over me. *I wonder what he told her?*

I spotted her sitting at a table when I walked in.

"Hey, Waverly, it's great to see you." She stood up and gave me a hug. Her blonde hair looked a little lighter than usual, and I wondered if she'd highlighted it for her trip to Vermont.

"It's, um, it's good to see you too." I was at a loss for words, a rare experience. *Does she know? Does she know I know?*

She pointed to the counter. "I just ordered a hot chocolate. Want one?"

"Sure, sounds good." I took off my coat and sat down at the table. *Oh lordy, this is awkward.*

A minute later, she handed me a hot chocolate and took a seat. "So how was your weekend with my cousin? I hope she didn't get herself arrested."

I laughed. "Thankfully, no, although she did drag me to a club in the Meatpacking District."

"You did *not*."

"I *did*. Do you know how *old* that made me feel?"

"I haven't been to a club in years. I can't imagine dealing with that scene now. Too many prepubescents in slutty clothes for my taste."

I pointed at her. "Exactly! It was a total scene. The stars of the scene were prepubescents in slutty clothes, and I was an extra who never should have been hired in the first place. I kept waiting for the director to show up and kick me out."

She laughed. "Please, I'm sure you added a much-needed touch of class to the establishment."

I took a sip of my hot chocolate. "You are way too nice. But we had a great weekend. McKenna, the third Musketeer, so to speak, surprised me and came out with Andie."

"She's the one who just had the baby, right?"

I nodded. "She rallied to fly all the way across the country for a girls' weekend."

"Sounds like the three of you are tight."

"Yeah, they're pretty much the sisters I never had."

She stared at the paper cup in her hand for a moment, and I was sure she was about to say something about Gary.

I held my breath.

What am I going to say back to her?

But then she appeared to change her mind—and the subject.

"So hey, I know you're swamped with taping, but I wanted to debrief you on the rollout plans for the orders at Jordan Brooke and Bella's Boutique. Those two accounts alone are going to keep us really busy, so I've found a couple students from FIT to do a work-study next semester."

I raised my eyebrows. "FIT? As in the Fashion Institute of Technology?"

She nodded.

"You got students from *FIT* who want to do a work study for *Waverly's Honey Shop*?"

She nodded again. "Why not? They're smart, eager, and willing to work for super cheap to get some experience in the business."

"I guess I associate FIT and 'the business' with runway models and couture, not girly tees and tote bags."

She smiled. "Don't sell yourself short, Waverly. Once Jordan Brooke and Bella's Boutique start carrying your stuff, a *lot* of people are going to be jumping on the Honey bandwagon."

"You really think so?"

She nodded. "You're a trendsetter, my dear."

I laughed to myself as I thought of the chocolate stains on my pajamas. *Trendsetter. Ha.*

Paige filled me in on her plans for bringing down our production costs and streamlining the ordering system. As she neared the bottom of her checklist, I glanced at a clock on the wall. I'd have to leave soon to get ready for my next taping.

You have to say something, *Waverly.*

I knew I had to ask her about her weekend with Gary. If a friend goes away with a guy for the weekend for the first time, you *have* to ask about it.

When she was done with her list, I forced the words out.

"So how did it...go with Gary?"

For a second I thought I saw a look of distress in her eyes, but then it was gone, and she smiled.

"It was good. We had a really nice time."

"What did you do?"

"Nothing too exciting, really. We window-shopped, took long walks, went to dinner, your standard bed-and-breakfast weekend."

"That sounds fun."

"It was." She smiled again, but I could tell something was off. She looked back at her notebook, as though she didn't want to make eye contact with me.

Does she know he's married? Does she know I know he's married? And that I work for his wife?

My mind raced, searching for what to say next. I thought of Kristina's advice to stay out of it, of Jake's advice to stay out of it. Of my own desire to stay out of it.

Stay out of it, Waverly!

I knew it wasn't my business. I knew I should just let it go.

But I couldn't.

Not entirely. Not yet.

I watched her body language for a clue. Maybe she wanted to open up but needed a nudge to unlock the door. Maybe I could give her a key?

"So, um, do you want to talk about it?" I asked softly.

She looked up from her notepad. "What?"

"Do you want to talk about it?"

She narrowed her eyes slightly. "What do you mean?"

I studied the look on her face. *If she knows he's married, she must know I know too. Does she know?* The thoughts were running around in circles inside my head, clamoring to get out.

One finally burst free.

"He must have told you I know," I blurted.

"Know what?" She took a sip of her hot chocolate and made eye contact for a second, then glanced away.

"Paige…" I paused because I didn't know what to say. I knew I should have kept my mouth shut, but I'd shown my hand.

She knew.

And she knew that I knew.

We sat there in awkward silence for a moment, and then she finally spoke.

"I don't really want to talk about it, OK? I care about him and he cares about me, so let's just leave it at that."

She knows. Oh, my God. She totally knows.

"So you're going to keep seeing him?"

She ignored me. "Listen, I don't want to talk about it, OK? And I have to go now anyway. I'll be in touch after the holidays. We're going to have to hit the ground running when I get back." She gathered her things and stood up.

"Are you sure you don't want to talk about it?"

She shook her head. "Thanks, but no."

"Are you *sure*?"

"Life doesn't always go the way we planned, Waverly."

I looked up at her. *Why are you acting so weird? Don't you know I care about you?*

There were suddenly so many things I wanted to say, but I just sat there, silently stunned.

She gave me a quick hug before turning to leave. "I need to run now. Happy holidays. Have fun with Jake's family."

"OK, thanks." My mouth hung half open.

She was nearly out the door when she stopped and turned to face me. "Oh, I almost forgot." She reached into her purse and pulled out a set of keys. "Here's your set. On January first, Waverly's Honey Shop starts a whole new chapter."

Before I could even respond, she was off again. She blended into the busy sidewalk outside, and I stood there, staring at the keys in my hand, thinking of the key I'd tried to give her.

Life doesn't always go the way we planned.

I thought of the way Gary had grabbed my arm at the holiday party. He wanted me to stay out of it, and now Paige was telling me to mind my own business as well.

Paige. Sweet, smart, *kind* Paige, who deserved to be with someone who deserved her.

Someone who wasn't already married.

I rubbed my fingers over the keys and wished they could unlock the hold he clearly had over her.

chapter twelve

The week continued at its frenetic pace, and by Friday, I could barely keep my eyes open. And I wasn't the only one. Early that morning, before yet another double taping in front of a live studio audience, we had our last staff meeting before everyone scattered for the holidays. The strain from the workload showed on everyone's faces, but none more so than Wendy's. Small bags were visible under her eyes, which looked a little bloodshot, and for the first time I could see tiny crow's feet at the corners.

Scotty clapped his hands to start the meeting. "OK, people, I know it's Christmas Eve, and I know everyone has been working double time to keep us covered over the holidays. I want you to know how much I appreciate all your hard work. Especially you, Wendy. Staying cheery for hours on end in front of the bright lights of a studio audience isn't easy, but you've done a remarkable job of holding it together."

Wendy nodded and chewed at her fingernails.

She looks awful, I thought. *Did she find out about Paige?*

"One more show, and then everyone is free for a few days. Do you have it in you?" He looked like a cheerleader up there. *He should get a job at Southwest Airlines,* I thought. Those people are always freakishly happy, no matter how crowded their flights are.

Wendy smiled and nodded. "I have it in me. Just let me stop by makeup, and I'll make the audience fall in love with me."

I looked at her. *You're totally right.* Bizarre as she may be behind the scenes, Wendy was the consummate professional before an audience. She was full of charisma, and her fans adored her.

"Waverly, you're on this afternoon's show, right?" Scotty said.

I looked up at him. "Excuse me?"

"You're doing a studio appearance on the show today, right?"

"Huh?" I definitely didn't remember that.

"On the two o'clock taping. Wendy said we'd scheduled you to talk about *Honey on Your Mind*, sort of a holiday-themed wrap-up?"

I looked at Wendy. "Did we schedule that?" I knew *I* certainly hadn't. If I had, I wouldn't have booked a four o'clock train to Boston. My suitcase was all packed and ready so that I could leave for Penn Station right from the office.

She sighed and rolled her eyes. "Yes, Waverly, we did."

I opened my mouth but didn't speak. *Huh?* Although I had zero recollection of scheduling anything with her, with everyone in the room staring at me, I caved. "Um, I'm sorry; I must have forgotten to make a note of it."

Scotty gave me a look that made it clear he didn't know what to believe but didn't have time to get into it. "OK then, Waverly, looks like you'll be joining Wendy in makeup."

"You could use it, my dear," Wendy said under her breath.

• • •

I called Jake as soon as the meeting broke up, but he was already on a plane to Boston from Atlanta, so I had to leave a message about my change in plans. If the taping ended on time, which was never a guarantee, I might get out of the studio by three-thirty. That would *probably* give me enough time to catch my train.

Wendy was already in makeup, so I settled into an empty conference room to prepare for my appearance on her show. What was I supposed to do at the last minute? If I'd had proper notice, I would have pulled together a fun montage of my favorite clips with a soundtrack and graphics, but there was no time for that now. Clearly, I just was going to have to wing it and talk. About *what*, I had no idea. I wondered why Wendy hadn't told me about this earlier. Was she trying to ambush me again? Was she more upset about the holiday party than she'd let on?

Scotty had already left, so I couldn't check in with him. I scribbled a few notes and tried to think of what to say on camera. *This could be a Honey on Your Mind segment on its own,* I thought. "*So what's on* your *mind, Waverly? Wondering how to deal with a lunatic boss, that's what.*"

I chewed on a pencil and stared at the page in front of me.

I am so screwed.

I let out a loud sigh and put both my hands on my head.

Ugh.

"You doing all right, Waverly?"

The sound of a voice startled me. I looked up and saw the skinny intern standing in the doorway.

"Are you OK? I heard that sigh all the way down the hall," he said.

I offered up a weak smile. "Oh, hi, Ben. I'm fine, just preparing for the show this afternoon." I covered the sheet of paper with my hand, not wanting him to see that it was nearly empty.

He laughed and pointed to my hand. "It's OK, I'm not going to steal your answers to the history midterm. Or is it the SAT?"

I looked at the paper and laughed too. "Sorry, I have no idea why I did that."

He sat down across from me. "Let me guess. You're brain-storming ideas for what to say on the show…because you didn't prepare anything…because Wendy never told you about it?"

I pointed at him. "Bingo." This was the most I'd ever heard him speak.

"Why not read some of those hilarious e-mails you've shared with us in the staff meetings?"

I chewed on my pencil again. "You think so? You like those?"

He nodded. "I love them. They keep me from falling asleep when Wendy starts droning on about her latest shopping spree on Fifth Avenue."

I laughed. "I hadn't thought of that. What a great idea."

"I think the audience would really enjoy it."

"Thanks so much, Ben, really. You may have just saved me from completely humiliating myself on national television."

"My pleasure, Waverly. Happy holidays."

As he sauntered down to the break room, I ran to an empty workstation and logged on to my e-mail account. It wasn't a video montage, but within seconds, I had a pile of potential material staring back at me.

Score one for the intern.

• • •

"Waverly, it's so nice to have you join us on the set like this. It's been awhile." Wendy beamed at me from her plush chair.

I smiled back and shifted slightly in my intentionally not-as-plush seat. "Thanks, Wendy. I'm glad to be here."

She clapped her freshly manicured hands together and looked out at the audience. "So, my friends, I know you've all enjoyed Waverly's *Honey on Your Mind* segment, so I thought it would be fun to invite her on stage for a little behind-the-scenes gossip." She turned to me again. "Waverly, can you share with us some of the moments that didn't make it on camera? It would be a *hoot* to see some bloopers."

Like a seasoned politician, I deflected her question to focus on the answer I had prepared. "Actually, I thought I'd do something a little different." I looked out at the audience. "What do you all think? Mix it up a little?"

As a small cheer erupted from the crowd, I could feel visual daggers coming from Wendy's direction. At least I was ready for them this time. I turned to face her with a forced smile. "Does that sound OK to *you*, Wendy?"

Her own phony smile was even bigger than mine. "Why *suuure*, Waverly. That sounds wuuunderful. What did you have in mind?" *Wow, she's a genius at being fake*, I thought.

I sat up a little straighter and turned back to the audience. "Great. Well, as you know, on my segment I talk about things that are on *my* mind as well as on the minds of people on the streets of New York."

Wendy nodded, as did the audience.

"However, I also receive a lot of e-mails from viewers across the country who like to share with me what's on *their* minds."

More nods.

"So I thought it would be fun to share some of the, um, more *colorful* ones, with you today."

Wendy raised her eyebrows and tilted her head slightly to the side. "That sounds like it could be a little...shall we say...*dangerous*." She turned to the audience and winked. Everyone laughed.

I laughed too. "This is true. I definitely get some e-mails that aren't fit for public consumption. However, the majority of them are very entertaining." I held up a piece of paper and looked out at the audience. "I've got some fun ones here. Anyone interested?"

"Yes!" the audience shouted.

"Well there you go," Wendy said with a smile that could melt steel. "Let's hear them."

"OK, here goes." I cleared my throat and began to read:

"Dear Waverly, I just saw a lady pushing a dog in a baby stroller. A dog. No baby in sight. What the hell? That's what's on my mind, why people are such idiots."

Laughter from the audience.

"Hi, Waverly, you know what's on my mind? Bumper stickers. *I'm of the opinion that the number of bumper stickers on a person's car is roughly the same as the number of days that person goes between showers. Just thought I'd share."*

More laughter.

"Dear Waverly, why is there never enough parking in Chicago? It drives me crazy. I even saw a sign in front of a church the other day that said, THOU SHALL NOT PARK HERE. *At least God is laughing with us, not at us."*

More laughter.

I glanced over at Wendy. She was nodding and smiling and truly seemed to be enjoying herself. *This is going really well.*

I kept reading.

"Hi, Waverly, here's what's on my mind: I'm recently divorced and decided to give the online dating thing a try. The first woman I had a conversation with seemed nice, so I asked her out to dinner. She accepted, but then immediately sent me another message that said, and I'm quoting verbatim here, 'You do make more than $400K a year, right?'"

The audience totally cracked up at that one, so I felt good as I entered the homestretch.

"Dear Waverly, I could stand to drop a few pounds, so ever since college I've been joking about how I need to 'lose my baby fat.' Now that I'm in my thirties, I've unfortunately realized that I can't do that anymore. The last time I said it, the person I was speaking to asked me, 'How old is your baby?'"

"Oh my," Wendy said, putting her hand over her heart.

I laughed and looked at her. "I know. Brutal, huh?"

"Oh yes, just *awwwful*. Actually, that reminds me, Waverly, wasn't having a baby on *your* mind?"

I looked at her.

What?

I hoped my jaw hadn't visibly dropped.

"I'm sorry?" I said.

"Weren't you talking about having a baby soon?"

I didn't reply. I wanted to, but my mouth was frozen.

What?

Before I could speak, Wendy put her hand on my arm and laughed. "I'm just joking, my dear. I know you're not even *close* to being married." She held up her ring finger and kissed it. "True love like mine doesn't come around every day, but maybe one day *your* prince will come. I'm holding out hope for you."

I still didn't say anything. I willed my brain to kick into gear and come up with a clever comeback, but all I kept thinking was, *What?*

As I sat there like a stone, Wendy smiled out at the audience. "Well, I'm sorry to say, folks, but it looks like we're out of time. Waverly, luuuv, thanks so much for visiting us. You were *veeery* entertaining, as always. Ladies and gentleman, let's give a big round of applause for Waverly Bryson!" She put her hand on my shoulder and gave me a little squeeze, then clapped her hands enthusiastically.

The audience erupted in applause.

• • •

As soon as the director cut the scene, I stood up and yanked off my microphone with such force that I nearly broke it. *Is she kidding me?* I couldn't bring myself to look at Wendy, who was still seated on the couch with a strange grin on her face. *What is her problem?* The audience, clearly enamored despite her psychotic behavior, was already lining up for autographs (hers not mine). I just hoped I wouldn't get caught up in the traffic as I tried to make a gracious exit. If I was going to make my train, I needed to sprint out of there faster than the lifespan of a celebrity romance.

No such luck.

"Waverly, Waverly!"

Frick.

I turned my head and saw two women waving frantically at me with huge smiles on their faces. They looked so excited that

I couldn't just ignore them, much as I wanted to. Then I remembered that fans were the only reason I had my job, so I decided to stop for a minute and be friendly.

I smiled and turned in their direction. As I approached them, I realized they looked familiar, but I had absolutely no idea where I'd seen them before. I smiled and put my hands on my hips. "Well hello there, did you enjoy the show?"

The shorter of the two held out her hand. "Waverly! It's Marge and Evelyn, from Chippewa Falls, Wisconsin? Do you remember us?"

Chippewa what?

She squeezed my hand. "We met you in Chicago, remember? We were at the scrapbooking convention?"

Suddenly it clicked. How could I forget Marge and Evelyn? How could I forget Marge's banana clip? I stole a glance at their fingernails, which were still pink, acrylic, and square. How could I forget pink, acrylic, square fingernails? The two of them looked like they'd been cut and pasted from a Sears catalog, but they were so friendly that it was impossible not to like them.

"Ah, Marge and Evelyn, of course I remember you. How are you? What brings you to New York?"

"Our silly husbands," Marge said. "They're best friends and wanted a boys' getaway to play poker and smoke cigars, so in return they sent us on a girls' trip to the Big Apple. We can't believe we're really here!"

"We've been *everywhere*," Evelyn said. "The Statue of Liberty, the Empire State Building, Central Park. We even saw a show on Broadway last night." She looked at Marge. "But *this* has been our favorite activity so far, hasn't it Margie?"

Marge nodded. "Oh yes, of course. Seeing Wendy Davenport in person? We're just tickled pink."

"Yes, she's really something." I looked over at the huge line of fans clamoring for Wendy's attention. *If you only knew.*

"And of course it's great to see you too," Evelyn said. "We still love *Honey on Your Mind.*"

I smiled. "Thank you. So how long are you in town? Are you spending Christmas here?"

"Oh no, we fly out tonight," Marge said. "Can't miss Christmas at home."

I smiled and grimaced at the same time. If I didn't make a run for it soon, I wasn't going to catch my train.

"What about you?" Evelyn said. "You're not spending the holidays with your family?"

"Um, well, actually, I'm trying to catch a four o'clock train to Boston."

Marge's eyes opened wide. "A four o'clock train? And you're standing here gabbing with us? Sugar, you need to get a move on." She held up her wrist to show me her watch.

"Scoot!" Evelyn said, shooing me away.

"I'm so sorry to run," I said. "I don't want to be rude."

Marge shook her head. "Young lady, you're not being rude. It's Christmas Eve, for gosh sake!"

I smiled. "Thanks so much for understanding. I hope you'll keep watching the show?"

"We never miss it," Marge said.

"Now skat." Evelyn shooed me away again. "We're going to wait to meet Wendy."

I took another look at the pack of eager beavers before Wendy. The line wound all the way around the studio back up into the seats.

• • •

Once outside the building, I ran over to Seventh Avenue and tried to hail a downtown taxi, but apparently, everyone in Manhattan had the same idea. The street was a sea of yellow vehicles, *all* of them occupied. As I watched cab after cab fly by me without stopping, my hopes of catching my train dwindled.

Frick.

Finally, I spotted an empty cab and flagged it. I jumped into the back seat with my carry-on bag, not bothering to put it in the trunk. I leaned forward, told the driver where to go, then fell back against the seat, and hoped for the best.

Traffic crawled along, and when we finally got to Penn Station, I handed the driver some money and jumped out without waiting for change. I ran to the escalator and sprinted down the moving steps, nearly knocking over an old man in the process.

"Sorry!" I yelled as I flew by, not turning my head. I wondered if I'd just officially become a rude New Yorker. I'd certainly become a rushed New Yorker.

When I made it to the center of the terminal, I was out of breath and sweating despite the cold weather outside. I looked up at the huge monitor to see which track my train was on. I scanned until I saw it:

BOSTON, 4:00 P.M.
STATUS: DEPARTED

No!

I scanned the board for other departures to Boston. The next was in an hour, so I could jump on that one. I'd be late, but at least not disastrously so.

Still catching my breath, I decided to sit down at a bar and have a glass of wine. *God knows I could use a drink right now.*

I looked around and spotted a tiny bar to my left. I grabbed the handle of my suitcase and made my way there.

"What can I get you?" the cheery senior behind the taps said as I sat down on one of the three stools.

"Do you have a wine menu?"

"We have red, and we have white. We're in Penn Station, my love."

I laughed. I deserved that.

"OK, I'll have a glass of red. Thanks."

As he set a glass in front of me, I looked out at the terminal floor. Frantic passengers rushed to and fro in every direction, everyone in a hurry to get somewhere else.

"Where you headed, love?" the old man asked.

"Boston. I missed my train, so I'm going to hop on the next one."

He raised his eyebrows. "The next one? On Christmas Eve? You sure about that?"

"I thought once you had a ticket you could jump on any train."

"If there are seats available you can, but do you know how crowded those trains are this time of year?" He gestured to the chaos outside.

I pressed my hand against my forehead. "Oh my God, I didn't even think about that." *Because I am the stupidest person alive.*

"You need to head over to customer service." He pointed across the room. My eyes followed and landed on an office with an open door…and a line about fifty people long snaking out of it.

I turned back at him. "You've got to be kidding me."

"Welcome to New York at the holidays, my love."

Did I mention I was the stupidest person alive? I gulped down the rest of my wine and braced myself for a long wait.

• • •

I finally made it to the front of the customer service line at 4:50 p.m. I had ten minutes to catch the next train.

I handed my ticket to the woman behind the counter. "Hi, I missed the four o'clock to Boston and want to see if there's room on the next train?" *Again with the statement as a question, Waverly?*

She looked at the ticket and raised her eyebrows. "Are you serious?"

I cleared my throat. "Um, yes?"

She laughed. "Sweetheart, every train in and out of here is booked solid. If you want to get to Boston, your best bet is the bus."

"The *bus*?"

She nodded. "The bus."

"How do I take the bus?"

She pointed to the exit. "Most of them leave on the corner of Thirty-Fourth and Eighth. They leave on the hour to Boston, DC, and Philly."

"So I just stand on the corner and wait?"

She laughed. "You're not from here, are you?"

"Was it my French accent that gave me away?"

She laughed again. "You got a smart phone?"

I nodded.

"Buy a ticket online. They fill up quick, but they have departures late into the night, so you might get lucky and find one with a seat left." She wrote the names of a few bus companies on a piece of paper. "Good luck, sweetheart. Now I need to attend to the next customer." She winked, and then gestured to the man behind me to approach the counter.

"Thanks." I sighed and walked slowly back to the bar.

"Any luck?" the bartender asked.

I shook my head.

"You want another glass of wine, love?"

The shake turned into a nod. I'd already missed the five o'clock *bus*, so why not? I pulled out my phone and looked up the first company on the list, and then did a schedule search for New York to Boston.

Every time slot was booked.

I tried the next name.

Booked.

I tried the third name.

Booked.

Oh crap.

I tried the fourth name.

Booked.

Holy frick.

There was one more name on the list: the Fung Wah Bus out of Chinatown. I punched in the schedule search and held my breath. I closed my eyes for a moment, and then looked back at my phone.

Seats available!

On the ten o'clock bus.

Arriving at Boston's South Station at two in the morning.

Nice.

I reluctantly bought a ticket, and after finishing my wine and saying good-bye to the sympathetic bartender, I decided to return to NBC. Instead of hiking all the way back to Brooklyn,

I figured I'd bring dinner to the office and hang out for a couple hours until it was time to head down to Chinatown. I called Jake on the way and told him about the delay. He said he'd set his alarm to come pick me up at the bus station.

As I walked back to NBC, I thought briefly about renting a car but decided otherwise. From the looks of the traffic snarled all around me, just navigating out of Manhattan might take several hours. *Ugh.* What was Jake's family going to think of me? Missing my train and showing up in the middle of the night? *Way to make a good first impression, Waverly.*

• • •

When I got back to the office, the building was practically deserted. Except for the security guards and a few random techies from the editing department, everyone had taken off to spend Christmas Eve with friends and family. I rolled my suitcase into the kitchen and set my chicken pad Thai on the table, then opened the fridge to grab a bottle of water.

Just then, I heard someone moving down the hall. I quietly closed the fridge and tiptoed toward the door.

Wendy was walking slowly, alone, toward the big conference room.

What is Wendy still doing here?

The last thing I wanted to do was spend Christmas Eve with Wendy Davenport, but the big conference room had a huge flat-screen TV, and that's where I'd planned to eat my dinner.

I decided to eat in the kitchen.

After I was done, I glanced up at the clock on the wall. I still had more than two hours to kill before it was time to head down to Chinatown. I stood up and walked to the sink to refill my bottle from the tap. As I watched the water level rise, I thought about Wendy. Over the past few months, I'd gradually learned how to deal with her, even when I didn't want to. Maybe I could deal with her now? She'd been off her rocker this afternoon, but maybe she'd be in nice-Wendy mode now? Nice Wendy was actually almost fun. Crazy Wendy was, well, enough said. And I couldn't help but feel bad for *anyone* who was spending Christmas Eve alone. My evening hadn't exactly gone according to plan, but at least I had somewhere to go.

I left my suitcase in the kitchen and tiptoed down the hall toward the big conference room, looking left and right as I walked.

Every office was empty.

I stopped in front of the conference room door and poked my head in. Wendy was sitting alone at the huge table.

With a bottle of vodka in front of her.

The lights were on, but the TV wasn't. She held a full glass in her hand.

Before I could step away, she looked up and saw me.

"Hi, Wendy," I said softly.

She quickly glanced at the bottle, but it was obvious that I'd already seen it.

"Hi, Waverly," she said with a sigh. Her eyes were bleary.

Is she drunk?

I wasn't sure what to do, so I stood where I was.

"Are you doing OK?" I asked.

She sighed again. "I'm drunk."

I looked at the floor. *OK, I guess that answers that question.*

"I'm drunk a lot lately," she said quietly.

I looked up at her. *What?*

"You are?"

She nodded and wiped a tear from her face. "Ever since *she* entered the picture."

What?

"Don't tell anyone, OK?"

My mind began to race. Was she talking about Paige? If so, when did she find out?"

I sat down at the table across from her.

She refilled her glass. "Do you want some?"

I shook my head. "No thanks, I'm good." My mind began to race with questions. *Have you been drunk at work before? Is that why you're so erratic? Is that why you never told me I was going to be on your show today?* It had never occurred to me that she might have a drinking problem. I'd just assumed she was a bitch.

"You sure? No one likes to drink alone." She laughed, but it clearly wasn't funny.

I swallowed but didn't say anything.

"It would mean a lot to me if you joined me, Waverly. It's Christmas Eve, you know."

I thought about it. I'd rather drink a glass of gasoline than straight vodka, but I didn't want to upset her, so I nodded. "OK, maybe a small one."

She reached toward the cabinet behind her and pulled out another glass, then poured me a drink. I thanked her and took a sip, hoping the alcohol wouldn't burn a hole through my esophagus.

I felt like I should say something, but I had no idea what. For a moment, we sat there in awkward silence.

"Do you want to talk about it?" I finally asked.

She shook her head and took a huge gulp of her drink.

"Things don't always work out the way you think they will, do they," she said. It wasn't a question.

I took a tiny sip of my drink and made a face as it stung my insides.

"Do you want a mixer with that?" she asked.

"You have one?"

"There's orange juice in the fridge. I'll get it."

She stood up, a bit unsteadily, walked out of the room, and returned a few minutes later with a carton of orange juice. She leaned over and poured some into my glass, splashing some on the table as she did so.

"Oh, I'm sorry, let me clean that up." She wiped the table clumsily with her hand. It was a bit sad to watch.

I stood up. "Let me get a napkin." I was nearly out the door when I heard her say something.

"You're a nice person, Waverly." It came out as a whisper.

• • •

An hour later, I was still nursing that one drink. The last thing I wanted to do was get drunk around Wendy Davenport, even if *she* was drunk. If loose lips sink ships, I certainly didn't need any vodka prying mine open.

"You really missed your train because of me?" she said.

I nodded.

Her shoulders slumped. "I'm sorry, Waverly. I thought I'd told you I planned to have you on the show today. I really... thought I had." She stared behind me at the wall, or maybe at nothing. It was hard to tell.

"It's OK, we all make mistakes." God knows I'd made enough of them myself. I wasn't angry anymore, especially after seeing her this way. Now I just felt sorry for her.

"So you're not getting to Boston until two?"

I nodded. "Looks like it. It's OK, though. Jake is picking me up at the bus station."

She kept staring at the wall behind me. "I'm sorry for being so hard on you, Waverly."

I didn't say anything.

"I'm sorry for making fun of you on the set today. I...I don't know why I did that. And when I first met you on the *Today* show, I was really a pill then too. I'm sorry for that as well."

Again, I didn't speak. She wasn't looking at me, but I got the sense that she wanted to keep talking, so I quietly started tearing up a napkin.

"I get like that sometimes. I'm just...*mean*. I don't intend to be. I really don't." She took another sip of her drink and stared at it. "Living a lie, it's not easy."

I looked up from the pile of napkin bits.

Living a lie?

I didn't know what to say, so I kept silent.

After a few moments, she finally looked up at me. Her eyes were glassy. "Trying to be something you're not, have you ever done that?"

I thought back to my days in sports PR, when I'd faked my way through meetings, trying to care, wanting to care, pretending like I cared.

"Yes, I guess."

"Did it make you a little...*crazy*?" she whispered.

It hadn't, but I didn't think that's what she needed to hear, so I nodded. "A little."

"What did you do about it?"

"I quit."

"You quit?"

"Yeah, I quit. My job. It wasn't a fit for me anymore, so I quit."

She shook her head. "I can't do that."

Is she talking about her marriage?

"So, um, why are you here this late anyway?" Paige was away visiting her parents in Maryland for Christmas, so shouldn't Wendy be with Gary and her kids?

She didn't appear to hear my question. Or if she did, she ignored it. "It's like my whole career...the show...it's all...it's all based on a lie." She took another gulp of her drink.

One thing I did know was that no matter how crazy Wendy could be—and at times, her elevator *clearly* wasn't going to the top floor—she was definitely good at her job. Very good.

I| shook my head. "That's not true, Wendy. You're great at what you do. People love your show. They love *you*."

She didn't appear to hear me. She finished off her drink and set the glass on the table. "My marriage...it's fake," she whispered.

I caught my breath. *Oh my God. She does know.*

Suddenly, despite all the horrible things she'd said to me since we'd met, I felt overwhelmed by compassion for her. I reached across the table and squeezed her hand. "I'm sorry, Wendy."

She smiled but pulled her hand back. "Thanks, but you can't help me with this."

I nodded, unsure what to say.

After a few moments, she spoke again. But she didn't make eye contact.

"Damn her," she whispered.

I wanted to make her feel better, but I didn't know how. My mind scrambled for something to say.

Unfortunately, a Waverly moment was the result.

"She's a nice person," I blurted.

Wendy looked up at me. "What?"

I bit my lip. *Damn it.*

"What are you talking about?"

Oh my God.

She doesn't know?

Then why did she just say that? And why did I just say that? What is wrong with me?

The thoughts bounced around inside my head.

I swallowed. "Nothing. Forget I said anything."

Oh sweet Jesus, just shut up, Waverly!

"Waverly, what are you talking about?"

I stood up and looked around the room, wishing someone else were there. Talk about loose lips. "I should probably go now, I'm sorry." *You suck, Waverly.*

"You don't know what you're talking about," she said, the edge suddenly back in her voice. Mean Wendy was back. "You don't know anything." She reached for the bottle. How many drinks had she had?

I grabbed my purse off the chair next to me. "I think it's time for me to catch a cab down to Chinatown. I'm so sorry."

She calmly refilled her glass, not making eye contact. "You don't know what you're talking about."

"Happy holidays, Wendy." I dashed out of the room.

chapter thirteen

I slept most of the way to Boston, though I couldn't breathe for
the first hour because of the overpowering aroma of fried chicken
engulfing the air space around me. The guy sitting in front of me
had a huge bucket of it on his lap, and yes, he ate the entire thing.
With his hands.

When the bus finally rolled into Boston four hours later, the
city was dark and quiet. Weary and rumpled, I filed out with
the other passengers, retrieved my luggage from the storage com-
partment, and then stumbled into the South Station terminal.
As I walked through the doorway, I scanned the crowd milling
around the entrance. When I spotted Jake leaning against the
check-in counter, I could feel my tired face brighten up.

"You have no idea how happy I am to see you." I smiled
and set my purse on the ground. He was wearing plaid pajamas
bottoms and an old Atlanta Falcons sweatshirt. Even in tattered sleepwear, he looked good. (I, however, look homeless in
tattered sleepwear.)

"Welcome to Boston." He walked toward me and opened his
arms for a hug. "And merry Christmas. It's the twenty-fifth now."

I gave him a quick kiss and then hugged him tight. I pressed
my cheek against his chest and inhaled deeply. Jake always
smelled indescribably...*good*.

"For the record, I know I look super gross right now, but I
don't care," I said.

He laughed. "You've definitely looked better. But I'm in my pajamas at a bus station in the middle of the night, so I shouldn't talk."

"Do I smell like fried chicken?" I looked up at him.

He laughed again. "What?"

I pressed my face against his chest again. "I'll tell you later. Can we go to the hotel now? I'm exhausted."

He gave me a squeeze, and then reached for the handle of my suitcase. "Of course."

• • •

Jake had booked us a room at a bed and breakfast a few blocks from his sister's house in the Boston suburb of Waltham. As we drove in his rental car through the dark streets, I couldn't help but remember the last time I'd been there, nearly a year ago, in my *own* rental car. In what could generously be described as a momentary lapse in judgment, but perhaps more accurately as an episode of temporary insanity, after months of emotional hedging, I'd flown across the country—uninvited—to finally tell Jake how I felt about him. After about ten hours of travel, I'd shown up unannounced at his sister's to declare my feelings, just like they do in the movies, only to learn that he'd left town a few days earlier. Oops. Talk about a Waverly moment. I cringed at the memory and wondered what I'd say to his sister and her husband the next morning at brunch. God knows what they thought of me after that display of semi-stalker behavior.

On the ride, I recounted the night's events to Jake. He was fascinated. I had to admit, it *was* pretty good gossip, even though I didn't consider our conversation as "gossiping" because I was talking to my boyfriend, not posting the scoop on Facebook.

No matter how awful she'd been to me, I wasn't about to throw Wendy under the bus and blab to anyone who knew her.

"Straight vodka, huh? So you think she's been drinking at work?"

I nodded. "I think so. She let it slip that she's been drunk a lot lately, and she kept talking about living a lie. She was messed up."

"That doesn't sound good."

"It makes sense, now that I think about it. She's super erratic, and while she's usually very professional on camera despite her weird personality, she's been forgetful lately. I thought she was just nuts, but at least now I know the reason behind it all."

"That's really sad."

"I know. It was disturbing, to be honest. She was clearly hurting, and I had no idea how to help her."

"Does she want help?"

I nodded. "I think so. At one point it seemed like she wanted to open up, but then I made everything worse by bringing up Gary's affair."

He didn't say anything, which totally said something.

I frowned. "Exactly. I suck. Why did I do that? And why did I let on to Paige that I knew Gary was married? Why do I do these things, Jake? Why can't I just keep my big mouth shut?"

He laughed and briefly lifted his hands from the steering wheel. "There is no safe response to that question, and you know it. So I will respectfully decline to answer."

"OK, maybe you're right about that." I shrugged.

He laughed. "Oh, I know I'm right about that."

I yawned. "I can't believe it's like two thirty in the morning. What time do we need to be at your sister's house tomorrow?"

"Brunch is at eleven. Think you can make it?"

I covered my eyes with my hands. "I can't believe I'm going to meet your parents in a few hours. What if they don't like me? What if I have huge bags under my eyes? What if I say something totally inappropriate? What if—"

He put his hand over my mouth. "What if you stop worrying and we get a good night's sleep?"

I spoke into this hand. "OK. You smart. Me not so smart. Have I ever told you that?"

He laughed again as he parked the car. "You're a lot smarter than you think, Miss Bryson. And that's just one of the reasons I adore you."

I looked at him. "You still adore me?"

He reached over and touched my cheek. "Even more than I did yesterday. Now let's get some sleep."

● ● ●

"Waverly, wake up."

I felt the tap on my shoulder and slowly opened my eyes. "Huh? What?"

Where am I?

Why are the drapes paisley?

"It's ten thirty, we need to leave in like twenty minutes."

I bolted upright in bed. "What?" I put a hand on my hair, an unnecessary gesture because I already knew it was going to be a rat's nest.

"We're supposed to be at Natalie's by eleven."

I threw the covers to one side. "Why didn't you wake me up earlier? Now I won't have time to wash my hair."

He laughed. "I tried to wake you up twice. You don't remember?"

"For real?"

"For real. You were *out cold*. The first time you begged me to let you sleep for another half hour, and the second time you promised you'd be up when I got back from my run."

My eyes got big. "Wait a minute. You already went for a *run*? And I just woke *up*?"

He nodded. He was showered and fully dressed. He looked like a Ken doll.

"Are you trying to make me hate you right now?" I narrowed my eyes at him.

He laughed and kissed my forehead. "I have something for you." He handed me a square box wrapped in shiny silver paper with a white bow on top.

"For *me*?" I fluttered my eyelashes.

He nodded and sat down on the bed next to me. "For you. Merry Christmas, Waverly."

"If it's another plastic plant, I'm breaking up with you." I slowly unwrapped and opened the box.

Inside was an antique silver clock.

"Oh, Jake, it's beautiful." I held it up to admire it. It was a little smaller than a tea plate, with a white face and black numbers. Its *ticktock* sound made me think of Captain Hook.

"You like it?"

"I *love* it. It's gorgeous. Thanks so much."

He put his hand on my leg. "Given how fast things are moving for you these days, I thought this might help you slow down once in a while."

I looked at him and shook my head. "How are you so perfect all the time?"

He laughed and tucked a strand of hair behind my ears. "I'm hardly perfect. I'm just learning what makes you…tick."

I smiled at him. "Perfect *and* witty. I have a gift for you too." I jumped up and darted to my suitcase. I rummaged around until I spotted the green wrapping paper, then returned to the bed and handed him a small box.

He opened it to reveal a wooden apple.

"I know it's not *big*, but that's supposed to be New York," I said. "You know, the big apple?"

He smiled. "Cute."

"There's something inside," I said.

He removed the top half of the apple and pulled out a set of keys.

"Are these…what I think they are?"

I grinned. "That's so you don't have to crash at Shane and Kristina's the next time my flight is delayed."

"Wow, I'm honored."

"Be careful with those." I rumpled his hair. "Only three other boyfriends have a set."

He gave me a look I hadn't seen before, then slowly leaned over and kissed me. "Thank you," he said softly. He put his hands on my shoulders. "You now have fourteen minutes. My mom is weird about punctuality, so we should get on a move on."

"OK, OK, I'm moving." I hurried into the bathroom and pulled my hair into a bun before turning on the shower.

As the hot water ran over me, I tried not to think about that look, but I couldn't help myself.

Was it a good move to give him the keys?

Or…does he think I'm getting too serious?

Am I getting too serious?

Or maybe he's getting serious too?

Did we just take a big step forward?

Or did I just…make a huge mistake?

• • •

We pulled up to Jake's sister's house at 11:21.

"Is your mom really going to be upset that we're late?" I unbuckled my seatbelt. "You've got me totally freaked out now, you know."

"Maybe."

"You're joking, right?"

"Maybe."

I squinted at him. "Are you trying to make me hate you right now?"

He winked at me as he opened his door. "It'll be fine."

We walked hand in hand toward the front door, my mind once again recalling last time I'd been there, nearly a year before.

Oh, how things have changed, I thought.

One thing that hadn't changed was how nervous I was. Although it was for a different reason this time, my stomach was still doing somersaults.

I squeezed Jake's hand as he rang the bell. Behind the door, I heard the sound of human feet, dog paws pattering on the hardwood floor, and the shrill voices of little kids.

The door opened, and I immediately recognized Jake's sister, Natalie. She shared his striking blue eyes and dark brown hair, although hers was long and pulled back into a low ponytail, as was mine. *I bet she washed hers*, I thought. *And I bet hers doesn't smell like fried chicken.*

"Hey, little brother, welcome back." She hugged him, and then turned to me with a friendly smile that immediately put me at ease. "Waverly, it's *so* nice to see you again. Please, come in."

I smiled back and handed her the bottle of wine I'd brought as a gift. "Hi, Natalie, thanks so much for having me...um, again." I laughed awkwardly.

She took the bottle and gave me a one-armed hug. "We're thrilled you're back." She helped us off with our coats and hung them on the rack in the foyer. We followed her into the living room, where we were instantly surrounded by two little girls.

"Merry Christmas, Uncle Jake!" they yelled in unison, tugging at his pant legs.

"Hi, Zoe. Hi, Lucy. Merry Christmas. Do you want to meet my friend Waverly?"

"Merry Christmas, Wa-ber-ly!" they yelled in unison.

"Well, hello there," I said, leaning down. Then I turned to look up at Jake. "Do little kids shake hands?" I whispered.

He shrugged. "It's worth a try."

I held out my hands to the girls, but they looked at me like I was crazy and ran away.

"Well done, Waverly. Well done." I stood up and put my hands on my hips.

Natalie waved her hand dismissively. "They'll love you soon enough, don't worry. So who wants a mimosa?"

I looked at her. "A mimosa? Really?"

She smiled. "Sure, why not? It's Christmas. Plus you're about to meet Mom, so I thought you might want one."

I narrowed my eyes at Jake. "Do I need a mimosa to meet your mom?"

He nodded. "I'm having one."

I looked back at Natalie, but before I could say anything, she started walking toward the kitchen. "She and Dad are in the family room with Brett and Michele and Tim. I'll bring you each a strong one," she called over her shoulder.

"I remember liking her before, but I *really like* her," I whispered to Jake.

"She's the best. So is my brother, you'll see. Are you ready for the McIntyre shark tank?"

I looked at him. "Did you just say the *shark tank*?"

"I'm kidding. Come on." He took my hand and led me through the large house toward the family room in the back. As we walked down the hall, I could feel my heart begin to beat faster. Soon it was pumping like a piston, and I wondered if the palpitations were visible through my top.

I took a deep breath. *Keep it together, Waverly.*

From the hall, I could hear several loud voices engaged in lively conversation. But as soon as we walked in, everyone stopped talking and looked at us.

I smiled and suddenly felt like I'd forgotten to put on my pants.

"Hey, Jake!" His brother gave him a bear hug. "It's good to see you."

Jake hugged him back, and then gestured to him and the woman standing next to him. "Waverly, this is my brother, Brett, and his wife, Michele." Brett was even taller than Jake, who was a hair over six-three, and Michele looked to be about five eleven. Suddenly I felt awkward and shrimpy, even at five-eight.

"It's nice to meet you both." I shook Brett's hand, and then held mine out to Michele, but she hugged me instead.

"It's so nice to finally meet you! I have twin toddlers, so I'm home with them and watch you on TV when I can catch a breather. I just love your segment, it's so much fun."

I could feel my cheeks go red. "It's nice to meet you too, and I'm glad you enjoy the show." *Shark tank? Huh? Could these people be any friendlier?*

Jake gestured toward the others in the room. "Waverly, I believe you've met Tim, Nat's husband?"

"Of course. How are you?" I swallowed and nodded as I held out my hand. I hoped he wouldn't bring up last year's ill-timed cross-country expedition in front of everyone. I was sure that discussion had already taken place when I wasn't around, which was mortifying enough.

"Welcome back to Boston," he said with a sly smile as he shook my hand. "We're happy to have you."

Then Jake gestured toward the couch, where his mom and dad were seated. "And, Waverly, these are my parents, Ava and Walt."

The moment the words were out of his mouth, it hit home that I hadn't been introduced to a boyfriend's parents since the time I'd met my ex-fiancé Aaron's, several years earlier.

I nervously turned my eyes to meet theirs and smiled.

"It's so nice to meet you both," I extended my hand first to his mom, who wore her dark hair in a crisp, chin-length bob. She too had pretty blue eyes.

"Happy holidays," she said with a polite smile. She held my hand briefly in hers, but didn't shake it back. She also stayed seated. *Uh-oh.*

Trying not to freak out, I turned to face Jake's dad and offered my hand. "It's so nice to meet you too, Mr. McIntyre."

"Please, call me Walt." He stood up and took my hand in both of his, smiling warmly. "We're just thrilled to have you here, my dear. Can we get you a drink?" *At least* he's *nice*, I thought. He was about Jake's height with a similar build, but his dark hair was streaked with gray.

I laughed and shook my head. "Actually, I think Natalie may have that covered."

"Indeed I do." Natalie appeared out of nowhere and handed me a mimosa. "Here you go, hon."

I took the glass and smiled. "Thank you so much."

She winked and mouthed the words *I told you*.

• • •

After a half hour or so of anxious small talk (anxious on my part, at least), Natalie announced it was time to eat, so we all migrated to a huge table in the dining room. I was still nursing my first mimosa, determined to make it last most of the day. The last thing I wanted was to get tipsy in front of Jake's entire family and blurt out something stupid. God knows I do that often enough when I'm sober.

As we passed through the living room, I admired the enormous and beautifully decorated tree in the corner. My Christmas trees were always pretty, but they had always been small, if not outright puny.

This is a real home, I thought.

As soon as we'd settled into our seats, Natalie appeared from the kitchen and directed us to the buffet lining the back wall. "Serve yourselves, everyone. I don't want to feel like I'm running a restaurant here. Plus I need to make sure the kids are still alive." She laughed and shooed us along.

Jake's mom put her hand on her heart. "Serve ourselves?" She looked horrified.

"Yes, Mom, serve yourself. You can do it." Natalie rolled her eyes, and Jake laughed and nudged me.

"Let's go, captain," he said, standing up.

I looked at him. "Did you just call me *captain*?"

He laughed again. "I must have picked that up somewhere."

"Apparently, my proclivity for assigning nicknames is contagious."

He put a hand on my head. "Apparently it is."

Suddenly I was starving. Everything on the buffet looks delicious. Croissants, ham, turkey, steak, mashed potatoes, scrambled eggs, French toast. I couldn't decide what to eat, so I served myself a bit of everything, and then made my way back to the table. When I sat down, I noticed that I had more food than Jake did. There was literally no room for daylight anywhere on my plate.

"Oh my God, do I look like a pig?" I whispered to him.

He looked at my plate and laughed. "Hungry much?"

"Oh my God, I totally look like a pig," I whispered again. "What should I do with all this food?"

"How about eating it?"

I tilted my head to the side. "Thanks for that, you're really helpful. Have I ever told you that?"

Still whispering, he laughed and pushed a strand of loose hair out of my face. "You look beautiful today. Have I told you that?"

I laughed too. "Damn you. You're impossible to get mad at."

We settled into brunch and were soon engaged in light and funny conversation. I was impressed by how witty everyone was, especially Brett. Twice he said something so out of left field that I nearly spat out my French toast laughing.

Just when I was finally feeling comfortable, Jake's mother took a sip of her orange juice and gave me a polite smile.

"So, Waverly, tell us a little more about this television job of yours. I understand the show is quite popular."

I broke out in a cold sweat and gave her a smile of my own, albeit a nervous one. "Oh, um, well, it's a daytime talk show called *Love, Wendy*. Wendy Davenport, the host, interviews a lot of interesting people, um, you know, celebrities promoting their movies, authors promoting their books, that sort of thing." I cleared my throat and reached for my water glass.

"It's a fun show, Ava" Michele said. "I watch it all the time."

I stole a glance at Michele. *I wish I were as composed as you are around this woman.*

I swallowed and looked back at Jake's mom. "So, um, I do a semi-regular feature for the show called *Honey on Your Mind.* It's based on an advice column I used to write for the *San Francisco Sun.*

"Advice?" She ran her fingers over her pearl necklace. "What kind of advice?"

I nodded and hoped no one had noticed the sweat mustache I was sporting. "The column was mostly dating advice, but, um, the TV show is a little different. It's sort of expanded to a lot of different things." *Good God, I sound lame right now.*

"She does a lot of man-on-the-street interviews," Jake said. "You know, taking the pulse of the city, that sort of thing. They're really funny."

I looked at him, so grateful that he spoke up. "You really think they're funny?"

He put his hand on my head. "Come on, you know I do."

"I loved the one where you asked people if they were more annoyed by, let me see if I can remember your exact words." Michele used air quotes. "'Jackasses who yap on their cell phones in restaurants or people who immediately post results of sporting events on Facebook.' I think that was my favorite one."

I blushed. "I remember that one. I definitely got a little carried away that day. I hope I didn't come across as too mean."

"Oh God no, it was fantastic. People drive me nuts all the time doing stuff like that, so it was great to see someone speak up in an effort to stop the madness," she said.

I smiled. "Thanks."

"I liked the one where you stopped people and asked them to tell a joke on the spot," Natalie said. "Those people were terrible!"

Jake looked at me. "I didn't see that episode. Is that where you get your material?"

"Hey now." I narrowed my eyes at him.

"Waverly likes to tell jokes," Jake said to the table. "Although I'd use the term 'jokes' lightly, so as not to offend the professionals."

I put my hand on his arm. "Be nice. If not, I may have to tell you my newest one."

"Oh no," he said.

Brett rubbed his hands together. "Lay it on us."

Jake held his palms up. "Don't say I didn't warn you. I take no responsibility for this."

The oldest Mr. McIntyre took a bite of his scrambled eggs. "I love jokes. Let's hear what you've got, young lady."

I quickly scanned the table, making eye contact with nearly everyone, and I was surprised to realize that instead of feeling freaked out, I felt…comfortable. As an only child whose one serious romantic relationship had been with another only child, I'd never attended such a big family gathering.

This is kind of nice.

I smiled and nodded. "OK, sure." I took a breath and paused for just a moment.

"What do you call a cow with only two legs?"

They all looked at me.

I tilted my body to one side. "Lean beef."

Everyone, or more accurately, everyone but Jake's mom, chuckled.

"What do you call a cow with *no* legs?" I said.

They all kept looking at me.

I hesitated before speaking again.

"Ground beef."

This time everyone genuinely laughed. Even Jake's mom, who was quietly folding and refolding her napkin on the table, smiled.

"That's pretty good," Michele said.

Jake's dad held up his plate. "I've got a cow with no legs right here next to my eggs."

I turned to Jake and playfully pushed his shoulder. "See? I'm not *that* bad."

"Nonpaying audience." He gave my shoulder a squeeze, then stood up and excused himself.

"How do you come up with the ideas for the show?" Brett asked me. "Do you make them up yourself?"

I nodded. "For the most part. We have a weekly staff meeting to bounce ideas around, as well. Plus I get a lot of e-mails from viewers through my website, and I have some funny friends, so I have a lot of material to choose from."

"Sounds so fun," Natalie said.

I smiled. "It *is* fun. It's nice to be able to laugh at work, you know?"

Brett coughed. "I'm an attorney. Our laughter masks internal pain and suffering."

Michele elbowed him. "Oh please, you love your corporate job. You'd wear a suit to the dentist on a Saturday." She looked at me. "Brett loves the suit thing, and if you hadn't noticed, he *loves* the preppy thing. His favorite color is Nantucket red, which I say is just a fancy word for pink."

"It's manly," Brett said in a deep voice as he patted his plaid sweater vest.

"So you're serious about this career, then?" Mrs. McIntyre said to me. The chilly tone of her voice sucked all the jovial feeling out of the air.

I looked at her. "Serious?"

Natalie stood up and started to clear plates. "Oh, Mom, leave her alone. Now who wants another mimosa?"

Everyone but Mrs. McIntyre raised an empty glass.

Natalie laughed. "I figured."

"Can you just bring out the pitcher?" Brett asked.

Tim stood up and started clearing dishes too.

"Can I help?" I asked him.

"Absolutely not," he said. "You're our guest."

Jake's mom excused herself to use the restroom. I chewed on my fingernail as I watched her walk away.

• • •

The Knicks were playing the Jazz that day, so after brunch, Jake, Brett, Tim, and I gathered in the family room to watch Shane take the court. Michele, Natalie, and Jake's parents stayed in the living room to chat and watch the kids play with their new toys.

As the Knicks streamed out of the locker room, Brett lightly smacked Jake on the back of the head. "That could have been you. You could have been our *meal ticket*, little brother."

Jake didn't turn around. "I averaged four points a game at Duke, older brother. Shane averaged thirty. You never *were* very good at math."

"A man can dream," Brett said. "What about you, Waverly? Jake tells me your dad used to play pro baseball. Are you a jock too?"

I shook my head. "Unfortunately those genes drowned in the pool."

He laughed. "Nice. Anyone need a drink? I'm thirsty." He stood up and smoothed his perfectly pressed pants with his hands.

"I'll take a beer," Tim said.

"Oh my God, that reminds me," I said.

"What reminds you of what?" Tim look confused.

"Being thirsty," I said. "That reminds me of something."

Jake looked at me. "Uh-oh, I sense a joke coming on."

Brett stopped walking. "Another joke?"

"Well, it's not really a joke. More of an observation," I said.

Brett wiggled his fingers inward. "Let's hear it."

"Well, I was just thinking about the cows I was talking about earlier. If you were a farmer and owned a brown cow, don't you think a cool name for it would be *Chocolate Milk*?"

Brett laughed. "OK, then."

"Ouch," Tim said.

"I told you," Jake said, shaking his head.

I put my palms up and looked at all of them. "What? What?"

Jake put his arm around me. "I'll take another Bloody Mary. And bring a muzzle for my little friend here."

"Or some chocolate milk!" I added, laughing.

• • •

At halftime, I got up to find an empty room where I could call my dad and wish him a merry Christmas. On the way down the hall, I heard the sound of voices in the kitchen.

"I'm just not sure I see a future there, that's all. I'm sure she's a lovely girl."

I froze.

It was Jake's mom.

Is she talking about me?

Then I heard Natalie's voice. "You don't know that, mom. A lot of things could happen. He might not even take the job."

"He told me she'd never move to Los Angeles. And you heard her in there; she basically said her TV career is more important to her than he is. So to me, that means there's no future. Jake has already said as much to me."

Los Angeles? Take the job?

What job?

What?

Mrs. McIntyre's voice continued. "Holly would never choose a career over Jake."

I felt like I'd been kicked in the stomach.

Holly.

Holly, his pretty ex-girlfriend.

Holly, his pretty ex-girlfriend who wants him back.

Jake had told me things were over with Holly, and I believed him.

But I still felt…sick.

I remembered the look in his eyes after I gave him my keys. He'd looked so pensive and serious, but in a *good* way.

Or so I had hoped.

Did I have it all wrong?

Is this not what I think it is?

I needed to get some air. Immediately.

I tiptoed past the kitchen into the foyer and quickly sifted through the coats on the rack to find my jacket and purse. At that moment, I felt like walking out of the house and never coming back. *She doesn't want me here…I have to get out of here…*

Hoping they wouldn't hear me, I opened the door and slipped outside. I quietly closed the door behind me, then pulled my hat and gloves out of my coat pocket and put them on. I hurried toward the sidewalk. Within seconds, tears were streaming down my face.

No future?

Is that true?

Is Jake just leading me on?

What job in Los Angeles?

He and I hadn't ever really talked about "the future," and we hadn't been dating seriously all that long. But I loved him, and he loved me. Wasn't that enough, at least for now?

I dug my phone out of my purse and started walking. I removed a glove for a moment to call my dad. It was freezing, but I couldn't go back inside.

He answered right away. "Baby, hi there, merry Christmas!"

"Hi, Dad, how are you?"

"I'm doing just wonderful, thanks for asking. Betty just made us a tasty Christmas breakfast, and we're getting ready to open our presents. How are you?"

I closed my eyes for a moment and smiled. This was the first time I'd been away from my dad for Christmas, and I was so glad he wasn't spending it alone. I wondered if Betty would ever know how grateful I was to her for coming into his life. I felt more tears stream down my cheek. Why couldn't Jake's mom feel that way about me?

"I'm good, Dad, a little tired from working so much, but I'm good." I wiggled my glove back on and hoped my shaky voice wouldn't betray me.

"You having fun up there in Boston?"

"It's a little overwhelming meeting the whole family at once, but they're really nice." *Most of them.*

"I'm sure they love you, baby. How could they not love you?"

For a moment, I was tempted to tell him what I'd just overheard, but then I decided to change the subject.

"So, um, how are the wedding plans going?"

"So far, so good. Betty's a whiz at organizing. I tried to help a few times, but I just ended up in the way. So in the end we decided that she'll tell me where to be and when, and I'll show up in a tuxedo. I figured as long as I don't screw *that* up, everything else will be OK."

I laughed. "I like your style, Dad."

"You're still coming, right?"

"Of course. I wouldn't miss it for anything. Andie and McKenna want to come too, if that's OK with you."

"Sure, baby, Betty would love to meet your friends. She's so proud of you, you know. She just loves watching you on that show of yours. She always says how she can't believe her soon-to-be daughter is on TV."

Daughter? Wow.

I thought of the year before, when I'd driven to Sacramento to spend Christmas with my dad in his small apartment, right before he started dating Betty. The day had been nice, but quiet, and a bit melancholy, as holidays always were with just the two of us. I'd shown up with Santa hats for us to wear, and we'd spent the afternoon watching basketball on TV.

"Dad?"

"Yes, baby?"

"Can you do me a favor?"

"Anything, baby."

"Do you still have those Santa hats I brought to your house last year?"

"Sure do."

"I know this may sound strange, but would you and Betty wear them today?" I could feel a lump forming in my throat. "It would… it would make me feel like a part of me was there with you."

"Why, of course we will. I'll get them out of the closet as soon as I hang up."

Suddenly I started to cry. "Thanks, Dad."

"Are you OK, baby?"

"I'm fine, just a little…cold. Will you please tell Betty I said merry Christmas?"

"Of course. She's right here if you want to tell her yourself."

I wiped the tears away with my glove. I could fool my dad, but Betty would know I was upset. "No, um, I really should be heading back inside now. But would you, um, would you please tell her…" My voice began to crack, and I fake sniffled to hide the fact that I was crying. "Um, will you please tell her…that I'm glad…that I'm glad she wants to be my…mom?"

"Will, do baby. She'll be thrilled to hear it."

"Thanks, Dad. I should really be getting inside now. They're going to be wondering where I wandered off to."

"OK, thanks for calling. You take care now, OK?"

"OK. Merry Christmas, Dad."

"Merry Christmas, Waverly."

I hung up the phone. *I love you, Dad.*

I stood still for a few moments, trying to absorb the conflicting emotions I was feeling. Love. Pain. Fear. Loneliness.

I looked back at the house. I wasn't ready to go back inside, so I decided to take a walk around the block. As I slowly wandered through the festive neighborhood, I studied the pretty houses lining the streets and wondered how the families inside were cel-ebrating the holiday. Was I the only one who was part of a big party yet felt a little bit alone?

When I made it back to Natalie's, I stopped on the side-walk and stared for a moment at the bright Christmas lights framing the front windows, then smiled weakly at the huge candy canes, elves, and sleigh decorating the snow-covered front yard.

It was probably the most welcoming home I'd ever seen.

I just wished I felt...welcome.

• • •

Back inside, Jake and the guys were still watching the Knicks game. The score was tied, so they were all focused on the screen. I sat down next to Jake and leaned back against the couch.

"Your dad doing OK?" Jake whispered, his eyes still on the screen.

I nodded. "Yeah, he's good." I was grateful for the close game. If Jake hadn't been so distracted, he would have seen that I was upset, and I just couldn't deal with that right now. How would I reply if he asked me what was wrong?

A few minutes later, the Knicks' coach called a time-out. By then I'd pulled myself together, so I forced a smile and put my hand on Jake's arm. "How's Shane doing?"

"He's got twenty-five already. That guy's a machine."

"I still can't believe how tall he is. How did he fit in the bed in the dorms?" I remembered when I'd first met Shane a cou-ple years ago, at a big tradeshow in Atlanta. He was there to do press interviews for a line of basketball shoes made by one of my clients, so we'd spent three days straight together. I'd never seen such an enormous man up close before. He made the media room look like something out of *Alice in Wonderland.*

"His feet hung off the end, that's for sure," Jake said.

"No joke. I thought I had big dogs, but that guy has some *gargantuan* dogs," Brett said. "They're like water skis."

We all laughed as the game came back on. I was grateful for the distraction and was beginning to feel a bit less rattled. Maybe later I'd get the courage to tell Jake what I'd overheard.

• • •

With less than a minute to go in the fourth quarter and the Knicks up by one, Shane leaped to block a shot. He landed awkwardly and crumpled to the floor, grabbing his leg.

Jake immediately stood up. "That wasn't good. Oh, hell. That was *not* good."

Tim shook his head. "That looked like it *hurt.*"

Shane lay there on the floor, still clutching his leg as his teammates circled around him.

"You think it's his ankle?" Brett said. "Or his knee?"

Jake didn't reply as he stared at the screen. The team trainer ran out to attend to Shane, who was visibly in pain, and then they cut to a commercial break.

We all sat there in silence.

"Damn it," Jake finally said. "That looked really bad. I hope it isn't his ACL."

I looked at him. "What's an ACL?"

"A major ligament in the knee."

"At his age, that could be career-threatening," Tim said.

Shane was thirty-four.

"Really?" I said.

They all nodded silently.

"Oh no," I added quietly.

Jake paced the family room as we waited for the game to come back on. When it did, the commentators said that Shane was being evaluated by team doctors.

"Let's cross our fingers for good news," Jake said.

It wasn't good news. Jake made a few phone calls, and we soon learned that Shane hadn't just torn his ACL, he had torn *all* the major ligaments in his knee. Surgery was scheduled for two days after Christmas.

There was no way around it; Shane's career was in jeopardy.

• • •

"Thanks so much for having me. I had a great time." I hugged Tim and Natalie at the front door several hours later. Jake's parents had left a few minutes earlier, and I was still defrosting from that good-bye. His dad had wrapped me a bear hug, but his mom had offered only another chilly, polite smile. I didn't want to offend her by going in uninvited for the hug or even a kiss on the cheek, so I'd just stood in front of her awkwardly until she'd turned away to get her coat. I'm sure everyone who witnessed it cringed.

Natalie hugged me back tightly. "It was our pleasure. I hope we see you again."

I hope so too, I thought.

"I really enjoyed meeting you," Michele said. "I'll be watching you on the show."

"You should tell one of your jokes on the show," Brett said with a laugh.

Jake poked his back. "Are you trying to get her fired?"

"If you don't watch it, I'm going to tell another one right here," I said.

As Jake and I drove back to the bed and breakfast, we mostly talked about Shane. I certainly wasn't happy he was hurt, but I was selfishly grateful for the diversion. Jake was clearly preoccupied, because if he'd been paying attention, he would have noticed that I'd barely made eye contact with him all afternoon.

• • •

Early the next morning, we said a rushed good-bye at the bed and breakfast. My train wasn't until ten, but Jake had to fly straight from Boston to Chicago to meet up with the Hawks, so he needed to leave at the crack of dawn to return the rental car and catch his flight.

I was still half-asleep when he left.

"I'll call you later, OK?" he whispered.

I nodded, my eyes half-closed. I still hadn't asked him about him about what I'd heard. I desperately wanted to, but I just… couldn't.

"I'm sure your mom hates me," I whispered back, then immediately regretted it. *Lame.*

He laughed and kissed my forehead. "Go back to sleep."

I put my hand on my forehead. "I knew it. She hated me."

"Hey now, I didn't say that. Don't worry, she'll warm up."

"I wish I could have washed my hair. I bet she totally smelled the fried chicken wafting off me. Smelling like dead fowl does *not* a good first impression make."

He laughed again. "You're nuts. I've got to run now. Are you going to visit Shane next week?"

I nodded. "Probably."

"I'm going to try him from the airport, but I may not be able to get through, so if he hasn't heard from me when you see him, tell him I'll track him down soon. I'm sure his voice mail is about to blow up."

I hoped that wasn't the only thing about to blow up.

He shut the door behind him, and I cursed myself for not having the guts to speak up.

You suck, Waverly.

chapter fourteen

On the train ride home, I had a hard time focusing. So many things in my life were changing, and I couldn't control any of them. As I watched the countryside roll by outside the window, thoughts flew around in my head like shrieking bats. The noise was relentless:

My dad is getting married!

Andie is moving in with her boyfriend!

McKenna is a mother!

Shane's career might be over!

My new career is just getting started!

My new business is opening in a week!

My boss drinks too much!

My friend is sleeping with her husband!

Jake's mother hates me!

I knew that last one was an exaggeration, but she was hardly warm and fuzzy. She'd definitely softened around the edges a bit as Christmas Day wore on, but it would be an overstatement to say she'd been outright *nice* to me. Thankfully, everyone else had been wonderful. But rising above the din and impossible to ignore, no matter how hard I tried, was what I'd overheard.

Is Jake moving to Los Angeles?

Why hasn't he said anything to me?

Why doesn't his mother like me?

She's his mom. *If she doesn't like me, does that mean we're doomed?*

Is what she said about our future true?

Was it a mistake to give him my keys?

I was still mad at myself for not talking openly with Jake, but I couldn't figure out a way to do so without it all turning into something bigger than I was ready for.

What was I supposed to say, anyway?

Blech.

The countryside kept flying by outside. So much change. So much movement. So little certainty.

On top of everything else, I kept thinking about Wendy and Gary. I couldn't shake that vision of Wendy, sitting alone in the conference room with a bottle of vodka. What had gone wrong with them? Was it Wendy's career ambition that had caused Gary to stray? Was that even a fair question to ask?

Is my career getting in the way of a future with Jake?

Is Jake's career getting in the way of a future with me?

I don't want to move.

I don't want to lose Jake.

Should I want to move?

It's hard enough now. How long could we make it with even more distance between us?

Ugh. I could hardly keep up with my present, much less envision my future.

I sighed and pressed my face against the glass to watch the changing scenery outside.

• • •

"Does it hurt?" I asked.

Shane shook his head. "It did for a couple days, but not anymore. They've loaded me up on painkillers. I'm actually feeling good right now."

It was a few days later, and Shane and Kristina and I were in their enormous, luxury apartment. Shane was resting in a recliner chair in the living room, his left leg propped up on pillows. Kristina was a few feet away, rolling out cookie dough on a granite island that separated the kitchen and living areas.

"Watch those painkillers," Kristina pretended to scold him. "I don't want you to end up in a back alley somewhere looking for your next fix. God knows I see enough of those types at the hospital. I certainly don't need to be living with one."

He laughed. "Got it, boss."

I watched them tease each other and wondered why they were in such a good mood. If Shane's career was indeed in jeopardy, as everyone had been saying, shouldn't they be upset? At least a little bit? Was I missing something?

"So what happens now? Are you already planning your big comeback?" I asked.

Shane took a sip of water. "I don't think so. I think I've had enough of life on the road."

"Really?"

He nodded. "It looks glamorous, but it's sort of a grind, as I'm sure Jake has told you."

I let out a small sigh that may or may not have been noticeable. *Please don't make me think about Jake right now.*

Shane shifted slightly in the recliner. "So I could probably try to come back, but I think it's time to hang it up and start a new chapter."

"Hang it up? Really? But what about winning a championship? Kristina told me you didn't want to retire until you had a ring."

He glanced at Kristina before looking at me. "I guess you could say my priorities have changed."

"Your priorities have changed?"

He nodded but didn't elaborate.

"Are you going to become a TV analyst?" Shane was smart and articulate, which made the transition seem like a no-brainer.

He nodded. "Yes, well, that, and…" His voice trailed off.

"That and what?"

Silence.

I raised my eyebrows. "*Hola?*"

"It's OK. You can say it," Kristina said to Shane.

I looked over at her. "Say *what?*"

"Go ahead, say it," Kristina said.

I looked back at Shane. "Say *what?*"

He smiled. "Yes, I'm going to become a TV analyst…and a dad."

I whipped my head toward Kristina. "*What?*"

She laughed. "Yes, it's true."

My eyes got big. "You're prego?"

She walked up behind Shane's chair and put her hands on her hips. "Officially knocked up as of seven weeks ago. Can you believe it?"

"No way! I thought you guys were going to wait until Shane's career was over to have kids."

"We were, but sometimes Mother Nature has her own ideas. So this injury, while unfortunate, has a silver lining." She leaned down and kissed Shane's enormous bald head.

I smiled. "Wow, that's so exciting! You must be thrilled."

Shane shifted again in the recliner and adjusted his leg. "*Terrified* is a better word for it. I have no idea what to do with a baby."

"Oh, shush," Kristina said. "You have good hands, and I'm a pediatrician. We'll be fine."

Kristina left to use the bathroom, and Shane turned to me. "So Jake's good?"

I nodded. "Why do you ask?"

He shook his head. "No reason."

He clearly knew something, but I let it go.

chapter fifteen

On the way home from Kristina and Shane's place, I couldn't stop thinking about the way Shane had described the major changes in his life.

It's time to move on to a new chapter.

I pulled the keys to my new office out of my purse and ran my fingers across them. *Honey on Your Mind* was still so new, and Waverly's Honey Shop was just finding its footing as well. New York was definitely a new chapter in my life, but in some ways, I felt years behind Shane and Kristina.

I also felt years behind McKenna.

In a way, I even felt behind Andie. At least she and Nick were moving *forward*. As his mother had so graciously pointed out, Jake and I didn't even live in the same state. The best I could say was that Georgia was in the same time zone as New York, which was closer than when I'd lived in San Francisco. Could we make it if he moved to Los Angeles?

I looked at my reflection in the streaked glass of the subway window. *Why do I keep comparing myself to other people?*

Suddenly I remembered something Shane said to me way back when I first met him. In a classic Waverly moment, I had blurted out something about feeling that I was missing the boat because I was nearly thirty and hadn't figured it all out yet as everyone else seemed to have done. He told me not to be so concerned about what other people were doing with their lives.

Life is not a basketball game, he said. *No one is keeping score but you.*

I turned to my reflection again...and reflected.

Look at all you've *done, Waverly.*

In a few short months, I'd started a brand new life, and who cared it if wasn't on the same track as my friends' lives. The truth was, I'd managed to go from carrying a subway map at all times to feeling like a bona fide New Yorker, all on my own.

I now had keys to my own office.

I had a good job at NBC.

I even had developed a growing disdain for tourists.

I squeezed the keys in my hand and smiled at the person in the window.

She might be a little neurotic, but she was doing just fine.

• • •

I called Jake after dinner. I rarely caught him live at this hour, so I was planning to leave him a voice mail while channel surfing, but he surprised me by picking up.

"Are your ears burning?"

I put the remote control on the coffee table as I sat down on the couch. "Huh?"

"Are your ears burning? I was just talking about you."

"You were? Good things, I hope?"

"Always. I was just going to give you a call. What are you up to?"

"I just got home from Shane and Kristina's."

"So you heard?"

I frowned. How did he know about the baby? Shane said he hadn't told Jake yet and gave me the green light to do so.

"Heard what?" Maybe he was talking about something else?

"Oh, just some NBA gossip."

Something in his tone told me he wasn't being entirely forthright.

I decided to tread cautiously. "You mean gossip about whether or not Shane's going to retire?"

He didn't answer for a moment, and I got a weird feeling in my stomach.

"Jake? You still there?"

"Sorry, got a little distracted. Yes, still here."

"Is everything OK?"

"Yeah, just got a lot on my mind right now. So what's up?"

I closed my eyes and decided to ignore the pit in my stomach.

"So, um, anyhow, when I was visiting Shane, he *did* share some big news, but it wasn't about basketball. Actually, he and Kristina shared the news together."

"Yeah? What did they say?"

I opened my eyes. "Kristina's pregnant."

"No way. For real?" He sounded genuinely surprised. *You really didn't know?*

"Yep, she's about two months along. They're thrilled."

"That's awesome. I need to call him. Things are just so crazy right now. Taking those few days off for Christmas really put me underwater."

His voice still sounded...*strange*, and I got the feeling he was itching to get off the phone. Or maybe *I* was the one itching. There was no denying the awkwardness between us, which seemed to have appeared out of nowhere.

"So I guess I'll let you go, then?" I intentionally posed it as a question. "You seem a little distracted."

He sighed. "Yes, I am. I'm sorry, Waverly."

The pit in my stomach tightened slightly.

"It's OK. I know you're busy," I said softly.

"Yeah, I'm swamped, I'm sorry. But listen, there's something I want to talk to you about. Just not now."

The pit turned into a massive sinkhole.

"You'd like to talk?" I whispered. *No one* wants to hear those words from a significant other, especially someone whose fiancé once broke up with her two weeks before their wedding by telling her they needed to "talk." Jake knew what had gone down with Aaron. He knew how afraid I was of getting hurt again. *That can't be what's going on here.*

It can't be.

He cleared his throat. "Yeah. But I think we should do it in person."

Do it? Do what?

I swallowed. "In person?" In-person talking is even worse.

"I was thinking of coming up for New Year's. Does that work for you?"

"New Year's? I thought you had that work party." The Hawks' owner was throwing a big bash and Jake thought it would be in bad form to skip it. Since I'd be working anyway, I'd encouraged him to go.

"I still can't make it for New Year's Eve, but I could fly up New Year's Day, probably in the afternoon."

"Um, OK, sure." Part of me wanted to just ask him what he wanted to talk to me about, but a bigger part was too scared to hear the answer.

"Listen, I've got to run now. I'll let you know when I book my ticket."

"OK." My lips felt numb.

"Bye, Waverly."

"Bye, Jake."

I hung up the phone and slowly placed it on the coffee table.

He hadn't said, "I love you," before hanging up.

I sat extremely still for a few moments, then quietly lay down on the couch and began to cry.

chapter sixteen

"He really said you need to talk?" McKenna asked.

"I think technically he said, 'I want to talk,' but you get the picture."

"And he didn't say about what?"

"Nope."

"Oh, sweetie, that doesn't sound good."

I frowned into the phone. "I know."

It was later that evening, and I was back on the couch, although now I was in my pajamas and eating an enormous bowl of chocolate chip ice cream with fudge sauce. I'd finally emerged from the Dark Ages and bought a Bluetooth earpiece, which made eating ice cream while chatting on the phone, something I'd struggled to master for years, much easier.

"Maybe he just wants to tell you about the job offer in person?"

"Call it women's intuition, but I don't think so. Plus, don't people usually give good news like that over the phone? It's the bad news they deliver in person, right?"

She didn't reply for a moment, so I knew she agreed with me.

"You think maybe he's going to ask you to move out there with him?"

I sighed. "I don't know. I want him to ask me, but I have a weird feeling about it all."

"Things went well at Christmas, right?" she asked.

I nodded. "Yes. His family was great, really great. Everyone except his mom. And if I hadn't overheard her like I did, I would have thought it went as well as it could have."

"She sounds a bit uppity. I bet she was wearing pearls. Was she wearing pearls?"

I laughed. "How did you know?"

"Just a feeling."

"She's a bit stiff, that's for sure. And I'm clearly not her version of the ideal girlfriend for Jake. Apparently Holly, otherwise known as *Miss Perfect*, has that title."

"Please, you know Jake loves you for *not* being perfect."

"I hope that was a compliment."

"It was. The way you describe Jake's mom makes me think of Andie's mom."

I sat up on the couch. "Oh my God, you're totally right. She's *just* like Andie's mom. A little cold, a little distant. Very traditional. I could tell she likes things just so."

"Is she a bitch?" McKenna asked. "Andie's mom is definitely a bitch."

"I really don't want to think she's a bitch. Maybe she's just hard to get to know?"

"Bitches are usually still bitches once you get to know them."

I laughed. "I think she's just old-fashioned. The fact that I have a career and live in a different city and am obviously not centering my whole life around Jake, it's like she's insulted or something. It's like she thinks I'm saying he's not enough for me."

"Did she ever work outside of the home?"

"That's a good question. Jake and I have never talked about it, but he has a sister and a brother, and raising three kids sounds like enough work on its own without having another job."

"Do you think that's what Jake wants too?"

I put my ice cream down and hugged my knees to my chest. "I don't know. I don't think so."

"So you've never talked about the future?"

"Not really. But I didn't think that was because we didn't *have* one. I thought things were going great. Do you think it's possible that I've been misreading things?"

"I can't answer that for you, Wave."

I sighed. "I know."

"Well, what if he asked you to move to LA. Would you do it?"

I bit my lip. "Do I have to answer that right now?"

"It sounds like you might have to soon."

"I just…it's just that I really like what I'm doing right now."

"I *love* what you're doing right now. I'm so proud of you."

I didn't reply. I just stared at the wall.

"Waverly?"

"What if he breaks up with me if I don't want to move?" I whispered.

"Why would he break up with you for that?"

"Well, think about it. We all saw how hard it was when I lived in California and he was in Atlanta, right?"

"Right."

"And it's much better now that I'm in New York, but it's still a challenge, right?"

"Right."

"So while taking a job there would be a step forward in his career, wouldn't it be a step backward in our relationship? A big step?"

Her voice suddenly sharpened. "Waverly, listen to me. First of all, you're just going to make yourself sick if you worry about that, OK?"

I nodded. "OK."

"And second, no matter *what* he says, you need to stay true to yourself, OK? You need to remember that this isn't all about what Jake wants, OK? What you want matters too. Will you promise me that you'll remember that?"

I kept staring at the wall.

"Waverly?"

I nodded. "OK, I'll try. But..." My voice trailed off.

"But what?"

"But what...but what if...I end up losing him?"

"Are you willing to give up everything you've worked so hard for?"

"I don't know. Maybe."

"But would you give it up *now*? Right when everything is just taking off?"

I looked at the boxes of Waverly's Honey Shop products stacked against the walls of my living room. One in particular caught my eye, the pink Honey Tee that said: I KNOW NOTHING, BUT AT LEAST I KNOW THAT.

How fitting.

"Waverly, did you hear me?"

"Yes, sorry. Spaced for a minute there."

"I know you love him, but would giving up everything, *now*, make you happy?"

I looked at the Honey products again and shook my head. "No," I whispered. "Not now."

"That's what you need to remember, OK? Your life is already in major upheaval, so it's not the time for you to be making any drastic decisions. I realize that Jake is a wonderful guy, and I really want things to work out between you two, but no matter how much you love him, you're asking for trouble if you give up everything you've worked so hard for. Please don't forget that, OK?"

"OK," I said slowly.

"Listen, I really hate to do this, but Elizabeth is crying for her bottle, and Hunter's at the hospital, so I need to go. I'm sorry, Wave."

"It's OK, I understand."

"I love you. You know that, right?"

"Yes. And thanks, Mackie. I love you too."

I hung up the phone and put my face in my hands.

Is this really happening?

Suddenly I thought of Paige, who was clearly sacrificing, in her own way, for love. Whatever she was dealing with couldn't be easy. Had I been too quick to judge her? Had I been wrong to judge Gary? Maybe he really did love her.

I stood and picked up the Honey Tee. It was the one that had landed me the Jordan Brooke account—the weekend we'd first met Gary in Chicago.

I really do know nothing, I thought.

• • •

I didn't sleep much that night, and when I finally opened my eyes the next morning, I had a thought I hadn't had in months.

I want to go for a run.

I looked at the clock on my nightstand. It was only seven, which gave me plenty of time before I needed to be at the studio. I jumped up and stripped off my pajamas, then dug through my drawers for a pair of running tights and a long-sleeved T-shirt. I put them on and topped off the outfit with the warmest fleece I had. I hadn't yet gone for a run in the winter cold of New York and had no idea if my makeshift getup would do, but I had to get outside and clear my head.

I grabbed a pair of gloves and my keys and was off.

I decided to run toward the Brooklyn Bridge. As I passed the subway entrances at Court Street and then Borough Hall, I watched people in their winter coats and scarves descend into the ground on their way into Manhattan. Despite my anxious mental state, I was glad to be in my own world for a bit and not about to join the underground rat race just yet. I turned left on Court Street and headed into frosty Cadman Plaza Park. While the sidewalks surrounding it bustled with people, the park itself was mostly quiet, its benches empty and still. The turf field at the center, normally filled with soccer players or friends tossing a football, was dusted with a light layer of snow.

I'd forgotten to put on a hat, and as I ran through the park, I could feel my ears beginning to freeze. I held my hands over them for a few minutes and wondered how much longer I could run before they chipped off.

By the time I reached the end of the park, I could barely feel my face. I was about to give up and turn around, but then I saw the entrance to the Brooklyn Bridge.

Should I keep going? Running over the iconic bridge had been on my to-do list since I'd moved to Brooklyn, but I just hadn't found the time to do it. Or, I hadn't *made* the time.

I'm going to do it.

I took the steps up to the pedestrian entrance to the bridge and set out west toward Manhattan. I looked up and took a quick breath in surprise. Since moving to New York, I'd crossed the bridge many times in a cab, but always at night, and the aboveground subway ran over the Manhattan Bridge farther north. This was the first time I'd been on the Brooklyn Bridge and taken the time to *look* at it–up close and personal.

It was beautiful.

"Wow," I stopped in my tracks and gazed up at the structure. It was truly stunning, and I felt foolish for having lived literally in its shadow for so long without taking the time to admire it properly.

I stood there for a few moments, my hands on my hips, breathing hard, looking up. It couldn't look more different from the Golden Gate Bridge, a symbol of my former life, but in its own way, the Brooklyn Bridge was just as beautiful.

I put my head down and kept running.

I'd read somewhere that it took fourteen years to build the Brooklyn Bridge. *Fourteen years.*

I thought about Jake, then about Aaron. They were the only two men I'd ever loved, and *combined,* those relationships hadn't even lasted three years yet.

I thought about how my dad had been widowed at a young age, how the future isn't ever certain, how fast things can change.

I thought about how in a few days the path I thought I was on might be upended right in front of me

I looked overhead again.

Fourteen years to build the Brooklyn Bridge.

Why can't life be more like that? Why does everything have to happen overnight? Why can't things stay the same for a while?

The last few months had been crazy and stressful, yes, but I wanted to enjoy the crazy ride I was on. It may not be traditional, but it was *my* life, and I wanted to enjoy it all.

I looked ahead to where the bridge connected with Manhattan.

Suddenly, I had an idea.

I scanned the skyline before me. To the left I could see the skyscrapers of Wall Street and the Statue of Liberty. To the right lay the Manhattan Bridge and the booming skyline of Midtown.

In between were buildings, cars, people, trees, *energy.* The entire city was covered in a thin layer of ice, but it was also bursting with life.

It was the dead of winter, but that didn't stop anyone from living.

When I got to the other side of the bridge, I stopped running, put my hands on my hips, and took it all in. I was terribly out of shape and breathing hard.

And taking in every moment of it.

Things all around me were in motion, but for a brief window, everything stopped, and for the first time in months, I could see clearly.

I finally had an idea for my New Year's Eve segment.

chapter seventeen

Although I was relieved to have come up with an idea for the New Year's Eve piece, I was still anxious. Hard as I tried to focus my mind entirely on the show, I'd be lying if I didn't say I was a little—if not completely—freaked out about Jake.

And it wasn't just the Jake situation that had me on edge. Since the *Love, Wendy* production team had decided to do the entire show on location in Times Square, they planned to incorporate *Honey on Your Mind* into the live show. Instead of including my usual prerecorded video feature, that meant I'd be doing my show *live*. And not just live on a quiet street, but live smack among the throngs of tourists from around the globe packed into the most touristy area in all of Manhattan on the most touristy night of them all: December 31. One wrong step, however tiny, and the whole world would see the damage unfold, reality-show style. Given how much editing my segments normally required to get them into the shape I wanted them to be, I was doubtful that I'd be able to pull it off without some sort of legendary Waverly moment ruining the whole thing.

A Waverly moment that would very likely be followed by a conversation with Jake that I desperately wanted to avoid.

Did I mention I was freaked out?

• • •

Three days before New Year's Eve, I entered the big conference room of the *Love, Wendy* office carrying an enormous cup of coffee that I hoped would compensate for the sleep I'd reluctantly left behind in my warm bed. I was the first one there, and as I was pulling my notebook out of my purse, Ben, the intern, walked in. Ever since that night when he'd finally acknowledged my existence, he'd emerged from his shell a bit more each time I saw him. I wouldn't exactly call us *friends*, but we were becoming chummy.

"Hi, Waverly, how's it going?"

I smiled. "Hi, Ben. I'm OK. I've got way too much on my to-do list, but I'm hanging in there. How about you? Did you have a good Christmas?" I went back to studying the notebook in front of me.

"Yep. I got a new phone. Life is good."

I glanced up from my notes and smiled. *To be that young again.*

People slowly began to trickle in and noisy chatter began to fill up the room. Wendy, the last to arrive, waltzed in casually. I hadn't seen her since that awkward encounter on Christmas Eve. It was only nine o'clock in the morning, but I couldn't help but wonder if she'd been drinking.

Without acknowledging me, she removed her cashmere wrap, hung it on the chair behind her, and patted her big hair. "Ben, dear, could you be a peach and fetch me a large, nonfat cappuccino from Argo?" There was a free cappuccino machine in our kitchen, but I'd noticed that Wendy rarely drank anything other than fancy cappuccinos from places like Argo Tea Cafe. Rarely drank her *coffee* from anywhere but there, I mean. The image of her sitting alone with that vodka bottle was still burned into my retinas.

"Sure, no problem." Ben stood up and looked around the room. "Anyone else want to throw in an order while I'm up?"

Every single hand in the room went up, mine included. We all laughed.

"I bet you regret asking that," I said.

Wendy shot me a look. "I bet you regret some things too," she said under her breath. It was just loud enough for me to hear but quiet enough that no one else could.

I looked at her, not upset, not...*anything*. A week earlier, I would have wanted to punch her for making such a spiteful comment, but now I just couldn't be angry with her. She had her demons, and they clearly weren't going anywhere anytime soon.

I forced a smile. "I'm sure I do, Wendy."

Scotty stood at the front of the table and clapped his hands. "OK, everyone, let's get started. This is going to be one busy day, and I can say with certainty that the madness is not going to end until the year is over. And by that I mean *every single day* until the end of the year."

We all laughed, and he took a bow.

"How long have you been waiting to use that line?" I asked.

He winked. "A magician never shares his secrets."

• • •

The next afternoon, Paige left me a voice mail that felt like a punch in the gut:

"Hi, it's Paige. I...I need to talk to you. I know we're supposed to get rolling with the new office January first, but now, well, things have changed for me, and I'm...I'm not sure it's going to work for me to be a part of Waverly's Honey Shop anymore. I'm really sorry. Please call me as soon as you can. Thanks."

I listened to the message three times, unable to believe her words were true.

She's quitting? I couldn't run Waverly's Honey Shop without Paige. What about the Jordon Brooke account? Or Bella's Boutique? Our office? Our interns? There was no way I could manage all of that with everything I had on my plate at *Love, Wendy.*

No way at all.

I'd created Waverly's Honey Shop, but Paige had taken it to a whole new level. Without her, I knew it would crash and burn.

Is this because of Gary? She doesn't want to work with me anymore because I disapprove?

I called her back but got her voice mail.

"Hi, Paige, um, it's Waverly. I just got your message and don't know what to say. I'm swamped preparing for my New Year's Eve show but want to talk to you. Can you please call me when you can? Or maybe we can just meet at the office on New Year's Day like we'd planned? I'll be there at eleven o'clock, um, like we planned. I hope you'll be there too. I...I really don't want you to quit."

I hung up and winced. I knew I didn't sound professional. The real question was did I sound pathetic? I certainly felt like it.

I closed my eyes and took a deep breath. Was it possible that within the span of a week both my boyfriend *and* my business partner were planning to leave me? Less than a week ago, I had the christening of my new office and a trip to meet Jake's entire family ahead of me. Could I really be losing them both because of my beliefs about what makes a relationship work? Was I really that wrong about everything?

I didn't know how my communication with both Jake *and* Paige had gotten so off track, but at that moment I had so much work to do for *Honey on Your Mind* that I could barely stop to eat, much less contemplate two major life changes at once. I didn't even have time to call Andie or McKenna. I didn't have time to do anything other than prepare for the show. If I screwed that up too, I couldn't even begin to think what that would mean for the future of *Honey on Your Mind*.

The future.

Ironic to think about, given what I had planned for New Year's Eve.

chapter eighteen

"You ready for the big show, princess?"

"Scotty, I can't believe you're technically my boss yet you still call me *princess.*"

"Would you prefer I call you *kitten?*"

I laughed and looked at Tad. "Isn't that violating some sort of sexual harassment policy?"

Tad nodded. "You should hear what he calls *me.*"

Scotty laughed too. "Well, *technically,* we're not on the clock right now, so *technically* I'm not violating any corporate policies, sweetheart."

It was the night before New Year's Eve. Scotty, Tad, and I were having dinner at Esca, a fancy Italian restaurant a few blocks from NBC. Scotty had seen how rattled I'd been all week, and he was determined to calm me down before I completely came apart at the seams. Until then, he'd assumed it was just the show that had me so stressed. While I was determined not to mention the Paige thing, I hadn't decided whether to bring up Jake.

I chose to take an indirect route.

I took a sip of water and smiled at Tad. "So, after you first met Scotty at that wedding and started dating, did you ever think he'd end up moving to New York to be with you?"

Tad laughed. "Are you joking? Never in a million years."

"Hey now, you know you wanted me to," Scotty said.

I shooed Scotty away. "I didn't mean that he wouldn't *want* you to, silly. I meant that moving to New York was a big deal for you."

Tad shook his head. "At first, I definitely didn't think he'd do it."

Scotty shook his head. "At first, I definitely didn't want to do it."

"But New York is so amazing, Scotty. Why *wouldn't* you want to live here?"

He pretended to remove a cowboy hat and tipped his head slightly. "I'm a Texas boy, born and raised, and you know what they say. You can take the Texan out of Texas…"

Tad laughed. "Don't buy it, Waverly. He likes New York more than he likes Dallas now. He just won't admit it."

"But it worked out great for your career, so that made the decision to move easier, right?" I asked Scotty.

He nodded. "True."

"But what if that *hadn't* been the case? Would you have moved?"

He gave me a strange look. "That's a good question."

I turned back to Tad. "Did you ever think of moving there?"

He coughed. "Oh God, no. Me? In Texas?"

"The South's a whole other world," Scotty said. "They say, 'Don't mess with Texas,' for a reason, you know." He gestured to the waiter and introduced dessert as a new topic of conversation, but I could tell he knew something was going on with me. He was too polite to pry in front of Tad, and I was grateful for his discretion.

● ● ●

I don't think I slept at all that night. For hours on end, I stared at the ceiling fan in my bedroom, my body ignoring my head's desperate pleas to *please, please, please* get some rest. To keep myself from completely losing it, I focused on what my dad used to say to me when I was a kid. "If you're lying still, your body is resting, and that's as good as sleep." I still didn't know if that was actually true or if it was just a trick he used to get me to take a nap when I didn't want to. But tonight, it was the only rope I had to keep me from falling into a pit of anxiety, so I grabbed hold and hung on.

My brain apparently believed the mantra, because the next morning I felt alert. My face had other ideas, however, as demonstrated by the huge bags under my eyes. I knew they'd de-puff eventually, but for the time being I resembled someone who might ask you for spare change on the sidewalk. I could only wonder what the well-heeled commuters on the subway thought about my haggard appearance. At least I was sure no one recognized me. *Now I know why celebrities wear sunglasses year-round.*

The hours flew by in a blur, with back-to-back meetings, prep calls, and run-throughs. At some point we stopped to grab lunch, but I was so focused on the evening ahead that when I finished my meal I stared at the plate in front of me and had absolutely no idea what I'd just eaten. *No idea.* That is sort of scary if you think about it.

Before I knew it, Tanya was performing her magic on my face. Normally she only did Wendy's makeup and had one of her assistants do mine, but every once in a while she took care of me. And because this was a special show, she wasn't leaving anything to chance.

I loved when Tanya did my makeup. No matter how stressed I was, she managed to calm me down. Her voice was deep and soothing, and when she told me stories it reminded me of my fourth-grade teacher, who used to read us *Watership Down* every day after lunch. One moment we'd all be running around the playground like feral cats, and the next we'd be sitting in front of her in silence, mesmerized.

"So you ready for the big show?" Tanya spread cool, creamy foundation over my face with a sponge.

I nodded with my eyes closed. "I think so. As ready as I can be, I guess."

"I'm sure you'll do great. Your segment is a lot of fun."

"Thanks. I hope it goes well. If I screw it up, Wendy will have my head."

She ran a concealer under me eye. "Oh please. She's not as bad as people make her out to be."

I kept my eyes closed. "Yeah, she puts on a hard front, but there's more to her than that. Maybe that's why she wears so much makeup, to keep people from looking too deep."

Tanya laughed. "Hey now, that's my livelihood we're talking about. There's nothing wrong with a little makeup." She lightly pressed powder across my forehead.

"Oh believe me, I know. I never used to think about it, but once I saw how much better you could make me look, I was ruined. Now I'm constantly, shall we say, *underwhelmed* by my natural appearance."

She laughed. "Oh please, you look great. You're a natural beauty. Everyone should be so lucky. Some people spend their whole lives trying to create an appearance that isn't who they really are."

I opened my eyes and looked at her in the mirror.

Are we still talking about makeup?

Just then, her phone rang. She dug it out of her purse and looked at the caller ID, then held up a finger.

"Waverly, I'm sorry, I've got to take this. I'll be right back, OK?"

I nodded. "No problem."

As she walked away, I couldn't help but think about what she'd just said.

• • •

"Can you hear me OK?" the voice asked.

"Yep." I put my hand over the tiny microphone in my ear and nodded into the chilly air. Then I glanced at the backup microphone, also tiny, attached to my coat in case anything happened to the microphone in my hand. Soon I'd be using it to interview New Year's Eve revelers on live TV. I could only hope I wouldn't choose anyone who'd been overly enthusiastically partaking in the pre-midnight festivities. One drunken slur and Middle America, not to mention the plug-pullers at the FCC, would utter a collective gasp. At the meetings all week Scotty—and Wendy— had drilled this into my head a million times. The screeners would preselect people for me to interview, but if I had any sense that the person speaking into the microphone was going to utter something that might upset our "core viewers" (code for uptight advertisers), I needed to pull the rip cord and move on to someone more...*wholesome.*

The assistant producer's voice was back in my ear. "We're going to count down from ten, and then Wendy will introduce you from her stage across the street, which you'll hear through your earpiece. Then we'll cue you that we're moving to a split screen so viewers will see her on one half and you on the other, understand?"

I nodded again. *I can't believe this is happening.*

"You two can chat a bit, and then we'll cue you that split screen has disappeared, and then it's all you. Got it?"

I nodded and tried not to think about the thousands of people swarming the streets around me, not to mention the millions of people who would be watching me from their living rooms.

I squeezed the microphone tightly.

You can do this, Waverly.

The cameraman nodded and held up ten fingers, then started counting backward.

Ten…nine…eight…

Don't freak out.

Seven…six…five…

It's just like the taped pieces you do all the time.

Four…three…two…one…

You can do this!

I closed my eyes and listened to Wendy's cheery voice in my ear.

"OK now, everyone, it's time to introduce a special live feature from one of our favorite parts of *Love, Wendy.* The always delightful Waverly Bryson is out here braving the cold with us to bring us her New Year's Eve edition of *Honey on Your Mind.*"

I opened my eyes and waited.

It's going to be OK. You can do this.

Wendy's voice came through the earpiece. "I know you're going to just luuuv what she's cooked up for you, so let's turn it over to her. Waverly, are you there?"

The cameraman gave me the thumbs-up sign.

I squeezed the microphone and smiled wide.

"Yes, Wendy, thanks so much for that kind introduction. I'm here, *freezing,* I might add, along with thousands of other happy visitors to Times Square on this crisp and clear evening." I rubbed my left arm with my free hand.

Wendy laughed. "The chill in the air certainly gives everyone out here a reason to look forward to that New Year's kiss now, doesn't it?" I couldn't see her, but I was willing to bet my life savings that she winked, charming the TV audience to no end.

I laughed too. "Indeed, it does. In fact, I've seen a few early kisses out here already. It looks like people are certainly in the mood for some New Year's cheer."

"Nothing wrong with a little smoochin' now, that's what we always say down in Tennessee. So Waverly, we're just *thrilled* that you're joining us live tonight. Personally I can't wait to see what you've got up that honey sleeve of yours."

"Thanks, Wendy, I think it will be fun."

"So we'll turn it over to you, while I get myself a hot chocolate. Bye-bye."

The cameraman spread his hands apart to indicate that the split screen was gone.

This is it.

I squeezed the microphone even tighter and smiled again. "Hello, everyone. When I began planning what to do for this New Year's Eve edition of *Honey on Your Mind*, I couldn't help but think about the obvious, which would be to ask people, well, *what's on their mind* for the coming year. After all, everyone makes New Year's resolutions, right?" I slightly shifted my weight from one foot to the other.

I held up a finger. "But...the more I thought about it, the more I realized how stressful it is to spend every New Year's Eve thinking about what's on my mind for the year ahead. I think about goals I'd like to accomplish. I worry about things I'd like to do better. I obsess over ways I'd like to improve myself. In fact, sometimes I spend so much time thinking about the future that I forget to think about the present. And why is that?"

The cameraman smiled and nodded.

I swallowed. "I thought about it a lot, and I finally came to realize that no matter what happens in the new year, there are so many wonderful things in my life *now* of which to be proud, for which to be grateful, for which to be *happy*, and I think it's important to recognize them…to *celebrate* them… before they're not here anymore." I thought of Shane's broken NBA career, my damaged friendship with Paige, my own precarious love life. "Life is short, right? And things can change so quickly, things you might never have truly appreciated because you just assumed they'd always be there."

The cameraman nodded again.

"So I thought a nice way to ring in the upcoming year would be to think about the past twelve months and what has made them special for us. The people, the experiences, the successes—however big or small—that have made our lives worth living. The things *on our minds* that keep us wanting to move forward on this crazy journey we call…life."

The cameraman kept nodding, so I could only hope I didn't sound ridiculous.

"So this New Year's Eve, instead of focusing on what you *want*, I urge you to appreciate what you already *have*. Don't take anything for granted…especially the people you love."

I took a deep breath.

"Now to give you an idea of what I mean, I'd like to start with me. I know I don't usually share personal details on the show, but my dad, who raised me all on his own, is getting married soon. I don't think his fiancé knows how grateful I am for how much joy she's brought into his life. He is literally a new man because of her, and seeing him so happy makes *me* happy." I smiled and wiped a tear from the corner of my eye with my glove. "So, Betty, if you're watching, I want you to know that *you're* on my mind this New Year's Eve. Thank you for everything you've done for me and my dad, and...well...I'm extremely honored to call you my stepmother."

The cameraman gave me a thumbs-up, and I smiled.

"So with that said, dear viewers, I'd love to find out *who* and *what* is on the minds of some of these lovely people out here tonight." I turned to face the first duo the crew had screened for me to interview. They looked to be in their sixties, a married couple from Detroit.

"Well, hello there," I said. "What are your names?"

Before they said anything, the woman surprised me by giving me a bear hug. "Your stepmother is one lucky woman," she said, holding me tight.

I laughed and looked at the camera. "Why, thank you. I hope she agrees with you."

"Come on, Marion, let her breathe." Her husband looked horrified as he pulled on her arm, and I laughed again. "I'm sorry, Ms. Bryson. My wife's a little emotional, as you can see. My name is Bob."

Marion broke away from me and nodded. "It's true, I cry at Hallmark commercials."

I laughed. "I do too!" I was about to ask her if she liked watching sappy movies on Lifetime when I realized we were on national TV, and I pulled myself together.

"So, Marion, Bob, welcome to New York. What is on *your* mind this New Year's Eve?"

Bob adjusted his glasses. "Well, I got a promotion at the factory this year. I work for General Motors. I haven't talked about it much, but the reality is that I'm darned proud of myself. Been there forty years, you know. It's like a second home to me."

"Forty years? Wow, that's wonderful. Congratulations, Bob."

"Thank you." He really did look proud.

I turned to Marion. "And you, Marion? What's on *your* mind?"

She smiled wide. "I adopted a cat."

"You adopted a cat?"

"Yep. Poor little thing had been left behind when its owners moved. I heard a few women at church talking about it, and I thought to myself *I could help*, so I did. I've never been a cat person, but damned if I haven't grown to love that darlin' cat as much as if it were my own flesh and blood."

"Marion, hon, your language? We're on *TV*." Bob again looked horrified.

"I just *adore* that damned cat. Now who would have *thought*?" Marion said.

I laughed as the crew whisked Marion and Bob away, and soon a shy, skinny teenager and her dad approached. Her beaming mom stayed off to the side.

"Well, hello there, and who might you be?" I said to the girl.

"Um, Monica." She could barely make eye contact.

"She's a quiet one," her dad said with a grin. "She's mortified I'm dragging her on TV, but she'll thank me one day."

I smiled at her dad and looked at the girl again. "Well, hello there, Monica. And what's on *your* mind this New Year's Eve?"

She adjusted her pink headband, still barely making eye contact. "Nothing, really."

"Nothing?"

"She made the varsity soccer team this year," her dad said. "She's only a freshman, and we want her to be proud of herself for that."

I smiled at the girl. "Varsity as a *freshman*? That's great! You *should* be proud of yourself, Monica."

She shrugged. "I didn't play much though, just for a few minutes in one game, actually."

"She was the only freshman on the team," her dad said to me.

I raised my eyebrows. "The *only* freshman?"

Monica nodded. I put my arm around her bony shoulder, which reminded me of a bird. "You should definitely be proud of yourself, Monica."

"You think?" she said softly.

I nodded. "Of course! God knows I never made a varsity team as a freshman. In fact, I never made a varsity sport ever. I'm not what you would call, well, coordinated."

She finally smiled, revealing a mouth full of braces, and for the briefest of moments, she looked me in the eye. "Thanks, Mrs. Bryson."

"You see, kiddo?" Her dad elbowed her playfully. "It *is* a big deal."

"Daaaad." She rolled her eyes, but I could tell something in them had changed. She looked a little less mortified, a little more...confident.

As I watched her walk back to her proud mother, I hoped our brief interaction would boost her self-esteem. I also tried to ignore the fact that I'd just been called *Mrs. Bryson* on national television. Ouch.

From there I did five more interviews without a hitch, including a grouchy old man who wanted to thank his grown children for putting up with him, a thirty-something English teacher who was proud of herself for finally having begun writing the novel she'd been thinking about for years, and a young married couple who had recently decided to adopt. As each of them walked away, they seemed happier than when they'd approached me, and I hoped my message would resonate with those watching at home too.

Before I knew it, it was time to wrap up the segment.

I smiled at the camera. "So there you have it, my friends. New Year's Eve is a great time to think about the *future*, but I don't want us to forget to appreciate what we have *now*. So celebrate the good things while you have them, and don't forget to tell the people in your life that you love them."

I'd planned to keep the summation short and sweet, but suddenly something happened. It was like I'd lost control of my own voice.

"Wendy, before I turn it back to you, I'd like to say something to the person in my life who is...well...who is always on *my* mind."

I moved the microphone from one hand to the other, squeezing it tightly.

"I'm not going to say your name, but you know who are. Even though I may act a little frazzled sometimes, I hope you know...I hope you understand...that no matter how long our future is, whether it ends in a week, in a month, in a year, or *never*, I hope you know how much I love you *now*. No matter what happens tomorrow, I will always be grateful for having had you in my life today."

I laughed a bit awkwardly and smiled into the camera. *What did I just do?*

"Happy New Year, everyone. I hope this little personal oversharing episode of mine encourages you to let those people who are on *your* mind know what they mean to you. Wendy, back to you." I kept smiling and waited for the cameraman's signal.

The cameraman held his hands out wide, then slowly brought them together, signaling that I was done.

"All clear," he said.

I dropped the microphone to my side and immediately made a face. "Was that awful?" What had come over me at the end? Why had I done that?

He shook his head. "I thought it was great. I'm sure Wendy did too. That's the sort of thing her audience loves."

"Really?"

He took off his headset. "Definitely. Good job. Now you look like you need a celebratory drink."

I laughed weakly. "Is it that obvious?"

He pointed to his left. "A bunch of us are heading over to The Perfect Pint on Forty-Fifth after we break down the equipment. Want to join us?" It was only eleven o'clock, but our part of the evening was done.

"Sure, sounds good. I'm freezing, and I could definitely use a pint, perfect or otherwise."

As I handed him the microphone, I felt a few snowflakes land on my nose.

• • •

The snow kept falling, but the show went on. An hour later, we watched—warm, inside and in front of an enormous television— the famous ball drop. The blissful crowd on TV celebrated in a white haze, seemingly undeterred by the weather.

I shook my head. "People are crazy. It's *freezing* out there!" I was sitting next to Ben on a barstool, looking up at the TV.

"You got that right. Cheers." He held up his glass to mine. "Happy New Year, Waverly. Here's to drinking indoors."

"Happy New Year, Ben." I clinked my glass against his. "It's been great working with you. Are you even old enough to drink? Or should I say to drink *legally?*"

He laughed. "Just barely, but I'm legal. Did you hear I'm going back to school in a few weeks?"

I raised my eyebrows. "Grad school?"

He shook his head. "Undergrad. I still have about a year left. I took a semester off for this internship, but I think I've decided that daytime TV isn't for me."

"Let me guess. You want to go work for a tech start-up?"

He looked shyly at the floor. "How did you know?"

I smiled. "I get the feeling that *Love, Wendy* isn't really your cup of tea. I'm guessing your parents set up this internship?"

"How did you know?"

I shrugged. "Just a feeling."

"I've always done pretty much what they want me to do, but I think it's time for me to strike out on my own a bit, see what the future holds for me, you know?"

I smiled. "Believe me, I know."

Scotty showed up at twelve thirty, weaving through the crowd and switching places with Ben, who wandered off in search of pizza.

"Waverly, love, I heard it went great."

"You did?"

He nodded. "Indeed I did. Well done, my dear."

I frowned. "I got a little emotional at the end. It was unexpected, and I think I sort of made a fool of myself."

"Ah, shush, people love emotional. Now what can I get you to drink?"

I held my hand over my glass. "I'm good, thanks. I have a big day tomorrow."

"A big day on New Year's Day? Who makes plans for New Year's Day other than to recover from New Year's Eve?"

I forced a smile, but all I could think about was Jake and the conversation I was dreading.

"Kitten, are you OK?" Scotty gave me a serious look."

"I'm fine." *Please don't make me talk about this.*

"Are you sure? You don't seem like yourself."

I was afraid I would start crying if I opened that door, so I changed the subject. "Where's Tad?"

He held eye contact for a moment, then let it go and looked at his watch. "He should be home by now. We left the last party right after midnight, and he dashed for a cab before the masses set in. Tad *hates* getting stuck on the streets after midnight on New Year's Eve. He likens it to being at Walmart during a half-off special on mayonnaise."

I laughed, and then glanced toward the door. "I hadn't thought of that. If I can't find a taxi, I guess I'll have to take the subway back to Brooklyn."

"Ah, look at you, still taking the subway. Your star is on the rise, my princess. Soon you may be too popular to take public transportation."

I laughed. "I'll believe *that* when I see it. As far as I can tell, ninety-nine point nine percent of people who have ever seen me on TV live far outside of New York City. And that's a conservative estimate."

He touched a finger to my nose. "Touché."

"Speaking of people *outside* New York City, I wonder what some of them are up to." I pulled out my phone to check my text messages. I'd sent Jake a note earlier, but he hadn't replied yet. If Scotty noticed the disappointment on my face, he didn't let on. He waited until I put my phone away to speak.

"So, sweetheart, I have some news."

I raised my eyebrows. "News?"

He smiled.

"About the show?"

He shook his head.

"Good news?"

He nodded.

"Does it involve me?"

He shook his head.

"Well? Are you going to just leave me hanging?"

He leaned in close and whispered into my ear. "I'm going to propose to Tad tomorrow."

My eyes got big. "No way. For real? That's wonderful!"

He grinned. "I know. Can you believe it? Me? I never thought I'd see the day."

"I never thought I'd see the day either."

"I just hope he says yes."

I pushed him on the shoulder. "Please. You know he will. He's completely smitten."

He laughed. "OK, you're right. I know he will. But still, I'm really nervous. And you know me, I *never* get nervous."

"See? You *do* have plans tomorrow."

"Ha. I guess you're right."

I pointed at him. "*Important* plans, I might add. I'm thrilled for you, Scotty."

"Thank you, kitten. I'm pretty thrilled too. Here's to new beginnings." He lifted his glass to mine.

"To new beginnings." I clinked my glass against his and could only hope his new beginning with Tad didn't coincide with the ending of Jake and me.

Scotty excused himself to use the restroom, and as soon as he was gone, I checked my phone again to see if Jake had replied yet.

This time he had:

Happy New Year to you too. Party fun but packed. See u tomorrow.

I studied the message for a few moments before tossing my phone back in my purse.

Ugh.

I could read the words, but nothing in between.

• • •

When it finally stopped snowing an hour or so later, we all streamed out of the bar and scattered every which way in a mad dash to find a cab. As I scanned the taxi-free streets, I was immediately jealous of Tad, cozy and warm at home.

Damn him for being so smart.

I wandered for a few blocks and was nearly back to the NBC building before finally spotting some empty cabs idling down the street. I quickened my step, and as I approached them, I saw two women doing the same thing from the other direction, about thirty feet away from me. They were holding hands and giggling, and not in a platonic way.

I froze in my tracks.

I watched them for a few moments, and then they hailed a cab and got in together.

I still didn't move as the taxi slowly pulled away from the curb.

One of the women was Tanya, the makeup artist.

The other woman was Wendy.

chapter nineteen

When I woke up the next morning, I had so much on my mind that watching the *Love, Wendy* show from the night before wasn't even on the list. I put on a pot of coffee, then sat on the couch in my pajamas and tried to process it all.

Wendy and...Tanya?

I couldn't shake the image of the two of them getting into that cab together. *Wendy is gay? Huh?*

It didn't make any sense. From the moment I'd met her, she'd bragged about having been with the same guy since high school, her wonderful *huuusband*, Gary.

The same man who was having an affair with Paige.

What?

I thought of that night I'd caught Wendy drinking in the conference room. What exactly had she said? Something about her marriage being a fraud? About another woman getting in the way?

I'd assumed she was talking about Paige, but apparently, I was wrong.

I covered my eyes with my hands.

She was talking about Tanya.

I stood up and poured myself a cup of coffee, doctoring it with half-and-half and sugar.

Wendy and Gary clearly had a troubled marriage, but it had never occurred to me that *Wendy* was the one rocking the boat.

I sat back on the couch and leaned into the cushion. *Does anyone else know?*

Suddenly, I sat up straight.

Scotty knows.

I thought of all the times Wendy had snapped at him, or said something critical for no apparent reason. He always let it roll off his back, which I admired. I'd just assumed she was homophobic.

That's why she is so mean to him. Scotty was living in the open about something she was clearly trying to hide. Did she resent him? Envy him? Was she projecting her own internal struggle onto him? I couldn't imagine what it would be like to live like that. To live, as Wendy herself had told me, a lie.

That's why Scotty cuts her slack. He knows what she's dealing with.

Scotty Ryan. Boss, friend, confidant, all-around stud, was also a world-class diplomat. They sure threw away the mold when they made that one.

• • •

At quarter to eleven, I left my apartment and walked over to the new office in Dumbo. I still hadn't connected with Paige and could only hope she would show up. The streets were practically deserted, the crisp air quiet and peaceful. Just as I reached Cadman Plaza Park, it started snowing again, so I pulled an umbrella out of my purse and opened it. I loved walking in the snow with an umbrella. It was one of those things I'd never even known that people *did* on the East Coast when I lived in San Francisco. Now it made me feel like a smart New Yorker. Like part of the club.

Fifteen minutes later, I arrived at the lobby of our building. I looked up at the number for a moment, then pulled off a glove and dug around in my purse for the keys. I hiked up to the third floor and unlocked the door to the new office of Waverly's Honey Shop.

It was small, but it was bright, open and inviting, with a hardwood floor, large windows, and freshly painted white walls. A small conference table sat in the center of the room with four chairs around it.

I took a seat and waited.

• • •

At 11:13, Paige walked through the door.

"Happy New Year," she said with a nervous smile. Even in the most awkward of situations, Paige was always kind. "Sorry I'm late."

I stood up and ran over to her, throwing my arms around her. "I'm so glad you came. I'm so sorry, Paige."

She hugged me back, and then held me away from her, her hands on my shoulders. "Whoa, down girl, are you OK? What are *you* sorry for?"

"A lot of things. I've been a little…confused."

She didn't say anything for a moment.

"Confused about what?" she finally said.

Now it was my turn not to say anything, because I didn't know what to say.

"Waverly?"

I looked out the window. "The name of this neighborhood is appropriate for me, don't you think?"

"Huh?"

I kept looking out the window. "You know, *Dumbo*? God knows I've acted like a *dumb ass* lately."

She laughed. "Waverly, what are you talking about?"

I turned to face her.

"I know," I blurted. *Ugh, so graceful.*

She raised her eyebrows but didn't reply.

After a few seconds of awkward silence, she finally spoke. "You know?"

I nodded.

"You know…what?"

I didn't want to say anything compromising. What if she *didn't* know?

I thought for a moment.

What should I say?

How can I put this without giving anything away?

I walked over to the conference room table and sat down, interlacing my fingers in front of me. Paige took off her coat and hung it over her chair as she took a seat across the table.

"Waverly, will you please tell me what you're talking about?"

I finally looked up from my hands and made eye contact.

"I saw her last night…with Tanya." I said softly.

A light went on in Paige's eyes.

"Wendy?"

I nodded.

"You saw Wendy with Tanya?"

I nodded again.

She scratched her cheek. "So you *do* know."

"Apparently so."

She smiled. "Things aren't always what they appear to be, are they?"

I put my hands on my forehead. "You can say that again. I'm so sorry for judging you, Paige. I had no idea."

She shrugged and pushed her hair behind her ears, and for a brief moment, she could have been Andie. "It's OK. You didn't know. And it certainly wasn't my place to tell you."

"So you just let me think you were a…home wrecker?"

She laughed. "What else was I supposed to do? He didn't want anyone to know. He *does* love her, you know."

And you must really love him, I thought. I was so impressed that she'd kept quiet about everything.

"So um, how long…or has it always been…" My voice trailed off.

She sighed. "I guess I can tell you the whole story now. Do you mind if I get some water first?" She looked over at the water cooler, our one piece of office furniture other than the table and chairs. A few paper cups were stacked on top of the plastic jug.

"Of course not. Go ahead."

"You want some?"

"Sure, thanks."

She poured us each a cup, then handed me one and sat down.

"So?" I said, my eyes getting big.

"From what Wendy has told Gary, it started in February, when she appeared on the *Today* show."

"You mean the Valentine's feature? When I first met her?" I'd never forget how awful Wendy had been to me that day.

She took a sip of her water. "Yep. Tanya did her makeup."

"Tanya did her makeup, and she suddenly became a lesbian?"

Paige laughed. "I don't think so. But that was the first time she *acted* on it, although apparently it was just a kiss, and they didn't start seeing each other until after she moved here for the

Love, Wendy job." She lowered her voice. "Gary and Wendy hadn't slept together in five years."

"*Five* years?"

She nodded. "Wendy always had an excuse. Too tired, need to get up early, have to help the kids, that sort of thing."

"For *five years*?"

"For five years."

"And he never suspected the real reason?"

She shook her head. "He thinks even Wendy didn't know the real reason, or that she'd buried it so deep inside that she couldn't bring herself to consider it. I mean, look at where she's from. They've been together since high school. She was head cheerleader, then Miss South Carolina, then a famous *relationship* expert with a huge heterosexual fan base, and a conservative one at that. What would happen to her world if it turned out she was gay?"

"I can't even imagine."

"Exactly. So anyhow, for a long time something was clearly wrong, yet Gary couldn't figure out what, and she wasn't talking. But after she came back from the *Today* show, he could tell something had happened, and he thought she'd been with another man. For a while, Wendy denied it, but then she finally broke down and came clean."

"And he agreed to stay with her?"

"She begged him. She'd just been offered the *Love, Wendy* gig, and she was afraid that getting divorced or even separated would ruin it for her. So he agreed to stick around and keep up the charade for a while, but only under one condition."

"What was that?"

"That if he met someone else, Wendy wouldn't get in the way."

"And then he met you?"

She nodded. "And then he met me."

"Wow."

"I know. Crazy, isn't it?"

"When did he tell you the truth about his situation?"

"The night I met him."

"No way. He really did?"

"He really did."

"But wasn't that jeopardizing Wendy? I mean, what if you'd never seen him again?"

She shook her head. "He didn't tell me her name or what she did for a living or anything, but he was completely honest with me. He's an amazing guy, Waverly."

I slouched in my seat. "Wow, and I was such a bitch to him at the holiday party."

"It's OK, he understands. We both know you've been in an extremely awkward situation. It's not like this has been a bowl of ice cream for anyone."

"I could use a bowl of ice cream right now."

She looked at her watch. "At eleven thirty in the morning?"

"Hey now, it's never too early for ice cream. So, you're sure you don't hate me?"

She laughed. "Of course not."

"And Gary doesn't hate me either?"

"Definitely not. How were you *supposed* to act toward him? You thought he was cheating on your boss *and* screwing over a good friend of yours. Why wouldn't you be a little rude to him?"

I smiled weakly. "So you still consider me a good friend?"

"Of course I do, Waverly. A very good friend."

I felt a few tears welling up. "When I got your message, I thought you hated me. I thought I'd totally blown it."

"I know. I'm sorry. When he told me you'd seen him at your holiday party, I didn't know what to say to you. So I just sort of retreated, which is how I tend to deal with things when they get uncomfortable."

I smiled. "Join the club." I looked around the office, then back at her. "So since you don't hate me, does that mean you're not quitting? This whole operation would fall apart without you."

She didn't reply.

"Please tell me you're staying."

She still didn't reply.

"Paige?"

She took a deep breath, and I held mine.

"The thing is…"

I stared at her.

"The thing is…" she started again.

"The thing is *what*?"

She looked at me. "I'm pregnant, Waverly."

"*What*? You're pregnant?"

She nodded. "Six weeks."

"Oh my God, Paige, what are you going to do?"

"I'm going to keep it."

"Really? So this is…good news?"

She finally broke into a smile. "It's not ideal, but I'm happy."

"So what's going to happen with Gary?"

She smiled wider. "Well…I *thought* I was going to end up moving to Nashville, but we've been talking about it, and he's moving to New York."

"No way. For real?"

She nodded. "For real."

"What about his kids?"

"The youngest graduates from high school in May, so as soon as he's off to college, Gary's going to pack things up and move here."

"And Wendy?"

"She's keeping her own apartment in the West Village. She's basically been living there all this time anyway, traveling back and forth to Nashville every other weekend or so."

"Are they getting divorced?"

She nodded. "He filed yesterday."

"On New Year's Eve?"

"He told me he wanted to start the year fresh, so he could focus on me and the baby."

"Are they going to make the divorce public?"

"Not yet, but soon. Wendy's worried about the news leaking, but she knows she can't keep up a front forever."

"You mean the news about the divorce or the reason behind it?"

"Both, but mostly the latter. Gary says she's terrified of coming out. She thinks her fans are going to turn on her."

"Maybe she'll be the next Ellen. *Everyone* loves Ellen, right?"

"That's what Gary keeps telling her. He still cares for her, you know, and he doesn't want to see her get hurt. But they both know it's time to accept reality."

It was no wonder Wendy had ended up turning to the bottle with the false facade she'd insisted on presenting to the world. *Maybe coming clean with the public will liberate her from* that, *as well,* I thought.

"I still can't believe all of this," I said.

"I know. It's a lot to swallow at once, isn't it?"

I took a drink of my water and nodded. "I'm so happy for you, Paige. I mean, I know this probably isn't the way you imagined it would all happen for you, but you seem really happy."

She smiled. "That's the way I look at it. It's definitely *not* your ideal 'how we met' story, but it certainly makes for interesting dinner-party discussion, or at least it will once everything blows over."

"You can say that again."

She stood up and looked around the bare room. "So anyhow, now that it's all out in the open, I guess you and Waverly's Honey Shop are stuck with me."

"Thank God for that."

She put her hands on her stomach. "Although it will be a little tricky down the road. I'll need to figure out a part-time schedule or something after I have the baby."

I smiled. "*Honey*, I'll take you any way I can have you."

We spent the next half hour talking shop, and I was so engrossed in all the expansion plans that for a brief window I stopped thinking about what was happening later that day. But that changed the moment Paige asked a question.

"So hey, with all this talk about Gary and Wendy, I completely forgot to ask you. How was it meeting Jake's family over Christmas?"

My stomach dropped. I ran to my purse and pulled my phone out to check the time. It was nearly two o'clock. There was also a missed call from Jake, plus a text message saying he was in a cab on his way to my apartment.

"Oh my God, I need to run. He's going to be at my apartment any minute!"

She laughed. "I'm glad I asked."

"I can't believe I almost missed him."

"Just goes to show how dedicated you are to your *own* baby," she said.

"My own baby?"

She gestured around the room. "Waverly's Honey Shop. You created all of this."

Suddenly, I felt like I was going to cry.

"Hey, are you OK?" she asked.

I walked over and hugged her. "Thanks for everything, Paige. None of this would have happened without you."

"Waverly, are you sure you're OK?"

I nodded and fought back the tears. "I will be. Listen, I really need to run. Will you lock up?"

"Sure thing. Scoot."

I put my coat and gloves on and grabbed my purse. "Thanks, Paige. I'm so glad you're not breaking up with me."

She laughed. "Breaking up with you?"

"You know what I mean. And congratulations on the baby. And, um, please tell Gary I said hi."

She nodded. "Will do."

I turned and bolted out the door.

chapter twenty

I ran all the way home. By the time I was a block away from my apartment, I was totally out of breath. *This is pathetic*, I thought as I rounded the corner. *I really need to join a gym.*

I was leaning on the front door of my building, trying to catch my breath, when I heard a car pull up alongside the curb.

Oh, no.

Please don't let that be Jake's taxi.

I turned around.

It was Jake's taxi.

Are you kidding me? I don't even have time to brush my hair?

Still a bit out of breath, I forced a smile as he got out and shut the door.

"Hey, you," I said. "Fancy meeting you here."

He set his carry-on bag down on the sidewalk as the taxi drove away. "Happy New Year, Miss Bryson."

I ran toward him and hugged him tightly. "Happy New Year, Jake."

Please don't break my heart please don't break my heart please don't break my heart.

• • •

Ten minutes later, we were sitting on the couch in my apartment, mugs of hot chocolate in hand. I was trying my best to act normal and had just finished telling Jake about Paige and Gary and Wendy.

He shook his head. "Wow, I did not see that one coming."

"You and me both. Wendy is the epitome of the boy-crazy girly girl. With her stiff, poufy hair and pancake makeup, it's like she's single-handedly trying to bring back the fifties."

"Just goes to show that you never know."

I nodded. "That's definitely been the theme of the year around here. You want some more hot chocolate?"

"Sure."

I stood up and walked to the kitchen, dreading the inevitable next phase of our conversation. "So you had a nice flight?" I said over my shoulder.

"Yeah, uneventful. People tend to be mellow on New Year's Day. It's like the whole world is operating in first gear."

"I definitely feel in first gear today, if not neutral. I'm exhausted." My hands shook as I ripped open the hot chocolate packet.

Please don't break my heart please don't break my heart please don't break my heart.

"So the show went well last night?"

I half-cringed at the memory. "I think so. Um, I haven't seen it yet." I knew he hadn't either because of his flight, thank God.

"My mom saw it," he said.

I froze.

"She did?"

"Yep. She called me about it, actually. Left a message when I was on the plane."

I slowly walked out of the kitchen holding two steaming mugs of hot chocolate. I handed him one and sat down next to him.

"What did she say?"

"She asked if I'd broken the news to you yet."

I dropped my mug. Hot chocolate splashed everywhere. "Damn it!"

Jake jumped up. "Are you OK?"

Suddenly I started to cry.

"Did you burn yourself?"

I shook my head through the tears and ran into the kitchen. "Let me clean that up before it sets." I grabbed a few rags and held them under the faucet, then rushed back to the living room to sop up the mess. I was still crying.

"Waverly, are you sure you're OK?"

"Will you get a few rags and help? They're under the sink."

"Sure." He stood up and backed into to the kitchen. "It's just hot chocolate. It will come out."

I was still crying.

If he didn't think I was crazy before, this ought to do it.

He returned from the kitchen and helped me mop up the rest of the hot chocolate in silence. Tears were still streaming down my face.

"Did we get it all?" he finally asked.

I nodded and stood up, my arms falling to my sides. "I think so."

He looked up at me. "Are you sure you're OK?"

I walked into the kitchen without replying. I just couldn't face him.

"Waverly?"

I stood at the sink, my back to him. Suddenly I started crying again, *really* crying. I put both hands on the sink, my shoulders shaking.

Soon he was standing right behind me.

"Waverly, what's going on?"

He turned me around to face him.

"Waverly, please talk to me."

Finally, I raised my eyes to his.

"Why are you here, Jake?"

He looked surprised. "What?"

"Why are you here? You said you wanted to talk to me, so why don't you just give me your...*news*?" I was surprised by the harsh tone of my voice.

He didn't answer.

"You said we needed to talk, so let's get it over with." I walked past him into the living room, but this time I intentionally sat on the love seat.

He looked at me for a moment, and then slowly sat on the dry part of the couch.

I held my hands up. "I'm listening."

"You sure you're OK?"

I wiped a tear from my eye. "Why *wouldn't* I be OK? Is it not OK that I want to give my business a chance? Is it not OK that I didn't want to throw away my career for a future that may not even happen?" The emotions from the last few days, weeks, months were too much to hold in any longer.

He gave me a strange look. "OK...I don't know where all that is coming from, but yes, I did want to talk to you about some news."

"So talk."

He paused for a moment.

"It's just that, well, something unexpected has happened."

I nodded.

"I've been offered a job as head of physical therapy and conditioning for the Lakers...the *Los Angeles* Lakers."

I nodded again. "I know."

"You know?" He looked surprised.

"So I guess you're moving to California?" I didn't mean to be cold, but I couldn't help myself.

"Well, um, that's what I wanted to talk to you about."

I didn't reply.

This is it.

He cleared his throat. "When I first met you, I never thought too much about geography, or where our jobs would take us, because none of that seemed important. At the time, I was more concerned about getting to know you than where you lived and what your career plans were."

I shifted in my seat. Not knowing if he was going to ask me to go with him was agonizing.

"And then when you moved to New York for the TV show, I thought it would be easier for us because you'd be closer to Atlanta. And while I think that's been the case, you can't say it's been…easy."

I nodded.

He glanced at the wall for a moment, then at me.

He sighed, clearly sensing the tension between us. "I know things are just taking off for you now, and it's not fair to ask you to uproot all that to be closer to me. I wouldn't *want* you to do that. Plus, you've made it clear that you don't want to move anywhere for a while."

I nodded again. *But ask me anyway! Ask me anyway!*

"So I'm not going to ask you to move."

The blood in my veins went cold.

I clenched my hands in my lap and stared at them. Was he really OK with *increasing* the distance between us?

He spoke again. "But the thing is…" His voice trailed off.

I looked up at him, full of hope. "The thing is what?"

This time, he was the one who didn't reply.

"The thing is *what*, Jake?"

"I just think that...at least for me, the distance thing isn't going to work anymore."

Oh my God.

My head started to hurt.

No!

Not again.

The tears started streaming down my face again. I couldn't believe this was happening.

Don't do this. Please don't do this.

He glanced at the wall again. "You know how much I love the outdoors, right? How much I love having a backyard and fresh air and being surrounded by things that are, well, *green*?"

I nodded, dazed. Suddenly, I felt like I'd gone back in time, back to the day Aaron had appeared on my doorstep and announced that he didn't love me...then called off our wedding. How could it be happening again? Hadn't I already suffered enough heartbreak?

I wanted to scream.

Don't do this! We can make it work!

But I was frozen.

I stared at the floor and tried to keep breathing.

Finally, he cleared his throat and spoke again.

"So..."

I kept staring at the floor.

"So...I guess what I'm trying to say is...that this job offer really got me thinking about things I hadn't had to think about before. And while I'd prefer the green in my life come from *trees*, it looks like for now I'm going to have to settle for...*walls*."

I looked up at him.

"What?"

He took a set of keys out of his pocket and looked around my apartment. "Various shades of green, actually. And some blue. I guess they'll have to do. For now."

"What are you…what are you saying?"

He stood up and touched the wall, then walked toward me. "I'm saying I turned the job down."

My stomach flip-flopped.

"You turned it down?"

He nodded and gave me a sly smile. "I heard a rumor that the Brooklyn Nets might be hiring, so I made a few phone calls."

The Brooklyn Nets?

He held up his set of keys to my apartment. "I thought maybe I could use these a little more often."

I opened my mouth to say something, but I couldn't find my voice.

Instead, I started crying again.

He put the keys back in his pocket, then reached for my hands and pulled me up to face him.

"Waverly? Are you OK?" He wiped a few tears from my cheeks. "Don't cry."

I coughed, and then tried to speak through my tears. "Are you saying…are you saying you want to move here to be closer to me?" It came out as a whisper.

He gently pushed a loose strand of hair out of my eyes. "That's exactly what I'm saying. The job here is mine if I want it. Assuming you want me to take it, that is."

"But I thought…I thought you were moving to Los Angeles… without me."

He shook his head, then put his arms around me and pulled me close. "I'm in *love* with you, Waverly. Don't you know that by now?"

I nodded into his chest and could feel my heart rate calming down. "It's slowly beginning to sink in."

He laughed. "*Slowly beginning to sink in?*"

"Have you ever noticed that I'm a little slow on the uptake sometimes?"

He smoothed my hair with one hand, the other still holding me close. "You're a little crazy. Have I ever told you that?"

"A few times. I'm OK with it." I smiled as my body began to relax against his.

We stood there holding each other, and soon my breathing returned to normal. He took a step back and looked down at me. "So how did you know about the Lakers job?"

I swallowed. "At your sister's house on Christmas…I…I overheard your mom say something about a job in Los Angeles; and then the other day, Shane said something about an NBA rumor, but now I'm not sure which rumor he meant."

"I bet he was referring to the job here in Brooklyn. Word travels fast in the NBA."

"I guess so."

"Why didn't you just ask me about it?"

I shrugged and half-smiled. "Have you ever noticed that when it comes to love I tend to assume the worst?"

He touched my cheek. "We'll work on that. So what did you say on the show last night that made my mom think I'd already told you about the Nets job?"

I swallowed. "I, um, I had a bit of a Waverly moment."

"A what?"

"Let's just say I acted like an idiot, and we can leave it at that." I wiped the remaining tears from my face. "To be honest, I don't really remember what I said, which is funny, because I think it was something about not forgetting. I thought you were going to break up with me, so I freaked out and over-shared, just like those people I hate on Facebook and Twitter."

He smiled and tucked another loose strand of hair behind my ear.

"Waverly, I'm not going anywhere, OK?"

"Promise?"

"Promise."

We stood there for a moment, just staring at each other. Then he slowly smiled and scratched his eyebrow. "So, I guess…I'm moving to Brooklyn?"

I grinned. "Apparently so." I pressed my palms against my forehead. "I can't believe I jumped to such a big conclusion. I was so…I was so…upset…" My voice trailed off again.

He leaned down and whispered into my ear. "Shhh, don't be upset anymore."

"I'm not upset anymore," I whispered back. "I'm not afraid anymore."

Then I hugged him tightly, determined not to let go.

epilogue

I never realized how many people get married on Valentine's Day.

Jake and I were sitting on a wooden bench in a hallway at Sacramento City Hall, surrounded by couples waiting to make it official. My dad and Betty were next in line, and Jake and I were the witnesses. They wanted to do something simple for the ceremony, so we were the only ones there. A few friends, mine included, were meeting us afterward for a late lunch and a small reception.

I leaned over and whispered in his ear. "Can you believe how many people are in here? I feel like we're at a chapel in Las Vegas."

"You think any of these people just met today?" He laughed and looked around. "I bet that's how a lot of people end up getting married in Vegas."

I nodded. "You've got to wonder what the average blood-alcohol level is at a twenty-four hour chapel."

A moment later, my dad approached us. He cleared his throat and clasped his hands together.

"Looks like we're up next. You kids ready? Betty's touching up her makeup."

I stood up and smoothed the skirt of my dress, then took a step toward my dad to adjust his tie. "Are *we* ready? Shouldn't we be asking *you* that?"

He grinned. "Can you believe your old man is getting hitched?"

"Yes, I can, and it's going to be great." I finished his tie and kissed him on the cheek.

"Thanks, baby, I appreciate that." He turned to Jake and held out his hand. "Thanks for making the trip out here. Mighty kind of you to come."

Jake smiled. "I'm just happy I got the invite, Mr. Bryson. Your daughter's a tough nut to crack."

"Oh believe me, I know," my dad said.

I pointed at both of them. "Hey now, no ganging up on me."

Just then, Betty appeared from the ladies' room. She was wearing a knee-length, cream-colored dress with a square neck and three-quarter-length sleeves, her blonde hair secured into a classic low bun. She could have been pulled straight from a Jackie-O photo collection.

I smiled at her. "Betty, you're *glowing.*"

She smiled back. "That's because I'm happy." Then she looked at my dad.

"Babe, you look beautiful," he said.

She winked at him. "So what do you think? Ready to go tie the knot?"

He held out his arm. "Sweetheart, you can't get me there fast enough."

• • •

After the ceremony, Jake and I drove back to our hotel to drop off the car, and then walked to a restaurant called The Firehouse for the reception. The moment we stepped inside, I spotted Andie and Nick sitting at the bar. They were playing rock-paper-scissors.

"Well, hello there, strangers." I approached them with my arms open wide.

"Hey, Waverly!" Andie stood up to embrace me.

"Bryson!" Nick followed with his own bear hug. "Welcome back to the left coast! We've missed you. Not as much as you've probably missed *us*, but we've missed you."

"Yes, I've missed you." I hugged him back, and when I could breathe again, I took a step away and gestured to Jake. "Nick Prodromou, this is Jake McIntyre. Jake, Nick and I used to work together at the *San Francisco Sun*."

Jake extended his hand. "You're the one who likes to wear T-shirts with clever sayings, right?"

Nick grinned and nodded as he shook Jake's hand. "I see my reputation of awesomeness precedes me."

"Are you wearing one under that dress shirt?" I asked.

He nodded. "Of course I am. Would I disappoint? Want to see it before this party gets started?" He unbuttoned his dark blue dress shirt to reveal a light blue T-shirt that said WORLD'S GREATEST...YOUR MOM'S NEW BOYFRIEND on the front.

I put my hand over my mouth. "Oh, good lord."

He buttoned his shirt and laughed. "Admit it. You miss me even more than you thought you did."

I laughed. "OK, I admit it. I miss you even more than I thought I did. Nice decision to wear that shirt to a *wedding reception*, by the way. And was that a giggle I just heard make its dainty way out of your manly throat?"

"Please, it was a hearty laugh. And what can I say? I'm a romantic."

"Giggle," I coughed under my breath.

"Hearty laugh," he coughed under his, then added, "Now what can I get you two to drink?" at a normal decibel.

"What are you having?" Jake said.

Nick held up his drink. "Scotch and soda. It's amazing."

"Vodka soda for me." Andie held up her glass and clinked it against Nick's.

I put my hand on her shoulder. "Thank God you're drinking. I was afraid you were going to announce that you're pregnant too."

She waved a hand in front of her face. "Oh, God no. Are you kidding?"

"Andie's anti-nugget," Nick said to Jake.

I looked at Nick. "Nugget?"

He nodded. "That's my new term for *little people*."

Jake raised his eyebrows. "Little people?"

I put my hand on Jake's arm. "That's his old term for *children*."

"I see," Jake said, nodding.

I laughed. "My friends take some getting used to."

"I don't have a *problem* with nuggets, I just don't want to *have* nuggets," Andie said. "Big difference."

Jake looked at Nick and nodded toward the bar. "Let me buy this round."

"Sounds amazing," Nick said. "Now if you'll excuse me, I need to use the facilities." He left to find the restroom, and Jake went to order the drinks.

Once they were both out of earshot, I leaned toward Andie and lowered my voice.

"So how is it, living in sin?" I whispered.

She shrugged. "So far, so good."

I laughed. "You enthusiasm is overwhelming."

"Hey now, for *me*, this is enthusiasm."

"This is true. So it's going well?"

She lowered her voice and pointed downward. "I've had to remind him about my one-V policy a couple times, but for the most part, yes, it's going well." She wasn't saying it aloud, but the bright look in her eyes told me everything I needed to know.

I laughed and hugged her. "I've really missed you, Andrea Barnett. Can I just tell you that?"

She hugged me back. "I've missed you too."

Jake returned and handed us our drinks. "What's with all the hugging? Did I miss something?"

"Just a little girl talk," I said, smiling.

Nick reappeared, and as Jake handed him a drink I pointed to the front door.

"Hey, speaking of nuggets, there's Mackie and the baby!" McKenna and Hunter had just entered the room. Hunter was holding little Elizabeth, who was dressed in a tiny, flower-print dress and wearing miniature, white, patent-leather shoes.

I waved my arm. "Hey, Mackie, over here."

She and Hunter joined us by the bar, and I gave them each a hug. "It's so great to see you guys. Hunter, you remember my boyfriend, Jake?"

Hunter nodded and extended his hand. "Of course. From our wedding. How are you?"

Jake shook Hunter's hand, and then put one arm around my shoulders. "I can't complain. In a couple weeks, I'm moving to Brooklyn."

"So we've heard," Hunter said. "You'll be working for the Nets?"

Jake gave me a squeeze. "That, and trying to keep this one out of trouble."

I laughed and looked up at him. "You be nice."

"Are you guys shacking up?" Nick asked.

I shook my head. "Jake's getting a place in Cobble Hill."

"Cobble what?"

"Cobble Hill. It's a super cute neighborhood in between where I live and the new Nets stadium. He'll be able to walk to work."

Andie pointed to me and then to Jake and back again. "I bet one of you does the walk of shame nearly every morning."

I glanced at her drink. "How many of those have you had?"

She shrugged. "God knows. We checked into the hotel early."

Nick put his arm around her. "That's my girl."

"Have you ever noticed that you two are amazing?" I said.

"Every day," Nick said. "We're like the royal couple of amazing."

Jake pointed to little Elizabeth. "Cute nugget," he said to McKenna.

"Huh?" she said.

Nick laughed and held his hand up to Jake for a high five. "I like you already."

Just then, my dad and Betty approached us. They were arm in arm and smiling ear to ear.

"Hey, Dad. Hey, Betty." I gave them each a hug, and then introduced them to the group. My dad had seen McKenna and Andie many times over the years, but he'd never met the men who had dated them along the way.

My dad smoothed his tie with his hand. "Thank you all for coming. It really means a lot to us to have Waverly's closest friends be part of our special day." He looked at McKenna and Andie. "You two girls are family to us, you know."

"We wouldn't have missed it, Mr. Bryson," McKenna said.

Andie nodded. "Couldn't keep us away."

"It's so lovely to meet you all," Betty said. She looked so happy I thought she might cry.

My dad cleared his throat. "Well, um, we have a little announcement."

I could feel my eyes get big. *An announcement?* I really didn't know if I could take any more announcements.

"What is it, Dad?" I glanced at Betty's stomach. *If she says she's pregnant, I'm going to lose it.*

He smiled. "After we get back from our honeymoon, Betty and I are going to open our own restaurant."

"Your own restaurant? Really?" I said.

He nodded. "Now it won't be anything fancy, you know, just a little café, actually. But we're excited about it."

Now I felt like *I* was going to cry. "Dad, that's wonderful." I thought of how far he'd come in just a few years.

"You made it happen, you know," he said to me.

"*I* made it happen?"

He nodded, and then turned to face the group. "Now, I'm guessing Waverly hasn't told any of you that she's been sending me money every month for quite a while now."

Everyone looked at me, and I could feel my cheeks go red. I looked at my dad. *Why are you telling everyone that?*

He put a hand on McKenna and Andie's shoulders. "You two know I haven't been the best about managing my money, but I've really turned things around."

McKenna smiled. "So we've heard." She and Andie had seen the progression over the years from gambling binges and get-rich-quick schemes to a stable job at a restaurant; from living in a double-wide in a dusty trailer park to renting a small yet respectable one-bedroom apartment.

He turned to look directly at me. "And now, because of *you*, Betty and I are going to have our own café, and I wanted to say thank you in front of your friends so they know how generous you've been to your old man."

"You don't have to thank me," I whispered. "You're my *dad*."

"Yes, I do have to thank you, and I *want* to. Will you let me have my moment here? It's my *wedding day*, for crying out loud."

I smiled and looked at the ground. "I'm just happy I could help out."

"Tell her, sweetheart," Betty nudged him with her arm.

I raised my eyes. *Tell me what? There's more?*

Everyone looked at my dad, who smiled coyly.

"Well?" Andie said.

"Don't leave us hanging, Mr. Bryson," Nick said.

I raised my eyebrows. "Dad?"

He cleared his throat. "Ladies and gentleman, we're going to name the café...Waverly's Place."

I swallowed. "Waverly's Place?"

He nodded. "What do you think? I think it has a nice ring to it."

"It definitely has a nice ring to it," McKenna said.

"I love it," Andie said.

For a moment, I didn't know what to say.

"What do you think, Waverly?" Betty said.

"It was Betty's idea," my dad said.

I walked over to Betty and gave her a hug. "Thank you," I said softly. "I love it."

"You're welcome." She squeezed me tightly.

Then I hugged my dad too. "Thanks, Dad."

"I'm glad you like the idea, baby. We wanted you to know that you'll always have a home with us, no matter where you're living."

"We've already picked out the space. You'd better come eat there next time you're in town, OK?" Betty said. "On the house, of course."

I laughed. "I think I can manage that."

My dad put his hand on Jake's arm. "You too, OK, Jake? Open invitation, anytime."

Jake nodded. "Thank you, sir. I appreciate that."

"What about us?" Andie said. "Are we invited too?"

I looked at her. "Andie!"

She held her palms up. "What? We'll totally pay."

Betty laughed. "You're definitely welcome, Andie. You're *all* welcome, any time." Then she turned to me and put her hand on my shoulder. "I just love your friends, Waverly."

I love them too, I thought.

· · ·

I had the window seat on our afternoon flight back to New York. It was delayed because of weather, so by the time we finally took off, it was dark outside. Once we were airborne, I stared out the window and wondered how cold it was back in Brooklyn.

Jake nudged me with his elbow. "Penny for your thoughts."

I turned to look at him. "Just a penny? That's all you got?"

He laughed. "You've been unusually quiet. You're *never* quiet. What's up?"

I leaned back in my seat. "Nothing's up. I'm just, I don't know, absorbing it all."

"The wedding?"

I nodded. "That and a few other things. There's definitely a lot of change in the air right now, you know?" I glanced out the window.

"I know."

Just then, the plane hit some turbulence, and I jumped.

"I hate turbulence," I dug my fingers into the armrests.

He put his hand over mine. "It's OK. We'll be fine."

I closed my eyes for a few moments, and soon the plane evened out again. The captain turned off the fasten-seat belt sign, and I opened my eyes.

"You doing OK?" Jake said. His hand was still over mine on the armrest.

I nodded. "I'm fine. I'm sorry, turbulence just really scares me. Doesn't it bother you at all?"

"Not a bit."

"You're lucky. It really freaks me out."

He smiled and gave me a funny look.

"What?" I said.

He laughed. "Nothing."

"Penny for *your* thoughts now," I said.

He unbuckled his seatbelt and nodded toward the flight attendants, who were preparing their drink service. "Can you use that penny to order me a Sprite when they come by? I'm going to the restroom."

When he left I looked out the window again. It was completely dark now. I pressed my face against the glass and tried to imagine what it would be like to be out there, flying through the clouds, hurtling through time and space.

The flight attendant snapped me out of my daydream to ask me for my drink order.

Jake returned a few minutes later. He sat down and picked up his drink, and just as he took a sip, I turned to him and put my hand on his knee. "Are you glad you decided to move?"

He looked surprised. "Am I glad I decided to move?"

I nodded. "It's a big change. I know that."

He scratched his eyebrow. "I don't look at it that way, actually."

"You don't?"

He shook his head.

"How so?"

"I don't know. I guess I just look at it as a step *forward* as opposed to just a change."

I glanced for a second out the window. "A step forward?"

He nodded. "Yep. Does that scare you?"

I didn't say anything.

He set his drink down, then reached for my hand, and interlaced my fingers with his. "Any step that brings me closer to *you* is a good one, as far as I'm concerned."

"It is?" I could feel my eyes well up with tears.

He nodded. "Indeed."

I smiled. "That's nice to hear."

"So to answer your question, *yes*, I'm *very* glad I decided to move."

"I'm glad too," I whispered.

"As long as you don't tell any more jokes about animals with no legs, we should be fine."

"Hey, that reminds me—"

He put his free hand over my mouth. "Please don't, OK?"

"OK." I laughed through his hand, then took it between both of mine and stared out the window into the darkness. I couldn't see anything, but I could feel how fast we were moving.

Life never stops, I thought.

Soon, I closed my eyes and lay my head against Jake's shoulder.

I didn't know where we were headed, but I finally felt settled enough to enjoy the ride.

Thank you!

As I write this, it's still hard for me to believe that a third Waverly Bryson book has sprung to life. Many of you have expressed that you enjoy spending time in her world, and I do too. Readers may be surprised to learn that each time I begin a new book, I have a general idea for how it will begin, but that's honestly about it. Instead of forcing a story on to the page, I've learned to (try to) be patient and let it gradually unfold in my head. I watch in wonder as this happens, and then I basically just write it down and hope people like it. The idea behind *Honey on Your Mind* was born on a pretty spring morning in the kitchen of my dear friend Alison Marquiss, the best sounding board a girl could ask for.

My superhuman mother, Flo Murnane (aka "Ma") was the first to read the initial draft of the manuscript. I value her opinion so much that I would have deleted the entire thing had she suggested it. She could also make a good living as a proofreader, although my dad (aka "Pa") has the edge on spelling and grammar…kidding. Thanks to both of you for your bottomless love and support, not to mention the occasional yummy care package.

Just like my other books, this one is sprinkled with anecdotes and insights from my own life, and once again, I'm grateful to have friends who provide me with a regular stream of material and expertise on a variety of subjects. This time around I extend a special thanks to the following people: Lindsay Barnett, Lauren Battle, Stu Berman, Steph Bernabe, Kerry Cathcart, Mary Clesi, Chris Conroy, Andrea Dershin, Carlos Escobar, Rosie Al-Saaid Mohammed FitzGerald, Heather Fraser, Val Hirota, Sean Lynden, Kirsty McGuire, Kara Mele, Mitch Miller, Luke Morey, Monica Murnane Morey, Mark Murnane, Immanuel "Manny" Palugod, Michele Murnane Sharkey, Danny Stoian, Liz Varland, Garett "MG" Vassel, and Charlie Wilson. I also want to thank Sarita Bhargava and Alberto Ferrer for their volunteer editing services. (Alberto, I can picture you counting each time Waverly bites her lip, and I love you for it.)

On the professional editing side, I was thrilled to work again with Christina Henry de Tessan. She manages to read my mind with her feedback and suggestions, essentially telling me what I wanted to think in the first place. I'd also like to thank Alex Carr at Amazon for being a self-declared and proud fan of books some might assume are just for women. Thank you as well to my agents, Mary Alice Kier and Anna Cottle, who are working tirelessly to bring Waverly to the big (or small) screen.

Finally, the all-around cheerleader award goes to Annie Flaig and Tami May McMillan. You two have no idea how much I appreciate your unwavering enthusiasm and encouragement. Thank you thank you thank you.

about the author

Maria Murnane left a successful career as a public relations executive to pursue a more fulfilling life as a novelist and speaker. Her own "story behind the story" is an entertaining tale of the courage, passion, and perseverance required to get her first novel, *Perfect on Paper*, published. (The sequel, *It's a Waverly Life*, was published in 2011.) Maria graduated with high honors in English and Spanish from the University of California–Berkeley, where she was a Regents' and Chancellor's Scholar. She also holds a master's degree in integrated marketing communications from Northwestern University. She lives today in New York City.